DON'T MISS THESE OTHER BOOKS
FROM **L.A. BANKS**

Available from
St. Martin's Paperbacks

ISBN 978-0-312-94302-8

SheLovesHotReads.com
Original Stories, Interviews,
Exclusive Content, and Much More!

L. A. BANKS

New York Tim...

"L. A. Banks takes on werewolves
and makes them her own."
—Kell...

PQT885332

FIRST
TIME IN
PRINT

LEFT FOR
UNDEAD

A CRIMSON MOON NOVEL

Praise For L. A. Banks #6

UNDEAD ON ARRIVAL

"The intensity and pressure continue in the Crimson Moon series as this briskly paced supernatural thriller races toward its climactic confrontation. For these protagonists, treachery and sabotage may spell their doom; for readers, they spell hours of pure pleasure. Banks rules!"

—*Romantic Times BOOKreviews* (4 ½ stars)

BITE THE BULLET

"The second book of Banks's electrifying werewolf saga [is] part special ops thriller, part supernatural adventure...Utilizing her storytelling flair, Banks imbues her characters with both nobility and kick-ass attitude. It doesn't get much better than this!"

—*Romantic Times BOOKreviews* (4 ½ stars)

"Tension, lots of action, and a current of sensuality...a novel that will provide hours of electric entertainment."
—Singletitles.com

"Filled with action, this fast-moving read is as powerful as the first, and will keep fans coming back for more."
—*Darque Reviews*

BAD BLOOD

"Super-talented Banks launches the complex and darkly thrilling new Crimson Moon series, which bursts with treachery and supernatural chills. The plot intri-

MORE...

cacies are carefully woven throughout, but Banks piles on the danger, making this one exciting thrill ride!" —*Romantic Times BOOKreviews* (4 ½ stars)

"Banks takes on werewolves and makes them her own...A blast to read." —Kelley Armstrong

"Shadowy, sexy, intense." —Cheyenne McCray

"An action-packed thrill ride!"
—#1 *New York Times* bestselling author Sherrilyn Kenyon

The Vampire Huntress Legend™ series

THE THIRTEENTH

"Wow! As usual, Banks blows your mind. This book is exciting from the first page, as all hell has broken loose...World religions, vampiric lore, and myths come into play, and overlying it all is a wonderful spirituality, as people of different cultures join forces to fight a pervasive evil. This powerful story makes you watch current events and wonder."
—*Romantic Times BOOKreviews* (Top Pick!)

THE SHADOWS

"Steamy and chock-full of action."
—Vampirelibrarian.com

THE CURSED

"A wild amalgam of Christianity, vampire lore, world myth, functional morality, street philosophy, and hot sex...fans couldn't ask for more." —*Publishers Weekly*

THE WICKED

"A complex world of Good vs. Evil...The story is so compelling, the whole series must be read."

—*Birmingham Times*

THE FORSAKEN

"Readers already enthralled with this sizzling series can look forward to major plot payoffs."

—*Publishers Weekly*

"In the seventh book in her incredibly successful series... Banks presents interesting myths—both Biblical and mythological...with prose that's difficult to match—and most certainly just as difficult to put down."   —*Romantic Times BOOKreviews* (4 ½ stars)

THE DAMNED

"All hell breaks loose—literally—in the complex sixth installment....stunning."   —*Publishers Weekly*

"In [*The Damned*], relationships are defined, while a dark energy threatens to destroy the entire squad. Banks's method of bringing Damali and Carlos back together is done with utmost sincerity and integrity. They have a love that can weather any storm, even when dire circumstances seem utterly overwhelming. Fans of this series will love *The Damned* and, no doubt, will eagerly await the next book."

—*Romantic Times BOOKreviews*

THE FORBIDDEN

"Passion, mythology, war, and love that lasts till the grave—and beyond....Fans should relish this new chapter in a promising series."   —*Publishers Weekly*

"Superior vampire fiction."   —*Booklist*

"Gripping."   —*Kirkus Reviews*

THE BITTEN

"Seductive...mixing religion with erotic horror dosed with a funky African-American beat, Banks blithely piles on layer after layer of densely detailed plot...will delight established fans. Banks creates smokin' sex scenes that easily out-vamp Laurell K. Hamilton's."

—*Publishers Weekly*

"The stakes have never been higher, and the excitement and tension are palpable in this installment of Banks's complex, sexy series."   —*Booklist*

THE HUNTED

"A terrifying roller-coaster ride of a book."

—*Charlaine Harris*

"The well-conceived and intricate rules of Banks's vampire-inhabited world provide endless opportunities for riffs on the meaning of power and sex that will please lovers of similar...philosophical musings found in the vampire tales of Anne Rice and Laurell K. Hamilton." —*Publishers Weekly*

"Hip, fresh, and fantastic."

—Sherrilyn Kenyon,
New York Times bestselling author of
Dark Side of the Moon

THE AWAKENING

"An intriguing portrait of vampiric society, reminiscent of Anne Rice and Laurell K. Hamilton."
—*Library Journal*

"L. A. Banks has taken her huntress series to another level; the action, adventure, and romance have readers tingling with anticipation...I find myself addicted to this series." —Book-remarks.com

"Again, Banks brilliantly combines spirituality, vampires, and demons (and hip-hop music) into a fast-paced tale that is sure to leave fans of her first novel, *Minion*, panting for more." —*Columbus Dispatch*

MINION

"Banks's mastery of character creation shines through in the strong-willed Damali...a sure-fire hit...pretty dramatic fiction." —*Philadelphia Daily News*

LEFT FOR UNDEAD

L. A. BANKS

St. Martin's Paperbacks

This is a work of fiction. All of the characters, organizations and events portrayed in this novel are either products of the author's imagination or are used fictitiously.

LEFT FOR UNDEAD

Copyright © 2010 by Leslie Esdaile Banks.

Cover photograph © Barry Marcus

For information address St. Martin's Press, 175 Fifth Avenue, New York, NY 10010.

ISBN: 978-0-312-94302-8

Printed in the United States of America

St. Martin's Paperbacks edition / October 2010

St. Martin's Paperbacks are published by St. Martin's Press, 175 Fifth Avenue, New York, NY 10010.

10 9 8 7 6 5 4 3 2 1

Many thanks to all of you who have joined me on this adventure and have followed this series, as well as followed my Vampire Huntress Legends series. You all made it so worthwhile and it has been an awesome journey into the realm of imagination and fantasy with wolves and pack alliances, lovers and Fae, vampires and witches, and good ultimately triumphing over evil. Thank you for the wild and wonderful ride!

Special acknowledgment goes to: My agent, Sara Crowe (an awesome lady!), my editor Rose Hilliard, and the St. Martin's team. Of course, I can never fail to mention my dedicated Street Team, the backbone! Plus special thanks to Police Officer Jerry Patterson of Grand Prairie, Texas, for your wonderful expert assistance in helping me understand weapons and ballistics—couldn't have done it without you, Jerry!

Thank you all!

PROLOGUE

New Orleans . . . Fall

Fae archers stood at the Sidhe wall and trained their arrows toward the tree line as a slow, unseasonable frost overtook the branches. A sudden hard chill sliced through the humid air all around them, keening their senses for a potential Unseelie onslaught.

The Captain of the Guards held up one hand, silently cautioning his archers to wait until they could tell the true direction of the enemy's approach. Skilled eyes remained focused on the minute changes in the flora as they picked up on a telltale clue. Thicker ice was forming on the branches that faced the glamour-hidden golden path to the drawbridge. But as the captain lifted an arrow from his quiver, a regal female voice rang out.

"Friend, not foe! I beseech you—I have come to seek asylum from Sir Rodney!"

The entire garrison exchanged confused but

skeptical glances. Again using hand signals, the captain sent his men into better positions, while cautioning them with his eyes to look alive and not to fall for a possible Unseelie ambush.

"Then show ye-selves!" the captain shouted around a stone pillar. "All of you!"

The stone path instantly glazed over with a thin covering of ice and Queen Cerridwen stood between two formidable-looking Gnome bodyguards. Her hands were concealed within a white mink muff and she was shrouded in a luxurious full-length hooded white mink coat that flowed out in a long train behind her. Perspiration rolled down her Gnomes' faces from beneath their heavy Cossack-styled hats and furs. But the queen's composure despite the Louisiana heat remained eerily cool as she simply pushed back her hood with ease, moving slowly so that the nervous captain could observe her hands. Not a platinum strand of hair was out of place as she turned her delicate face up to the captain's and made her appeal while her intense ice blue eyes beheld him.

"We have traveled far under dangerous conditions," she said calmly. "I need to confer with my husband on matters of national security to our Fae way of life."

"*Ex*-husband," an elderly disembodied voice stated bluntly. Within seconds Garth became visible as he joined the standoff on the fortress outer wall.

"No matter what you may think of me, dear Garth," Queen Cerridwen cooed, "in the end,

Rodney and I have a link that goes back as long as—"

"Too long," Garth snapped, cutting her off. He pulled out a wand with crooked fingers from the sleeve of his monk habit–styled robe; it was a thinly veiled threat—one that, wisely, neither Cerridwen nor her Gnomes responded to. "There are some things that our monarch may be blind to, but that I, as his top advisor, will always see."

Queen Cerridwen allowed a tight smile to form on her pale rosebud-shaped lips while she studied the ancient wizard. "Then see that I have come with limited guards and did not arm myself to match your rude challenge just now. My mission is much too important to be derailed at the foot of your monarch's drawbridge."

Garth arched an eyebrow and glanced at the Captain of the Guards, then let out a little snort of disgust. "This is not the Cerridwen I am used to. Something is clearly awry."

"There could be more of them in the trees awaiting an ambush," the worried captain murmured to Garth.

Garth nodded but spoke quietly: "But if we have their queen and a full garrison at our walls, then the odds that they will siege the palace are tremendously reduced."

As though reading their minds, Queen Cerridwen stepped forward. Using a simple hand signal, as one would command well-trained hunting dogs, she bade her guards to stay where they stood.

"I need to speak to Rodney," she said, never

blinking as she fixed her gaze on Garth. "It is a matter of utmost importance."

After a moment, the elderly Gnome gave a curt nod with his bald head, which was enough to signal the captain to lower the drawbridge.

"Only you," Garth said, addressing the queen.

Queen Cerridwen nodded and lifted her chin as she gracefully glided forward. "As only I would expect. But I thank you for your limited hospitality, nonetheless."

Her ice-heeled shoes clicked against the bridge, ringing out in the deafening silence as garrison archers kept their deadly arrows trained on her. The moment she was on the other side of the bridge, anxious guards quickly drew up the only access to the castle. Then, just as quickly, a phalanx of guards surrounded her.

"Your wand, Your Majesty," Garth said in a suspicious tone, then grudgingly gave her a courtesy bow before holding out his hand.

She calmly gave her muff to the closest guard beside her and then carefully reached into her flowing left sleeve with two fingers to produce a crystalline ice wand. As he cautiously accepted the queen's instrument of death, Garth nodded and silently dispatched a runner to alert Sir Rodney.

"I will show you to the war room," Garth said in a dignified tone.

Queen Cerridwen tilted her head with an amused expression. "But I was so hoping you'd show me to his private bedchamber." She released a melodramatic sigh with merriment in her eyes as the old

Gnome drew back, clearly shocked. "No matter, we'll wind up there sooner or later. You know Rodney almost as well as I do, and some of his notions of détente should be predictable by now even for you, dear Garth."

CHAPTER 1

Elder Vlad stood by the desecrated mausoleum peering down at the charred male corpse. Blue blood slowly blackened beneath the visible pulsing veins in the paper-thin skin of Vlad's bald head while his black irises completely overtook the whites of his eyes. The Vampires around him were quiet and still under the blue-white wash of moonlight in the cemetery, awaiting his permission to investigate. Fury threaded through his body like dark tendrils of hatred, although the ancient vampire remained stoic.

"Who did this?" His rhetorical question was uttered between his fangs with deadly calm. He already knew the culprits; his angry query was simply a command for external confirmation. Elder Vlad glanced up, holding his top hunter lieutenant's gaze, and impatiently waited for an answer.

"We believe it had to be Unseelie Fae, Your Excellency. Just like the others." Caleb dropped to one leather-clad knee, allowing his long spill of platinum hair to flow over his shoulders as he more closely examined the Vampire ash. The black leather coat Caleb wore dusted the ground, billowing out around him from supernatural fury.

"Undoubtedly death by daylight invasion," Caleb said, suddenly looking up baring fangs as his rage kindled. "I suspect that Monroe Bonaventure went to ground, sleeping here in his mausoleum for fear that since the mansions of so many others had been recently overrun that his might be as well. But they found the poor bastard anyway."

"He was my sixth and last viceroy in the region." Elder Vlad paced away with silent footsteps, beginning to levitate from his unspent anger, and then he turned quickly to speak in a burst of rage to the assembled hunters. "We are of the caste Vampyre! We are the eternal night! That we fear *anything* is sacrilege! We are the definition of fear in the supernatural world! It is our kind that has always been at the top of the food chain for millennia! By all that is unholy, I vow that there will be merciless redress for this offense. Tell me, dear Mara, what clues have you uncovered, before I formally declare war. . . . Transylvania will want to know why and I shall give them indisputable proof."

Mara traced the edges of the broken door hinges and locks around the opened crypt with her fingers. Only her long brunette hair moved in the gentle night breeze as she stopped for a second to peer at Elder Vlad, remaining momentarily eerily still.

"This metal was fractured by sudden freezing . . .

temperatures so cold that a mere tap would have shattered them," she finally said. Her smoldering dark gaze beheld Caleb's ice blue stare for a moment before returning to Elder Vlad. "Our local Seelie Fae do not work with such extreme temperatures," she murmured, her voice sounding like a seductive forensic expert's. "Nor do the wolves."

Elder Vlad narrowed his gaze and looked off into the distance. "No, they don't, do they."

Mara shook her head. "Sir Rodney is many things, but a fool he is not," she said with a low hiss between her fangs.

"Your orders, Your Excellency?" Caleb asked, rising to stand with his head bowed before the ancient leader of the North American Vampire Cartel.

"Fix this," Elder Vlad murmured. "Make sure the Unseelie have a list of names for which we demand blood restitution. And do be sure to let Queen Cerridwen of Hecate know how very displeased I am."

"Queen Cerridwen of Hecate," Rupert announced, bowing before Sir Rodney as he entered the war room with Garth and a formidable retinue of palace guards.

"Cerridwen," Sir Rodney said in an even tone, offering her a slight bow while refreshing his Fae ale. "And to what do I owe the rare pleasure—especially at this hour, unannounced, and well after I have declared war on you via Fae missive for your treason of siding with Vampires against my kingdom?"

"I was set up, Rodney. Purely and simply." Queen Cerridwen casually shed her mink coat and walked forward, allowing it to pool on the floor behind her. "I received your missive and I suspect that you received mine stating that all is forgiven. We are not at war . . . what has been between us has been a bitter disagreement at times—something that occasionally happens amongst evenly matched rivals—but never war. However, we are now under siege."

"Rivals," he said flatly, his sapphire gaze holding hers for ransom.

"Among other things," she said softly. "Is that not sometimes the outgrowth of passion . . . for lovers to become rivals?"

"Or enemies."

Her cool gaze warmed him as it slowly raked him from head to toe.

"You don't mean that," she murmured. "I have known you a long time, my summer prince. Your warmth always belies the coldness of your words."

Sir Rodney glanced over her head at his men who rimmed the room in protection, noting how they bristled at the queen's blatant attempt to lure him into complacency with feminine charm.

"And your coldness always belied your warmth, Cerridwen. Therein always lay the conundrum."

"Touché. Evenly matched in words and wit, as I said." A sad smile overtook her face as she walked closer to stand before him. "We may have fought, but the one thing you never lost was my respect."

He nodded. "And I never lost respect for how dangerous you can be when crossed, Cerridwen. Forgive my hesitancy to simply allow bygones to be bygones. I have felt your wrath, and men died behind it. We did not fight as a couple; we went to war. So let us not play games tonight. State your cause or leave my castle."

"Very well," she said, lifting her chin. "I have traveled long to come here before nightfall, as have my guards. Surely hospitality is not so lacking that you would see us unsheltered against Vampires in the dead of night?"

"Rupert, please bring the lady refreshment and have her men placed in the dungeon under heavy guard—albeit with food and ale."

"Thank you," Queen Cerridwen replied in a tight voice, keeping her unblinking gaze on her ex-husband.

"Aye." Sir Rodney waved his hand before her to motion for her to be seated at his round table. A chair drew itself away from the table, waiting for her to fill it, but she declined.

"There is no need for me to sit here and break bread with you, Rodney, as I am clearly not trusted. Should you cough from swallowing your food too quickly or somehow accidentally choke on a quail bone, your men would have my head thrust in the guillotine. Therefore, as long as my guards are fed, I am fine. But the information I have brought you is vital to our Fae way of life."

She kept her eyes on her ex-husband's back as he walked away from her with a cup of ale in one hand and the other clasped in a fist at his spine. Despite the years and all the raging water under the bridge between them, it was hard not to study his regal posture and broad shoulders or the way his dark brown hair spilled over them. That sight was almost as compelling as his deep blue eyes and his strong jawline.

"You make me sound like such a lout, Cerridwen . . . and yet trust is hard to come by between us, for good cause." He turned away from the window and stared at her.

"Yes, it is, Rodney," she said in a gentle tone that lacked its usual bitter edge. "I thought we would live a long and passionate existence together—you ruling the summer and I ruling the winter—but after the first century you grew bored of me and the nymphs and human conquests were too much of a temptation. I do know about trust becoming a difficult commodity to own."

"Back to that again," he said, taking a slow sip of ale and sending his gaze toward the window once more.

"It never left that," she said more coolly than intended.

"It never does . . . but there were other things, too."

"Yes. Like your weakness for the human condition and my disdain of it."

He looked at her hard, ale held mid-air. "Have you not learned from what we have recently experienced that there are those of that species that have honor?" He paced to the round table and set down his ale, waving Rupert to set down the silver-domed tray of refreshments he'd brought in for the queen. "They are weak; they own no magic but rush in anyway to do that which is heroic. Some of my men would not be here were it not for the humans that Sasha Trudeau led into battle with us against Elder Vlad and the horror he conjured up from the demon depths."

"Time improves vision and perspective," Queen Cerridwen said carefully, and then released a weary sigh.

"Not understanding that, taking such an intractable line against the humans . . . allowing your subjects to harm them with foul tricks for sheer amusement is what drove me from your bedchamber, Cerridwen—not my so-called wandering eye. I do not claim sainthood, but I was indeed yours without rival for a very long time . . . until my opinion no longer mattered and I began to feel as though I, too, was one of your subjects."

Both monarchs looked away and crossed the room in opposite directions, oblivious of the uncomfortable guards who stood stone still during the emotional exchange.

"Milord," Garth finally said, diplomatically trying to restore order. "There is a matter of state business that Queen Cerridwen has brought tonight . . . and mayhap we should learn more about this potential Vampire threat?"

Queen Cerridwen lifted her chin as she faced

Sir Rodney's top advisor. "Word has traveled to my castle doors like wildfire that someone has opened Vampire graves to daylight invasion and has made it appear to be me, using permafrost as a signature. I was left a list of names of the sun torched and given twenty-four hours to answer for my actions. The last grave that was opened was that of Monroe Bonaventure, Elder Vlad's sixth viceroy."

"Your calculated coldness is legendary, Queen," Garth said evenly, his sarcasm biting as he thrust his shoulders back. "Permafrost befits your methods. We well remember the dead roses in the outer gardens, not to mention the dead guards. If you have gotten yourself into a dilemma with your previous cohorts in crime, you may well be in too deep for our assistance. You were *in bed* with the Vampires at one point. We, the Seelie, also have long memories and we fail to see what this has to do with us?"

She spun on Sir Rodney, tears of anger and frustration glittering in her pretty eyes. "All of that nasty business of temporarily siding with the Vampires was a matter of court record, and you learned that in the swamps of this godforsaken land! I was duped by Elder Vlad, coerced into an arrangement with him against you, thinking you had attacked one of my vassals in retribution for what happened with a rogue member of my court. But once I learned of his duplicity, I promised him that the Fae had *very long* memories and there would indeed be a cold day in Hell for him to pay for ever making me raise arms against you. However, someone beat me to that promise and has now forced my hand, and, therefore, I suspect, his."

"Aye . . . the Fae do have long memories," Sir Rodney said quietly.

"Can't you forget the past and understand that we, the Unseelie, are soon to be under attack in the northern country? How long before the Vampires attack the Seelie as well?"

"I cannot forget the past, Cerridwen, any more than you can."

Her ex-husband's voice was quiet and sad, like a low rumble of rolling thunder that she felt in her belly. Just the sound of it and the tone of it made her clasp her arms about herself.

"No, I guess we cannot ever forget the past, can we?" she said, swallowing hard. "I should not have come here seeking an ally. My apologies for imposing. Upon first light, my guards and I will be gone."

"Leave us," Sir Rodney said, turning away from Cerridwen to stare at his guards.

"What? . . . ," she murmured, horrified. "Now? At night with Vampire patrols in the hundreds with a bounty on my head? Do you hate me that much, Rodney, that you would—"

"Not you, Cerridwen. . . . Garth, Rupert, clear the room so that I may speak to my queen privately. Thank you."

"Milord?" Garth said, glancing at Rupert and the others in sheer disbelief.

"What about my request was unclear?" Sir Rodney said, growing agitated. His gaze remained steady on his men until Garth conceded.

"As you wish, milord," Garth said in a tight tone of voice, and then bowed and withdrew from the great room, taking the rest of the men with him.

Stunned silent, she watched Rodney's men leave, now better understanding the part of the past that Rodney was referring to and clearly couldn't forget. For a moment, she hadn't been sure he'd remembered what they'd once shared; it had been so long ago and his initial reception of her was so distant. He'd seemed so angry when she first arrived, his voice and remarks still lingering with old hurts from wounds that had cut bone deep. It was the same part of their past that she could never fully divest herself of, either; the hurt and the passion was all intertwined, and something that neither his old advisors nor hers would ever fully comprehend.

"Have you eaten?" Sir Rodney asked quietly as the large double doors closed, then went to the table to pour her a goblet of wine.

"Not since yesterday," Queen Cerridwen said in a soft tone as he brought her the chalice. She accepted it from him, allowing her fingers to gently graze his. "Thank you."

"You're welcome . . . but that is not good. We must rectify your nutrition before you waste away. My kitchen staff is at your disposal, if what Rupert has brought isn't satisfactory."

Only a few inches from him, she looked up and took a slow sip of wine. "You're right. It isn't good and I'm sure that what has been brought will suffice. But this inexplicable thing between us has always been the best sustenance for me, Rodney. . . . It's the one thing that could always revive me . . . and it was always good."

He nodded and touched her cheek gently with the back of his knuckles. "We may war, but I would never allow Vampires to brutalize you or your Sidhe, Cerridwen. Never."

She closed her eyes and turned into the warmth of his caress. "I swear to you this is no game or ploy. I have not done that which they hold me liable for. I would not involve you in my mischief, were it thus."

"I believe that," he said quietly, allowing his hands to slowly cover her soft, creamy shoulders. "Maybe because I want to believe it as much as I need to believe it."

She closed the gap between them, letting the chalice dissolve away with a sparkle of magick. "Can we forget the past and start anew just for tonight . . . on this beautiful autumn eve—this halfway mark between the end of summer and the beginning of the winter? Shall we meet in the middle and join as one?"

Tracing the edge of her delicate jaw with trembling fingers, he lowered his mouth to hers. "What past, Cerridwen?" he murmured, gently tasting her lips. "When we've just truly met for the very first time tonight."

*   *   *

New Hampshire's woodlands were in full fall
color, their breathtaking splendor made even more
glorious by the light of the brilliant moon. Hunter
turned quickly and protectively pressed his naked
body against Sasha's as a sparkling multihued Fae
missive parted the fall foliage, whizzing through
the branches like a heat-seeking missile. It terminated with a loud thunk into a birch tree, narrowly
missing them, its silver tip deeply embedded in
the ghostly wood under the full moon.

Slowly peeling his skin away from Sasha's,
Hunter reached out and yanked the arrow out of
the tree trunk with annoyance.

"Two inches closer and we would have spent
the night trying to recover, instead of enjoying the
moon or each other," he said with a growl.

"Something's gotta be wrong, baby," she murmured, touching his clasped fist as she gazed up
into his amber wolf eyes. "Usually their missives
just find us and hover. This one was sent with a lot
of extra topspin on it."

"It had better be a matter of life and death."

Hunter's voice filled the glen in a low rumble as
he flung the arrow away from them, clearly still
peeved that Sir Rodney had sent a missive that interrupted a full-moon wolf run. But she tried not to
smile as she gently caressed the five o'clock shadow
that graced Hunter's jaw, tracing the lush contours
of his lips while waiting for the kaleidoscope-like
missive to open and unfurl the message it contained.

Leaning into his warmth, she could understand his frustration. His massive six-foot-five frame was still burning up from a near shape-shift, and the chase erection he owned was still angrily bobbing up and down with every deep inhalation and exhalation he took. Waiting to be with him required every ounce of discipline she had. Her body was also on fire from the promise of the pleasure his would surely bring as he possessively held her and nuzzled the crown of her head against his cheek.

Her breasts ached with anticipation as she remained pressed against him. Damn, Sir Rodney has lousy timing. Her hand traveled down Hunter's stone-cut chest to trail over his amber and silver clan medallion, loving the feel of his dark skin beneath her fingertips. She wore the mate to it, and she could feel his body heat almost soaking into the metal and exquisitely etched talisman. For a moment she was driven to near distraction, almost forgetting that there was even a Fae missive hovering mid-air in front of them until it suddenly opened. She'd have to gently remind Sir Rodney one day not to send urgent requests during the full moon; it was just not good form when dealing with Shadow Wolves, or even Werewolves for that matter.

Quickly sensing Hunter and Sasha for authentication, the missive released silver glowing letters into the air before them—a standard protective measure to keep its contents safe from demon or Vampire interception.

*There may be foul play at the Sidhe—stop.
Queen Cerridwen of Hecate has arrived
with news of Vampire graves being daylight
invaded—stop. The queen claims no Unseelie involvement, despite her permafrost
signature being found at the destruction
sites—stop. The last invasion murdered
Monroe Bonaventure, Sixth Viceroy of Vlad.
Sir Rodney could be compromised by his
own emotions and must not know that I
have asked you to return to New Orleans to
both investigate and support him, should he
be lured to ally with the Unseelie—stop. I
may have said too much—stop. But this is
a matter of Seelie Fae national security—
stop. She is with him tonight—stop. Do you
understand—stop. In the morning, when
cooler heads prevail, he will need to speak
to those he respects who can reason with
him—stop. This is not our war—stop.*

*Respectfully requested,
Garth*

"Whoa . . . ," Sasha murmured as the message disappeared and the arrow flamed. "Garth sent a missive behind Sir Rodney's back—about his ex-wife the ice queen . . . who is at the Sidhe as we speak—on the run from Vampires?" Sasha dragged her fingers through her hair and looked out into the distance, thinking for a moment. "What the hell happened in the coupla months we were gone on vacation?"

Hunter just stared at her for a moment, taking in how her gorgeous gray eyes reflected the moonlight and the way her dark, tousled tresses hung about her shoulders. His gaze swept her full, kiss-punished mouth and he unconsciously wet his lips with the tip of his tongue as his eyes slowly followed the length of her throat, over her fragile collarbone, to linger at her pendulous breasts. His palms ached with the need to touch her there, to feel her lithe torso beneath his and to feel the gentle swell of her hips in his hands . . . or the tight lobes of her delicious ass and the way her long, shapely legs wrapped around his waist to anchor him in deep.

"Hunter—what are we going to do?"

"Huh?"

"Did you read the missive? Do you see what's going on?" She shook her head and paced away from him to get her bearings. "You have to do better than 'huh?' Come on."

He smiled and rubbed his jaw, then flung his long ponytail over his shoulder with a shrug. "Brain blood loss. It is a gender condition. Repeat the question."

"Are you serious?" Sasha opened her mouth for a moment and then closed it, and suddenly began to laugh. "Oh, my God. We have potential World War Three about to happen and—"

"How long have you known me?" he asked with a sheepish grin.

"Long enough to know that you were serious when you said, 'Repeat the question,'" she said, smiling.

"I read and comprehended that Garth said we should speak to Rodney in the morning, when cooler heads prevail. Yes?"

"True, but . . ."

"Worrying all night serves no purpose and we are too far away to save him from the queen in his bedchamber, if she is there to poison him or to do him harm. Yes?"

"Yeah . . . but—"

"And I am in no condition for war."

Sasha's smile broadened. "True."

"Then, may I make one request?" he murmured, slowly stalking her.

"Maybe . . . ," she said, beginning to laugh. "Depends on what it is."

He smiled, now showing wolf canines. "It's very simple, I promise you."

She tilted her head and sidestepped his quick lunge, taunting him. "What?"

His smile faded and his voice deepened to a sexy rumble. *"Run."*

CHAPTER 2

"It still feels pretty weird," Fisher said as he hauled another crate of equipment into their new make-shift lab.

"Change is always weird, dude," Winters shot back without looking at him.

Fisher wiped the perspiration forming on his brow with a lanky forearm and then dragged his fingers through his damp blond hair after he set down the heavy load. "Yeah, but for as long as I can remember I've been in the military. I don't know jack about this entrepreneur crap. Two months out and I feel like a . . . well . . . yeah . . . like a fish out of water. Get it?"

"Fisher being a fish out of water, aw, man . . . bad pun." Clarissa shook her head and offered Fisher a reassuring smile. "Me, Winters, and Bradley have been government contractors for years. Even Doc Holland has after coming out of uniform. So don't worry. It's almost the same as having a lifetime job, as long as we don't screw up."

She pushed her heft out of her chair and went to

help Bradley arrange his dark-arts manuals and ancient texts on the wall-to-ceiling bookshelves. When she neared him, he brushed her mouth with a casual kiss and moved a strand of her short blond bob behind her ear.

"When you guys get to be my age, past forty, you learn to take things in stride and count your blessings." Bradley allowed his intense dark gaze to settle on Clarissa for a moment before he glanced over his shoulder at Fisher. "Like not having to deal with the possibility of coming under the command of another SOB like Colonel Madison, even though he finally came around. The next commander you got might not be as forward thinking as General Westford, you know."

"You don't have to tell me twice," Fisher said, giving Bradley a mock salute. "But as long as the POTUS likes our unit and is gung ho about this whole supernatural thing, dickheads like Madison won't be a problem."

"Until there's a change in administration, and then it's a crap shoot again." Bradley pushed his horn-rimmed glasses up the bridge of his nose, studying the binding of a text as he spoke. "Like Winters said, Fish—change is inevitable."

Winters nodded but didn't glance up from the computer he was installing. "It's gotta be bizarre, though, dude. Like, how long were you and Woods in the Service?"

Woods smiled and playfully ruffled Winters's shock of brunette hair as he passed him, sipping a longneck beer. "As long as you've been in diapers, kid."

Winters pulled back and then suddenly jumped up to play-box with Woods, who only responded with one hand, expertly maneuvering with his brew held mid-air. The matchup was so ridiculous that the other team members simply shook their heads. Winters was a skinny 150 pounds soaking wet, and his greatest physical exertion was wielding thumb strength on his computer games. Whereas Woods had been combat hardened for years, stood a full head taller than the poor kid, and weighed in at about 180, with less than 5 percent body fat, not to mention the fact that he owned a quarter compliment of wolf DNA, like Fisher did.

"Hey, no fair," Winters finally said, laughing, unable to land even one blow. "Between Delta Force training and freaking wolf DNA, I didn't stand a chance against you—but that's the only reason. My kung fu, under normal circumstances, is strong, bro."

"Yeah, okay. Save it for a hunt." Woods chuckled and polished off his beer, then hauled another crate over to the lab tables.

"It's cool. I got your back, lil' brother," Fisher said, grabbing a beer and heading toward Woods to roughhouse with him. "This ole country boy's got a little bit of the wolf thing going on, so—"

"So I wish you gentlemen would stop horsing around in here with all this expensive equipment,"

Doc Holland said, suddenly filling the doorway. Although deep frown lines wrinkled his dark, leathery face, amusement played around the edges of his mouth and hid in the gray stubble covering his cheeks, despite his gruff tone. "There's over a quarter-million dollars' worth of hard-negotiated-for Paranormal Containment Unit government-issued, *breakable* items in this room alone. How would you like it if I started yanking around in your artillery shed out back? Not to mention the cost that went into restoring this Spanish-style single and pulling strings to get the zoning, need I go on?"

Bradley offered Doc a half smile. "I told them if they come near my bookshelves with that nonsense, or knock into my crystal ball, I'll hex them. . . . Perhaps you need a ward for the computers and lab gear?"

Both Woods and Fisher let go of each other and downed their beers, laughing as they pounded each other's fists and pointed at each other to signify the fight game would resume later.

"Just because we're no longer in uniform doesn't mean all discipline goes out the window," Doc fussed. "I might take you up on the ward, though, Bradley."

"All right, all right, we'll be outside in the backyard," Woods said in a good-natured tone. "All this packing and moving is making me claustrophobic. Are we done yet?"

"It ain't the move to this big ole house in the French Quarter, bro," Fisher said, turning a beer up to his mouth and waggling his eyebrows. "The moon was a beaut last night and is even better tonight, feel me?"

Woods took up a beer from one of the six-packs on the table and clanked it against Fisher's. "That she was, brother . . . and that she is."

Doc released a weary sigh. "The guy working in the basement should be done within the hour. Once we get the alarm system installed, you gentlemen are off the clock. It's been quiet lately, but almost too quiet . . . so be careful when you head out, all right?"

"Most excellent," Fisher said, dodging away from another one of Woods's quick jabs.

Woods bobbed and weaved away from him, a beer in hand. "We'll be reachable by electronic leash—the old cell-phone method—but tonight . . . this dog's gotta hunt."

"Come on, guys, can I go to the bar with you this time?" Winters looked from Fisher to Woods with a plaintive expression. "Who wants to be stuck in here with Brads and 'Rissa? No offense, but you guys are like sickeningly in love. Or Doc, seriously no offense, but need *I* say more?"

"Take him with you before I kill him," Doc muttered. "I may only be half Shadow Wolf, but sometimes I swear I feel my canines coming in."

Winters shrugged. "Sorry, Doc."

Doc Holland released a long breath. "And note that he's Vampire bait alone, so do look after him, if you do take him to those houses of ill repute you gentlemen frequent."

"The strip club? We're really going tonight!" Winters was up and out of his chair again. "Like, seriously, you're not just messing with my mind?"

"Yeah, lil' bro. We'll hook you up, but once we get the ladies to say yes, the rest is on you. You've gotta handle your business—can't do that for you." Woods gave Fisher a wink and then turned up his beer and guzzled it.

"Cool," Winters said, enthusiastically heading for the door.

"You guys are off the clock once all this new equipment is installed and the alarm guy finishes the install," Doc said flatly, dampening all enthusiasm in the room. "So the faster you work, the faster you're out of here."

Clarissa shook her head. "There is entirely too much testosterone in here. I don't think I can take another month of this. Any idea when Sasha will be back?"

"You tell me," Doc grumbled, checking the microscopes for any signs of damage. "You're our resident psychic."

Clarissa smiled. "Yeah, but she left with Hunter, remember, and right now the moon is full. Some things I don't want to open my third eye to see— TMI, ya know." She dug in her jeans pocket and produced a cell phone. "But there are some old fallback methods that work just as well."

"You sure you wanna do this, man?" Bear Shadow leaned in close to his pack brother and kept his voice low. "You don't have to do this, if you don't want to."

Crow Shadow pulled away from the huge, linebacker-sized Shadow Wolf and lifted his chin. "Listen, I don't need you to be talking me out of this as my best man. I'm not gonna have my kid not know his dad . . . or leave Jennifer ass out to raise a kid all by herself."

Bear Shadow held two beefy hands up in front of his chest. "I make no judgments. It just seems hasty. Hunter doesn't know. Silver Hawk doesn't know, even your sister, Sasha, doesn't know . . . and neither does Doc, who would be the last person to have an issue with this, given he never knew you were made until you were grown. So, if there is no so-called family problem with this, then why are we standing in Vegas wearing tuxxes and—"

"Because I need to do this right now, tonight, before I change my mind," Crow Shadow said, squeezing his eyes shut. "Are you with me, brother?"

"Does she know what you are?"

Crow Shadow opened his eyes and stared at his friend without blinking. "Not . . . well . . . not exactly. Like, I tried to start her off easy, you know . . . telling her that there's genetic differences that our kid is gonna have. But she got all angry with me and said I was racist." Crow wiped at the perspiration on his brow and then laughed sadly. "She said she loves what's growing inside her no matter what color it is. But she don't know the half of it. If I actually show her, she might have a heart attack . . . or what if she miscarries or something, man? Like, who knows what could happen, and if I just tell her, she'll think I'm hitting a crack pipe and that's the real reason I don't wanna be there for her and the kid."

"You do realize that it's a full moon tonight and she's pregnant . . . and this will be your wedding night."

"Yeah, I know—that's why . . ." Crow Shadow's voice trailed off as sudden awareness slammed into his brain.

"You gotta go easy, that's all I'm going to say. She's a pregnant human female, and I can't even fathom how you'll be able to consummate this."

"Oh, shit . . . oh, shit," Crow Shadow said, beginning to pace in a tight line back and forth. "I can't just back out now, brother . . . like that would be so fucked up to do to her."

"Then marry her and deal, but just be easy, man. . . . I don't know what else to tell you."

The two wolves stared at each other for a moment.

"Thanks for having my back, no matter how crazy this shit is." Crow Shadow sighed hard and then shrugged. "I just wanted to man up, you know. I didn't want to do what a lot of other Shadows have done, leaving a hybrid kid out there never knowing why it was different, never knowing what its father was. We were lucky. We got raised by the pack, had the whole clan with us. I can't do to my kid what got done to Doc. His old man walked away and left him out there a half-breed to figure it out on his own. Then my own mom pawned me off on a full-blooded wolf to make me be accepted as a full-blood, you know. All that time I thought the man who raised me was actually my dad and he wasn't. Even though I understand why my mom did it for my own protection, the shit was wrong eight ways from Sunday, man, and once I found out I vowed I wouldn't be party to anything that foul. . . . Then this accidental scenario with Jennifer cropped up, all because I didn't understand human female cycles."

When Bear Shadow lowered his gaze to his shiny black shoes, Crow Shadow looked away and shook his head, shoulders slumping.

"I don't even love her, man. She's nice, she's cool, I like her, she's pretty—but I don't know her well enough to say all that I love her . . . but I have to do the right thing or else that makes me a hypocrite and a liar. Plus, the kid is gonna have a hard enough time in the human world, not only being genetically different, but it'll be part white, part Native American, and part black. Jen works as a cashier at a donut shop, understand? If I don't do my part, then what happens to our kid? Her people already disowned her for messing with a guy like me—I show up with canines and they call the dogs and start loading shotguns. Shit. I can't just leave her and my kid to all that. Am I making any sense to you, man?"

Bear Shadow released a long, weary sigh as from

the corner of his eye he glimpsed Jennifer entering the wedding salon. He landed a heavy hand on Crow's shoulder. "I'm with you, man . . . till the bitter end—no matter how insane this decision is. Honor is always the way of the wolf."

Elder Balog Kozlov opened his eyes and sat up slowly with an angry hiss. As he telepathically perceived Elder Vlad's impassioned message from half a world away, Elder Kozlov could feel that the sun had just gone down over his beloved Carpathian Mountains, shrouding his castle in darkness.

Unable to comprehend the sheer arrogance of the affront Elder Vlad described, Elder Kozlov rose from his black marble tomb, sliding the top off with ease to stand. Wall torches lit in the dank stone subterranean lair as he passed them while his dark crimson robe billowed behind him on a supernatural energy current.

"The Unseelie have been an abomination for centuries!" he exclaimed through lethal fangs. "They play with our food. They taunt our livestock—our humans! That has always been transgression enough for me to eliminate them from my territories." Imagine ranchers allowing wolves to run amuck to torture and stampede prize stock. What would the wise rancher do to protect his herd?

Elder Kozlov nodded, receiving the appropriate response from Elder Vlad. "Yes. He would kill the wolf to restore order. But if that wolf then got into his children's bedrooms and killed six of his beloved offspring . . . what would he do to the wolf, then?"

Elder Kozlov closed his eyes and nodded, making a tent with his long, spidery fingers before his mouth. "Yesssss," he murmured in a hiss. "We've tolerated them long enough . . . but this is unacceptable. We must find the parties responsible and make a display of butchery so severe that any remaining offenders that had not been routed out would smell the death of their kind on the land and fear to ever come near our property again."

When he opened his eyes, his pupils glowed red within the totally black orbs that had overtaken his irises. He nodded with satisfaction and then turned to set his powerful gaze upon the stone gargoyles around the crypt and watched the stone come alive ready to do his bidding.

"Elder Vlad," he murmured, going over to a fawning creature to pet it, "you may avail yourself of the resources from our central lair. New Orleans is an important holding. Let me know when you need reinforcements from Europe and it shall be so."

CHAPTER 3

Dawn broke across the sky at the same time a long, forlorn howl awakened her. She'd know that voice anywhere. What the hell was Hunter's brother, Shogun, doing in the states when he was supposed to be on holiday in China?

Sasha sat up, slightly panicked and ready to bolt toward the door when Hunter's log-heavy arm was slung over her lap.

"It wasn't a distress howl," Hunter muttered with his eyes closed. "Just a casual visit at a very bad time."

She lifted Hunter's arm off her lap and then got out of bed, quickly locating a discarded thermal undershirt, her panties, and her jeans. "Shogun doesn't do casual fall-by visits all the way from China."

Hunter rolled over and groaned. "Can't a man get a little peace?"

She chuckled and kissed his forehead. "You got more than a little piece last night. I'm going to find out what's wrong. Put your pants on."

Not waiting for an answer, she hurried to the bathroom to splash water on her face and to smear a glob of toothpaste in her mouth. The next howl was within a hundred yards of their cabin, which meant a shower was out; she barely had enough time to pee, wash her hands, and spit out the toothpaste and make it to the porch when she heard Shogun coming up the walkway.

She refused to acknowledge the butterflies that always took flight in her belly when Shogun was around. It was that unspoken thing that had gone down between them long before she knew he was Hunter's brother . . . long before Shogun or Hunter knew they were half brothers. But try as she may to put a long taxidermy pin in each butterfly when she opened the door, her breath silently hitched when she saw Shogun.

Rose pink dawn sunlight framed his golden complexion against a perfect backdrop. He'd let his hair grow long again and he stopped at the bottom of the steps staring at her with intense almond-shaped eyes. He looked good in the ivory sweater and jeans, looked healthy and like life was treating him well. That's what she told herself and that kept it safe. It didn't matter that there would always be some chemistry between them—that big "what if" question that they'd never know the answer to. What mattered was that they both had enough sense and enough love for Hunter to never act upon it. Still, the huge diamond, turquoise, and amber engagement ring she wore suddenly felt ostentatious. She hugged herself, hiding the ring after Shogun briefly appraised it.

"Sister," Shogun said, addressing her in the familial title that was his way to ensure mental safety. "I hope this morning finds you and my brother well?"

The small talk was killing her. That's when she knew Shogun was in distress. He'd retreated behind Asian formality and had not given the more gregarious wolf greeting one afforded dear friends.

"I'm well; so is Hunter," Sasha said quietly. "But how are you?"

He smiled and looked off into the distance. "I am."

She nodded. "I'll get Hunter."

For a moment she hesitated at the door, watching Shogun close his eyes against the sun. Then she felt the cool autumn breeze. God help her, she was upwind from him and had not showered. The moon was still waxing full, even though it was dawn . . . and Werewolves more than Shadows felt the lunar pull. Sex scent covered her from head to toe. Sasha bit her bottom lip and quickly spun to retreat from the porch but ran smack into Hunter's stone chest.

"Talk to him," she whispered. "I don't know what happened in China, but he needs you." Then she slipped behind the door.

Hunter looked after her for a moment but said nothing as he heard the shower turn on deep within the house. "Brother?"

Shogun turned and gazed at him. "Can we talk . . . while we walk?"

Hunter nodded, not needing an explanation. It was the unspoken understanding between them; his brother had to get away from Sasha's scent. Hunter knew his brother would always have feelings deep enough to swim in toward his mate, but his brother was a man of honor. More important, Sasha's honor was embedded in the very marrow of her bones. Hunter couldn't think of any way that she hadn't shown him how much she loved him, so he allowed the tension to slowly ebb as he descended the steps to join his brother at his side.

They walked awhile in companionable silence, each man caught up in his own thoughts. Women's intuition proved more accurate than radar, Hunter noted as he watched Shogun's body language. He was definitely in some sort of severe emotional distress, so much so that his normally fluid wolf pace was jerky and more like that of a human fighting against the underbrush.

As they continued their silent trek a hundred questions began to catch fire at the edges of Hunter's mind. How would he react if his brother made some kind of confession regarding Sasha that he couldn't handle? Soon Shogun's tension became Hunter's own. Once they found a ridge, Shogun stopped and motioned to the ground.

"Is this acceptable?"

Hunter nodded and sat down yogi-style, facing his brother. Shogun sat in one lithe motion, matching Hunter, and then let out a very weary sigh.

"I don't know what to do, Brother. You are the only family I now have, except my cousins, Seung Kwon, Dak-Ho, and Chin-Hwa."

Pure relief rippled through Hunter; whatever it was, it wasn't about Sasha. He let out an exhale and chose his words carefully. "Whatever the problem is, Brother, I stand with you."

"This is a delicate matter, one that has so many layers that I don't even know where to begin."

"Start at the beginning. That is always the simplest way."

Shogun sighed hard and looked out toward the multicolored tree line behind them. "I met all of Amy Chen's family while in China, and some of her parents' friends and family here before we left. They are decent people. Honorable people. They want me to marry their daughter . . . and I have no family for them to meet."

Hunter frowned. "I don't understand. You are the Southeast Asian alpha, leader of the Werewolf federation of clans in that region . . . no less than I am that for the Shadow Wolf clans of North America. There are hundreds of—"

"The clan elders will not hear of it," Shogun said quietly, returning his gaze to Hunter. "In my homeland tradition that goes back thousands of years in the human culture and is just as deeply entrenched in the way of the wolf there, I do not have an understanding set of elders or even one like your beloved grandfather, Silver Hawk."

"Aw . . . man . . . But just because the girl is human they—"

"Cannot cast their blessings on a union where a mixed-breed heir could jeopardize the House of Kwon-Yin. For centuries my ancestors ruled that region. A weak heir that is half human is sacrilege to them. Every son I sired with Amy Chen would constantly be battled in dominance challenges amongst the wolf packs. It would cause unrest and they are correct. Therefore, they have asked me to decide—I can either marry a suitable alpha she-werewolf and be free to do as I like or step down. But should I step down, and since I'd be dishonoring my family name, I would be shunned. Dead to them."

"Oh, shit. . . ."

"Yes, Brother. The choices are limited. I can almost hear my dead sister, Lei, along with my twisted dead mother, laughing from their demon ashes. They both hated mixed breeds and considered such a creation unholy. I thought if anyone could help me weigh my heart and my options, it would be you, dear brother. You have lived this hell as a child and as a man."

Hunter nodded. "But the union that created me was between my Shadow Wolf mother and our Werewolf father. Both were wolves. That was challenging enough, and after my mother perished with our father I was lucky enough to also have my grandfather, a tribe elder, there to stand behind me—as a full-blooded Shadow . . . yet if I had come out half human, I don't know if Silver Hawk would have been as understanding. The elderly are set in their ways."

Shogun nodded. "Yes, and that is the crux of my dilemma, but not all of it. They are affronted that Amy is Chinese and I am Korean, to add salt into the wound. After the loss of so many of our line in the clan wars, as well as from the demon contagion that affected my parents, losing me to Amy could put her life in jeopardy. I would not be surprised if they tried to kill her in order to bring me back to my senses and back to my leadership position. All the while, I have sent traditional Chinese wedding gifts to her family in a show of good faith . . . dragon and phoenix bridal cakes, male and female poultry—pheasants, sweetmeats, sugar, wine, tobacco, chai-li, tea presents."

Hunter wiped his hands down his face, rendered speechless for a moment. The problem was too complex, too filled with emotional drama, and way out of his league in terms of finding a quick solution.

Shogun allowed his head to fall into his hands. "What am I going to do? Her parents don't know that I'm not human. Amy knows; she saw us all in battle when we saved her life and she saw too much through my evil aunt's eyes when her body was temporarily possessed by Lady Jung Suk. . . . She's seen the sidhe, she knows of the supernatural world, and once that genie is out of the bottle one cannot force it back in."

"Have you spoken to Amy about any of this, Brother? She has to know—maybe she'll help your decision."

"It's the full moon!" Shogun shouted, and stood

in one move. "I can't be near her, Brother," he said, walking in a tight circle. "She's made like porcelain . . . fragile, her bones like that of a small bird'—and I'm a goddamned Werewolf!"

"Okay, okay," Hunter said, standing, trying his best to calm his overwrought brother. "Then wait until the moon is waning and—"

"Her parents went to the feng shui expert, the fortune-teller who picks auspicious wedding dates, and he chose a full-moon date, next month!" Shogun raked his hair, dragging the red silk tie out of his ponytail. "Chinese wedding ceremonies are very complicated. They install a bridal bed; your best friends who are lucky—mated with children, preferably—move it to add good luck and then throw red dates and oranges and peanuts and pomegranates on it. Children are supposed to fight over the ripe fruit in the bed to bring fertility energy to it. I am supposed to go to her parents' home and collect her in a red silk chair and bring her back to my home. . . . There's so much more that I cannot even explain it all. But at the ceremony, she and I are to kneel before our parents, our elders, and serve them tea as a sign of respect. There is a huge dinner. Her good-luck woman is to attend her in all things until she is given to me. But it will be on a full moon . . . when my people are most prone to violence and will most likely not just boycott our wedding, but crash it in full transformation."

"Okay," Hunter said, beginning to pace with Shogun. "What if you tell them your parents are dead, which is no lie . . . and that the bulk of your close-knit family is here in the states?" He waited until Shogun stopped circling and looked at him. "That, too, wouldn't be a lie, because I am here, Sasha is here, Crow Shadow is here, Bear Shadow is here, all of Sasha's human team is here . . . we could rally enough family, and if need be we could make sure there were guards."

Shogun closed his eyes and allowed his head to drop back, turning his face up to the sun. "I cannot touch her while the moon is in full phase. . . . I could hurt her. You know that. We never become intimate with humans while we're out of control, only our own kind . . . and she has such a gentle heart." Shogun straightened and walked away from Hunter, and then drew in a shuddering breath. "I would have to leave her for three or four nights every month . . . and after my lies wore thin, she would come to learn why. That betrayal would probably kill her faster than my own clan would. Any female that got wind of the fact that I had taken a human as my wife and submitted to a human ceremony would stalk her, hunt her, and if she didn't hurt Amy physically, she'd be sure to tell my bride why she could never expect fidelity."

"Man . . . you don't know that," Hunter said quietly. "Maybe . . ." His words trailed off, sounding hollow to his own ears. He did know.

"It's been two months," Shogun said in a shaking voice, keeping his back to Hunter. "I would not defile her by taking her before we were married, just in case the politics forced me to change my mind. . . . At least she'd be left with her virginity—

you may not understand it here in this land, but in lands that have traditions that go back for thousands of years, something like that could have the poor girl shunned to a decent marriage proposal."

Shogun let out a hard sigh and then drew himself up, as though each part of the problem he exposed was more painful than the last. "And to see if I could honor her with faithfulness, I haven't gone to where there are willing she-wolves. I love her. And then I thought, what happens when she is filled with my seed? What happens if she does become pregnant, with her fragile, porcelain body . . . and I want her? Do I stay and risk harm to her and our unborn child, my heir, or do I shatter her heart and leave her to be what I am—a wolf?"

"Brother, these are profound questions that only someone with the age and the wisdom of Silver Hawk can answer." Hunter studied the ground as he spoke, rubbing the nape of his neck. "No matter what you decide, I am here for you with the full force of the North American Shadow Clan. . . . We will always have a home for you, and we will not allow your home to be overrun or your wife attacked—should you decide to take that step. But the only other thing I can say is, talk to Silver Hawk and then talk to your betrothed. Tell her what the realities are and let her decide how much of this she can bear."

Shogun nodded and looked at Hunter with a sad smile. "Just knowing that I have family behind me helps a great deal. Thank you."

"No thanks every required for being your brother, man." Hunter extended his arm to clasp Shogun's in a warriors' handshake. "Talk to Amy."

Shogun shook his head. "Maybe someday. But she is young, still in college, and thinks love can solve all of this."

Hunter shrugged as he let go of his brother's arm. "I don't make assumptions any longer about female logic. But they do know a brand of magick that we will never own."

Both men paused, knowing they had just unwittingly stumbled into the delicate mental territory claimed by Sasha.

"Maybe she would talk to Amy," Shogun said quietly without directly mentioning Sasha's name.

Hunter nodded. "She has a big heart and would help, if you thought that would be best." It was a noncommittal response but the best one he could offer without discussing it with Sasha first.

Shogun nodded and walked more deeply into the underbrush, leaving just as oddly as he'd come. "Thank you."

"Be careful, Brother!" Hunter called behind him, and then jogged to catch up to Shogun.

Shogun stared at Hunter for a moment, his expression unreadable except for the sadness that haunted his dark eyes.

"We got a strange missive last night from Sir Rodney's castle. There are Vampire grave openings happening in New Orleans. The Vampires believe the Unseelie did it, and their queen is currently at Sir Rodney's Sidhe requesting an alliance."

"And what has this to do with the wolves?" Shogun's question was delivered with bland detachment. "We have only committed to ally with Sir Rodney."

"True," Hunter said, rubbing his broad palm across the new beard stubble covering his jaw. "But if Sir Rodney gets pulled into this madness, then it could be wrongly assumed that as his allies we're involved. Sasha and I are going to try to learn more, but in the meanwhile it would be best to stay in touch and keep a low profile. So watch your back."

CHAPTER 4

Sasha stared out the window as she held her cell phone to her ear. It was a hard thing to do, but she tried to focus. Just before the phone rang, she'd been mentally juggling a hundred possible scenarios at once. Her thoughts ricocheted between every conceivable reason Shogun had arrived and the plausible reality that Sir Rodney was once again under attack.

Now she was attempting to sort through all that while also seeming thoroughly engrossed in the early-morning conversation that had caught her off guard. In order to give Clarissa the full attention she deserved, Sasha knew she had to push Shogun's sudden appearance after the arrival of the strange Fae missive out of her mind. But that was only marginally possible while she listened to Clarissa's recounting of all the equipment installation antics and general office mayhem that had taken place over the last couple of months.

Forcing a smile into her voice, Sasha told herself there was no need to worry the closest female friend she had by sounding tense or as though she hadn't welcomed the call. Truthfully, she missed the entire team. Even without Clarissa's call, between the arrival of the mysterious Fae missive the night before and Shogun showing up on their cabin doorstep in the morning Sasha knew the little island of peace that she and Hunter had claimed was gone. It was time to go back to work. More important, it was time to come out of the lovers' cocoon and get back to friends and family—the real world, as she liked to call it.

It didn't matter that they'd been hunting demons, getting shot at, or battling rogue Unseelie factions and Vampires prior to escaping to their little getaway outpost in the woods. Everything had its season, and the home team was getting antsy. Truthfully, so was she. There was only so much rest and relaxation her normally hyper system could handle. Not that Hunter was a bad distraction. On the contrary. The man had a delicious way of making days and nights run together like a river until time simply didn't exist. But still. There was a new government contractor business, Containment Strategies, Inc., to get off the ground, now that all the equipment had come in.

The only thing keeping guilt at bay as she stared out at the beautiful fire red, gold, and neon orange foliage was the fact that she'd put in time prior to her getaway to ensure contracts got put in place, supplies were ordered, and her team had a comfy base of operation in the French Quarter. But she could tell that Clarissa missed her just by the tone of her friend's voice. They'd all been through a lot together as a team while formally working in the Paranormal Containment Unit. It felt weird that there was no deployment schedule, no brass to formally report to. Sasha felt free for the first time in her adult life, but that was also a terrifying thing. There was no regimen, no definites.

A pang of homesickness suddenly washed over Sasha. "I'll be home within a day or so." Sasha gave in to Clarissa's unspoken question as her friend finished the long litany of things that had gone wrong with the initial equipment orders.

"Good, because it's been a real challenge trying to keep Fisher and Woods from bouncing off the walls."

Sasha let out a sigh. "I've missed you guys."

Yeah, it was time to go home right after she made a pit stop to check on Sir Rodney and his Sidhe. That was the plan, anyway. The only issue was going to be breaking it to Hunter.

"Well, we've missed you, too," Clarissa said, perking up. "I know Doc and the guys are going to be so excited. You know you're the only one who can keep crazy Woods and Fisher on a short leash."

Sasha laughed. "Me? Are you kidding? Those guys are their own brand of special."

"Well, maybe they'll chill out when Hunter gives them the growl."

"One can only hope," Sasha said, laughing harder.

"We need you here," Clarissa added in a dramatic rush. "It's like having two big Labrador puppies constantly roughhousing all day long. Then when Doc pops the choker chain and lets them off the leash to run, oh . . . my . . . God. And they've totally corrupted Winters."

Sasha shook her head, smiling broadly. "I can only imagine."

"No, you can't, boss," Clarissa said, laughing. "But I am not going to interrupt your Zen by going into the gory details."

"Something tells me I don't wanna know."

"Trust me—you don't."

"Well, I'm still glad you called." Sasha's tone became slightly wistful as the full weight of being gone so long hit her. Her team was her family. Yeah, it was definitely time to go home.

"I'm glad I called, too," Clarissa said softly. "Really missed you, kiddo . . . even though I know it's gotta be tough to drag yourself away from the big guy."

"Uhmmm . . . in a word . . . yeah."

Both women laughed.

"Well, we can't compete with Hunter, but we've got a great comedy routine going on here when you get back."

"Can't wait."

Again, laughter filled the receiver and the cabin living room. She was so glad that Clarissa had picked this day to call her; psychic timing was everything. It had helped keep her from standing on the porch waiting for Hunter to come back and clue her in to what was going on with Shogun. But as Hunter was a man of few words, and this seeming like it was some kind of male-to-male bonding moment, there was no telling if she'd ever fully understand what was really up. So gabbing away an hour with 'Rissa was just what the doctor had ordered.

"Well, in the meantime,'" Sasha said, not losing a beat in the conversation, "please give everyone my love. Like I said, I'll be back in a day or so. But that also reminds me; I got strange word last night that Vampire graves were getting opened to daylight. You guys hear anything about that?"

"Whoa, Sasha . . . that's not something you just drop on somebody in an 'oh, by the way.' If we had heard something like that, it would have been the first thing I would have called you with—given our really bad relationship with them."

"True." Sasha gnawed on her bottom lip for a moment. Oh yeah, she'd definitely been gone too long and was slipping. "Well, we're going to make a few stops and do a little investigating on the way home. Something tells me that this might be our next big case—but I want you guys to keep a really low profile. Seriously. Because I don't have to tell you how our Vampire buddies will take it if they think we had any involvement in opening their graves. Not to mention, there may be possibly Unseelie involvement. I don't know yet. But those guys are just as deadly when provoked."

"You don't have to tell us twice, Sasha."

"Good." Sasha paced away from the window.

Man, where had her mind been? "Make sure you communicate that to the team, especially Doc. Tell Woods and Fish that playtime is over. They've gotta be on nighttime guard duty. If you see Bear or Crow, make sure you also give them the heads-up so they can let Silver Hawk know, too."

"Roger that, Captain," Clarissa said, returning Sasha to her old pre-retirement rank.

"Okay . . . listen . . . you look alive and stay alive. I'll be back as soon as I can."

"Big hug. I feel better already. Bye."

"Bye," Sasha said quietly as the call disconnected. The more she thought about it, the more alarmed she became. If the Vamps thought the ice queen had double-crossed them and had somehow gotten Sir Rodney's support, there'd be hell to pay—and possibly in the streets of New Orleans again. The one thing Vampires were known for was swift and decisive retaliation. And if Sir Rodney had gotten lured into the fight somehow, the vamps would no doubt assume his allies—the North American Shadow Wolf and Southeast Asian Werewolf federations—had his back. . . . "Shit!"

Sasha pushed the cell phone into her jeans pocket and walked out onto the porch. She needed air. More than that, she needed to talk to both Hunter and Shogun. She hoped that was what had Shogun concerned. Maybe that's why he'd shown up on their doorstep unannounced. Then again, if that was it, then why wouldn't he have simply spoken to both of them right on the porch?

Straining her gaze, she tried to penetrate the dense tree line more than a hundred yards away in search of Hunter and Shogun. No luck. Part of her mind said to just be cool and wait; nothing was going to happen at this very second. But the impatient wolf in her wanted immediate resolution.

By the time she saw Hunter coming toward the cabin, a full fifteen additional minutes had passed. Even though she hadn't run outside and accosted him on the porch, the wait had stripped her resolve not to rush him the moment he walked through the door.

Gone was the plan to calmly ask him if he wanted a cup of coffee to ease into extracting information on what was wrong. She didn't own that much self-discipline right now. The door swung open and she was right there, standing in the middle of the room hugging her waist.

"So, what happened?"

Hunter looked at her for a moment and slowly closed the door and then ran his palm over his hair. "Long story."

This man shit was going to drive her out of her mind.

"Want a cup of coffee so we can talk?"

"Yes, and no," he said, going around her body block to head to the bathroom.

He closed the door behind him and she stood on the other side of it pacing for a moment until she heard the shower.

"Aw, c'mon, Hunter," she said, cracking open the door a bit. "Is everything okay?"

"Yes, and no," he said flatly. "Give me a minute to figure out how to present all of this in a way that preserves my brother's dignity, all right?"

She quietly banged her head against the wall. "Yeah, sure . . . of course. I didn't mean to pry. I just wanted to know that everything was all right."

"No one is in mortal danger yet, so relax."

Sasha stared at the door. Yet? Before she could stop herself she was in the bathroom staring at the shower curtain and watching Hunter's dark-hued limbs splash color, soap lather, and water against it.

"You said yet?"

He released a long sigh and shut off the water valves. "How about that cup of coffee?"

"And we'll talk—not just this twenty-questions stuff?"

"Yes, Sasha," he said in a weary tone. "We will talk."

"You cannot be serious." Winters rubbed his palms down his face and scratched his head while the other members of the team yawned and slurped coffee.

"Wish I was joking," Clarissa said, scanning the group. "Look, Sasha was being low-key for my benefit, I'm sure. But the implications of what she said were really messy. If the Fae go to war with the Vamps as a united front, then that drags the wolves into it. Kinda like guilt by association."

"If you ask me, it's bad enough that the entire human world is constantly on the brink of the

Armageddon in the frickin' Middle East. But to know the supernaturals are now hell-bent on war just makes me wanna crawl into the nearest cave and wait it out." Woods shook his head and sucked in a huge slurp of coffee. "I mean, seriously—WTF."

"Dude," Winters said, and then pounded his fist.

Bradley leaned back in his chair and allowed his head to hang back with his eyes closed. "So, what are our options? We can either lay low and hope these two very strong forces annihilate each other, somehow bypassing us in the process—which isn't likely. Or we can do some investigating, like Sasha suggested, and to try to find out what the hell started all this hoopla."

Doc nodded and walked to the window nursing his cup of black coffee. "I'll get in contact with Silver Hawk and let him know what's going on. The Shadow Wolf Clan should be able to literally put noses on the ground and can probably move faster into some of the more dangerous areas than we can."

"Good plan," Fisher said, glancing around the team. "Maybe 'Rissa and Bradley can make a few house calls in Dr. Buzzard country, you know . . . see if some root workers and local psychics heard anything . . . while Winters and Doc try to interpret data coming in from the wolves?"

"We can do that," Clarissa said, glancing at Bradley.

Woods stared at Bradley as he sat up slowly. "We've got your back. This time we're not gonna let 'Rissa go in too deep alone. Nobody wants to put her at risk again, man."

Bradley reluctantly nodded but kept his troubled gaze fixed on Clarissa. "Just a simple fact-finding mission. No heroics."

"No heroics," she said softly. "I promise."

Crow Shadow leaned up on one elbow and stroked Jennifer's cheek. Her lashes fluttered for a moment and then she slowly opened her eyes.

"Good morning," he murmured, and then kissed her gently.

A gentle smile dawned on her face. "Good morning," she whispered, and then kissed him again. "I can't believe you did it."

"I told you I wasn't gonna leave you," he said in a quiet tone, watching tears begin to well in her eyes. He placed a warm palm against her belly bump. "We mate for life. We have a code of honor. Even though fate put us together maybe before we were ready, we have a whole lifetime to grow into whatever this is."

She touched his cheek with trembling fingers, searching his eyes through her tears. "You speak in the strangest way sometimes . . . use the most unusual phrases, like you're not from here. It's beautiful, but I don't understand why you would say 'mate' and not 'marry' for life as though . . . I don't know."

"We're not like Werewolves." He looked at her hand and clasped it within his own. "We're different."

"Of course I don't think your people are animals. Oh, my God, Crow . . . is that what you think I was trying to say?" She sat up, distressed, allowing the tears to slide down her cheeks. "I know my family is horribly prejudiced, but I'm not like that."

He shook his head and sat up slowly. "No, baby, you're not. You have a good heart and such a sweet soul. I know that's not what you meant . . . but it is what I meant. I am part wolf."

She bit her lip for a moment. "So, you're saying that, even though we're married, you're still gonna run around on me." She released a sad sigh and then got out of bed in search of her robe.

"No. That's not what I meant at all. I told you I'm not a Werewolf. But I am part wolf. Shadow Wolf, the highest totem of the tribes, next to the bear. I will protect you from all harm to the death as your mate. I will never take another as long as you're alive. My children I will defend with all that I am. We of the Shadow Wolf Clan define the way of the wolf."

"Oh," she said, slumping with relief and placing her hand over her heart. "I didn't understand . . . the Native American way of speaking about being a wolf. I guess there's so much we have to learn about each other's cultures and I'm just—"

"Sit down," he said quietly. "You still don't hear me. And it's my fault. I should have shown you this before . . . well, probably before everything."

She pulled on her robe and tied it tightly, clutching the ends of the tie. "You have something . . . a disease. Oh, Jesus Lord, and I'm pregnant. The baby . . ."

"I do not have a disease. I'm immune to everything. The child will be stronger than you can ever imagine." He patted the side of the bed. "Come sit. There's something I have to show you."

He waited until she nervously complied, and when she sat he stood and crossed the hotel room.

"Take two deep breaths and remember what I told you. I will never lay a hand on you, will never harm you. But I'm different."

"We're all different, baby. I don't understand?"

He put a finger to his lips and took in a deep inhalation and changed. Jennifer's scream could have shattered glass. Crow Shadow simply looked at her as she dropped back on the bed limp. Within minutes footfalls coming down the hall forced him to shift back into his human form and then grab the sheet off the bed to wrap around his waist. The inevitable knock on the door was from hotel security: He didn't have to be a telepath to know that; it just made sense.

Calmly opening the door, he looked at the two huge casino guards.

"Is everything all right in here, sir?" one guard asked, peering around Crow Shadow into the room.

"Yep," he said, releasing a sigh. "My wife saw something in here that sorta freaked her out, but she'll be all right."

"Can we come in and ask her about that, sir?" the other burly guard said.

"Sure." Crow Shadow walked over to the bed

and gently shook Jennifer. "Baby . . . hotel security came when you screamed." He turned to the guards. "Mind getting her a glass of water?"

One guard complied while the other gently patted Jennifer's cheek.

"Ma'am . . . ma'am, can you hear me?" The guard looked up at his partner as she slowly stirred. "Ma'am, can you tell me what drug you ingested?"

Jennifer groaned and then suddenly sat up, clutching the first guard for a moment, staring past him at Crow Shadow.

"She might wanna go with you-all and get this whole thing annulled," Crow Shadow said, and then found the chair on the far side of the room to plop down into. "It's cool. Not everybody can handle this, and I ain't mad at her."

"Ma'am, are you hurt in any way?" the larger guard asked, flexing as he glanced back at Crow Shadow.

"Uh, no," she replied, but still visibly shaken. "I just saw a mouse, is all."

The two guards looked at each other for a moment.

"If there's anything harmful going on here, ma'am, you can come with us. You don't have to stay here." The guard holding the glass of water offered it to Jennifer, all the while glaring at Crow Shadow.

"If you're scared in here," Crow Shadow said, "you can go with these gentlemen. All right?"

"No," she said, shrugging away from them and sipping the water she'd been given with a shaking hand. "It just caught me off guard. We're married; we've got a baby together. I . . . I . . . well, I guess I mate for life, too." She lifted her chin as two big tears rolled down her cheeks. "I ain't got no family, nowhere to go, so I'm staying."

"Ma'am, you don't have to stay here if he's hitting you, you understand. We—"

"Whoa now, just wait a minute," she said, swinging her legs around to get off the bed. "He ain't never laid a hand on me that way. Never."

"Okay, Miss," the guard standing closest to the door said, eyeing his partner.

" 'Ma'am' it is," Jennifer said, crossing the room to go stand by Crow Shadow. "I'm married."

The other guard released a long breath of annoyance. "If you say so."

Thrusting out her hand, she flashed her diamond chip at them as though it were a ten-karat stone. "I am 'Mrs.,' thank you very much—and I saw a mouse . . . and I want you gentlemen to leave. You should have an exterminator come next time instead of throwing terrible accusations against my husband."

Again the guards gave each other suspicious glances, but they nodded and moved toward the door, but not before one mumbled under his breath, "I wish this trash would do their drugs at home."

Crow Shadow just closed his eyes as the door slammed. He knew the flurry of questions was coming and he waited, feeling them building like the low-pressure system of a pending storm.

"Why'd you go and do something like that—show me something like that in a damned hotel!"

"Because if you had a heart attack or a miscarriage or wanted to leave me," he said in a quiet tone, "I wanted you to be around other humans who could immediately help you."

"Or were you trying to get me to leave you? Then that way your conscience would be clear."

"No. My conscience would never be clear, no matter what. Because you shoulda seen this before we slept together. It was my fault you got pregnant. . . . I didn't understand the human cycles."

"I didn't make you use no condom, so I can't put it all on you . . . and I shoulda known my own cycle."

"Water under the bridge now."

"But you kept your word, which is more than anybody in my own family ever did."

For a while they said nothing and he simply sat there with his eyes closed.

"Is our baby gonna be able to do what you did?" Her question came out in a frightened rush.

"Hopefully, if it's lucky."

He opened his eyes and stared at her, watching her hug herself and intermittently wipe away her tears.

"Okay, then I've got like a thousand questions more to ask you and I'm hungry and want to eat breakfast," she said after a moment. "Because after you get over the shock, that wolf thing you do is really pretty cool."

CHAPTER 5

Coffee mug pressed between her palms, Sasha closed her eyes and lowered her forehead to the kitchen counter as she wrapped her ankles around the legs of the stool. The situation with Shogun was so messed up.

"I know," Hunter said, getting up to pour more joe. "I felt the same way when he told me. This sucks."

"I'll talk to Amy as gently as I can, but . . ."

"Yeah, yeah, I already told him that it was better for him to sit her down and explain the differences between Werewolf and Shadow Wolf males. That should really come from him."

Hunter glanced over his shoulder at Sasha as she looked up.

"But the truth in this case could make him lose face." She pushed herself up with a weary sigh. "I mean, are they really that much worse than a Shadow male at the full moon?" She dragged her fingers through her hair.

"I don't know." Hunter paused for a moment and looked at her. "You tell me?"

Sasha opened her mouth and then closed it for a second. "Not fair. Not fair at all. I wouldn't know and you know that I wouldn't know!" She jumped off the stool and left her coffee on the counter. Oh, hell yeah, it was time to get back to New Orleans.

"All right, maybe that was uncalled for," Hunter finally muttered, now standing in the bedroom doorway, watching her pack.

"Ya think?" She didn't miss a beat slinging clothes into her duffel bag.

"All of this hits too close to home." He rubbed the nape of his neck and then pushed off the wall. "You'll have to allow me that."

She stopped packing for a moment and placed one hand on her hip. "So, every time your brother comes to town and whenever there's some personal whatever going on in the family, you're going to go back to something that almost happened but didn't—when nobody, not even you guys, knew you were related—am I hearing you right?"

"No," Hunter said in a low rumble. "What it is, is that I thought Shogun was settled, and he's not . . . and that unsettles me, all right. You want the honest answer, that's the honest answer. I told you when we first met that I was no liar."

"Unsettled, what the hell is that supposed to mean?" Both hands went to her hips as she dropped the duffel bag onto the floor.

"He's unsettled because you're still unsettled," Hunter said without blinking.

"That is such *bull*," she said, snatching up her duffel bag and walking deeper into the bedroom.

"Look me in my eyes and tell me it's bull and then I will leave this subject for dead forever."

"I'm not even going to dignify this wolf interrogation," she snapped, yanking clothes from the drawer to jam into the duffel with her back still turned.

Hunter nodded and crossed his arms, watching her jerky motions. "You and I are linked at the soul . . . when you're unsettled I feel it. My brother and I share DNA, and when he's unsettled I feel it. This doesn't mean I think anyone will act on what is there, but you will have to allow me my occasional growl for hating that it even exists—especially when you are so near phase and it is during the full moon."

She felt her face get hot as her motions slowed. What could she say? She couldn't look at Hunter as he quietly stalked out of the room and she straightened and closed her eyes, furious at herself and the whole damned situation.

"She knows?" Bear Shadow was incredulous as he sat up and pulled his body from beneath three casino beauties. He held the cell phone to his ear, speaking softly as he climbed out of bed. "What on earth possessed you to tell Jennifer while still in a hotel, little brother?"

Bear Shadow listened intently and then shrugged. "Seems like a logical explanation to me—but let's hope that delivering the message to Silver Hawk goes as well. You may want to call Sasha first."

Sasha clicked off the call and went to find Hunter, bags packed. What was with everybody today? Last night's full moon definitely wreaked havoc. Settled? Hell, what was that? The world had gone loco in the last twenty-four hours after months of serenity. Her brother had actually gone to Vegas and gotten married? Good for him, but sheesh.

But it was a great conversation opener, regardless—that is, if she could find Hunter and get him to sit down and have breakfast with her. She wasn't surprised that he'd left the cabin, just thoroughly disappointed. She dropped the duffel bag on the living-room floor with a thud, went out on the porch, and then leaned her head back and released a long, mournful howl.

For the first time that she could remember, her personal life was fully eclipsing a mission. This had to stop and it had to stop right now. Before, when she was in uniform, she had personal shit going on, but somehow having the uniform on kept her head on task. Now, with this new unfettered entrepreneurialism, finding a rudder was harder than she'd imagined. Where was the structure? Where was the brass that she had to report to? Where were the rules and regs to keep her on point? Everything that she'd once hated and had felt onerous was now feeling like a loss of control. Now she was the brass. Now she set the schedule and all of the rules of engagement. Damn.

Maybe once she stopped by the sidhe she'd go speak to Colonel Madison, just to give him a heads-up about the possible storm heading his way. Going to the NAS would be familiar. It would be good to get her feet firmly planted on a military base again. Would be good to see fellow soldiers. Maybe some of that would click her psyche into gear.

When Hunter didn't respond, she released another forlorn howl. All of this was such a waste of valuable time! More than anything, she hated that he'd been right. She also hated that this unspoken thing between her and Shogun even existed. The scarier part of it all was neither she nor Shogun had a clue as to how to make it go away. But one thing was for sure: Neither of them would act on it. That's what she repeatedly told herself. It was her mantra. It was a pledge. She loved and respected Hunter too much to go there. That was what had infuriated her, the insinuation that there was more to the story than she'd already divulged and that there may be some hint of impropriety just because of the phase of the moon.

Sasha released a hard sigh and then turned to go back into the cabin to gather her duffel, but something gave her pause. It was an eerie feeling preceded by an unidentifiable scent and a glimpse of something that flashed by her peripheral vision. The hair instantly rose on the back of her neck and along her forearms. Something clear had shot by her, almost as though the translucent form were a heat wave of some sort. Then it was gone.

"Hunter!" Her voice gave in to panic as she leaped off the porch and ran headlong toward the tree line. "Hunter!"

She saw him part the underbrush in his wolf form, a few seconds from a shape-shift. Standing three feet at the shoulders, he bounded out of the dense foliage, massive canines bared. His glossy velvet black coat was bristled and his eyes were angrily glowing amber. She didn't even have to ask. He'd seen it, too. She knew it; she felt it.

"What was it?" she asked as he shifted back into his human form.

"I don't know." Hunter looked behind him off into the distance. "I came out on the porch to cool off, and then I saw something out of the corner of my eye. It felt dark. Evil. And I knew it had no business being anywhere near the cabin or my mate." He turned and looked at her. "So I went after it, but it was invisible. . . . I could only track it by scent and through sensing. I had to come out of my human to do that."

Sasha nodded. "Let's get you some clothes and then head to Sir Rodney's. Vacation is over."

"Yeah, it definitely is."

It had been so long since she'd shadow-traveled that the first few seconds of doing so were disorienting. Hunter had said it was like riding a bike, but he'd been going in and out of shadow paths all of his life. This was still relatively new to her by comparison. Two months of serenity that was only interrupted by bursts of hot passion didn't prepare her for the feeling of vertigo that stepping into a shadow and racing through mist-filled caverns created. When they came out on the other side, Sasha clutched her large amber ward that dangled from a silver chain.

"Take two deep breaths and breathe into the amulet," Hunter said, stepping closer to her and placing his hands on her shoulders to ground her.

She just nodded with her eyes closed, feeling slightly nauseous, and let her duffel bag drop to the swamp grass. "Remind me to do a few shadow jumps before we engage an enemy target."

"I'll definitely do that," Hunter said, picking up her duffel and hoisting it on his shoulder with his backpack. "Once we leave the Sidhe, we should do a practice run through the bayou on the way to the French Quarter. I don't like how you look." He touched the side of her face with his fingers, gently stroking it. "You're perspiring, but your skin is cool."

Sasha dabbed her forehead with the back of her wrist. She did feel clammy, but once a soldier always a soldier, and she wasn't about to allow a little bout of the dry heaves take her off mission. She'd already gotten delayed enough, and now with something weird stalking her and Hunter she didn't have time to worry about all of that.

"I'll be all right. It's just the change from New Hampshire's morning frost to the Louisiana heat, and then throw in the shadow-travel distortion."

Hunter nodded but didn't seem convinced as he leaned his head back and released a howl to Sir

Rodney's Fae archers. Within moments they appeared high in the treetops with a friendly wave.

"Glad to see ya, laddie," one archer said, giving them a nod. "Sir Garth has been pacing the floors waiting on your arrival."

"We came as soon as we could," Sasha hedged. "Last night—"

"Was a full moon," another guard said, nudging one of his buddies with his elbow and making him smile.

"It was also inadvisable to travel at night, if there were Vampire hostilities going on in the region," Hunter said, giving the smiling archers a deadpan expression.

"Of course, of course," the lead archer said, retaining his good nature and sounding unconvinced. "Follow us."

Sasha let it drop and simply trudged along following the archers as they deftly leaped from tree branch to tree branch. It was a graceful aerial display that had to be the envy of every squirrel, but it was dizzying to watch as full-grown men jumped distances that were surreal and landed on limbs that shouldn't have held the weight of a bird.

Finally they stopped and turned to look at Sasha and Hunter. The lead archer took aim and then shot an arrow into what looked like dense foliage. But the moment the silver-tipped weapon hit its mark the entire Sidhe came into view, including its golden cobblestone path.

"Welcome to Forte Inverness, as always, my friends."

"Thank you," Sasha said, suddenly feeling the comfort of the familiar.

"Go fetch Sir Garth," the lead archer said to a subordinate, sending the young man scurrying toward the lowering drawbridge. "Meanwhile, come in and rest yourselves. 'Ave some ale and bread. I know he'll want to brief you before ye meet the king."

The thought of Fae ale on an empty stomach with bread to soak up the alcohol was surely going to make her hurl. However, the offer of hospitality was too genuine to ruin with particulars and requests. So rather than protest, she and Hunter just offered nods along with noncommittal smiles as they followed their exuberant host.

As expected, nothing had changed. The sidhe still looked like it probably had for the last several hundred years or more. Once past the drawbridge and closer into the center of town, the lively Seelie Fae community was bustling in what looked like a medieval open-air marketplace. Irritable Gnome vendors hawked everything from vegetables to pheasants, magical housewares, and all manner of garments. Small Pixie children dodged between the stands, causing adults to fuss as they chased after the multicolored Fairies that looked like iridescent fireflies. Cheerful Brownies called out, trying to lure Sasha and Hunter to their stands to sample tempting treats, while Elves worked hard at craftsman stands, creating unicorn horseshoes for the palace cavalry.

The long walk to the palace did Sasha good.

Here the air felt balmy and the breeze was welcomed. Sasha looked up with awe. No matter how many times she visited Sir Rodney's magical castle, the sight of it always stole her breath for a few seconds. Griffin Dragons circled the upper castle turrets that were so high they actually pierced the clouds. It never eased to amaze her how he'd created this piece of Scotland in the middle of the Louisiana bayou, below sea level at that, but with all of the trappings of the emerald highlands.

As soon as she and Hunter entered the castle courtyard, a familiar retinue of palace guards came out to warmly greet them.

"You're a sight for sore eyes, and have come none the sooner," a guard said, passing the word along the ranks to fetch Sir Garth.

"Glad to be here, as always," Hunter said, clasping the guard's forearm in an old-world warrior greeting.

"Ale and bread for our visitors!" an archer called out.

"Nay," Garth said, mysteriously appearing on the front steps. "These be wolves, laddie. Fresh-grilled meat to go with a lager."

"I stand corrected," the younger man said, his cheerful voice ringing out as he bowed to Garth. "This is why you are now in better hands."

"Indeed," Garth said, and then stepped in closer to speak more confidentially. "Please, come with me. You'll be refreshed from your journey, but we don't have much time. This is a delicate matter. You came here on your own volition, understand?"

Sasha and Hunter both nodded.

"Don't worry," she said. "We get it."

CHAPTER 6

Normally she wasn't one to turn down magick-grilled-to-perfection Fae meat and mead, but for some reason the smell of steak and ale made her want to hurl. Discreetly pushing the large stein away from her, she picked at her plate while Garth filled them in on the details.

"You gonna eat that?" Hunter asked, not waiting for her reply before cutting a huge hunk of rare sirloin off her plate and gratefully accepting her ale.

Sir Garth never missed a beat in his conversation as he paced around his dungeon magick workshop with his hands clasped behind his back. It was virtually impossible to keep her eyes on the small, ancient Gnome and eat at the same time. His elliptical movements around the room were giving her motion sickness.

"So you see the delicate nature of this endeavor," Garth said, and then stopped to close his eyes so tightly that his bushy white brows knit in the center as one.

"We get it," Hunter mumbled with his mouth full. "Sir Rodney cannot lose face with his subjects or his lover. . . . Thus we cannot accuse her of fraud—lest we lose a friend for life. But he also cannot afford to ally with Queen Cerridwen, if she is playing him."

"Nor can he afford to go to war with the Vampires over some bull that he wasn't even involved in."

"I love the way of the wolf," Garth said, now staring at them both with bug eyes. "Simplistic. Honest. Practical. Yes. That is what we are endeavoring to be here in the Sidhe—practical. But we cannot ever have it appear that we are attempting to undermine our monarch. . . . That is the last thing we would do. His top advisors have all sworn a blood oath."

"No offense, but didn't the last castle insider who betrayed him swear loyalty?" Sasha shrugged. "I'm not trying to be funny. . . . I'm just saying."

Garth frowned. "True, and after that we all created an irreversible spell that would explode a liar from the inside out if they ever tried to do anything but help Sir Rodney. When we say 'blood oath' here in the Sidhe, we mean it."

"My bad," Sasha said, impressed.

"Totally," Hunter said through a swig of ale. "All right, now that that's settled, we should talk to Rodney—that is, if he's, uh, available yet?"

"We'll rouse His Majesty," Garth replied, seeming annoyed at the situation. "Rupert can get him to receive guests."

Sasha gave Hunter a look. "Maybe I should be the one to explain our sudden, unexpected visit."

"I don't care who leads the conversation, but why—"

"I don't have silver in my aura like Hunter," Sasha admitted, cutting off Garth's question. "Normal Shadow Wolves can't, well . . . bend the truth. If they do, it's easily detectable in the silver energy of their auras. I was genetically engineered. I don't have the same limitation."

"Oh . . . ," Garth said quietly, looking from Sasha to Hunter. "Then, by all means, please lead the dance, milady."

It was not the kind of thing one wanted to admit in front of one's mate, especially if there were pending issues regarding the veracity of one's claims that nothing was going on with Shogun. She already knew that this lack of a silver truth barometer in her aura was going to come up in a future conversation with Hunter, but she couldn't worry about all of that now. What was paramount was protecting Garth's position within the sidhe and finding out whatever she could on Sir Rodney's behalf for his own good.

Monitoring the subtle tension in Hunter's stride as they left Garth's private chambers to head to the Roundtable Room, Sasha let her shoulders slump. Why was her life a series of extremes, either really jacked up or passionate euphoria? The ping-pong between those two states of being made her head hurt. She could just do even keel and dull right about now.

"I'll return with Rupert," Garth said, ushering them past the palace guards and into the huge state room. He waited until the massive round table pushed out a chair to receive Sasha, and then hustled back toward the door. "Please rest yourselves. Hopefully, we will return to you before too long."

The moment the door closed behind Garth, Sasha's attention snapped toward Hunter. "Before you say it, let me tell you the answer is 'no.'"

"I didn't have a question." Hunter crossed the room and went to stare out the window, giving her his back.

"Yeah, you did. I'm just saying that even though I don't have silver in my aura, I never lied to you about Shogun, okay?"

"This is neither the time nor place, Sasha. Besides, there are larger issues to consider."

"It's because there are larger issues that I want to get this out of the way, all right?" She pushed herself away from the table and dragged her fingers through her hair. "Listen, okay, I admit it, there was a time when something could have happened. But here's the important fact—it didn't. And it will never happen. Period. I know that. He knows that. You need to know that."

"I accept whatever happens, Sasha. I can't be your warden."

"First of all, that is probably the first lie you've ever told me. You do not accept any of this and I don't expect you to. Second of all, you can't be my warden and don't have to be . . . but if you are going to let Shogun's wistfulness for what could have been but what isn't jack your head around every time you see him sooner or later you guys are going to get into a confrontation that will forever change your relationship. I know you well enough to know you don't want that."

Hunter let out a long breath and continued to stare out the window. "No, I don't want that. But just like there are some stirrings in your gut that you cannot let go, then you must respect that there are some stirrings in mine that are not so easy to eliminate."

This time she fell mute. What the man said was too true. Her lack of an immediate answer made him turn around and finally capture her gaze.

"You're right. I accept that and respect that." She didn't look away, blink, or stutter when she answered him. "Just remember one thing: No matter what you feel or perceive . . . remember that I love you."

Hunter drew a breath as though about to reply, but the large oak double doors opened. Advancing ahead of Rupert and Garth, Sir Rodney strode into the room beaming.

"Welcome! You two are a sight for sore eyes! What a great surprise. What brings you? Not that you don't have a standing invitation."

For a moment Sasha and Hunter glanced at each other, and then she swallowed a smile.

"It's great to see you as always, Sir Rodney . . . uh, you look well."

Hunter cleared his throat.

"I am well," Sir Rodney said, gesturing broadly with his hands. "And you?"

"We are adequate," Hunter said carefully.

"Oh, come on, old buddy—you are more than adequate with a beauty the likes of Sasha as your mate." Sir Rodney laughed at his own joke and went over to fully embrace Hunter, who seemed slightly uncomfortable. "Now, really, what brings you to sidhe?"

"We have a bit of distressing news," Sasha hedged, making Sir Rodney's smile wane. "We've heard that Vampire graves have been daylight exposed, and just this morning Hunter and I saw something . . . well, not exactly saw something but rather felt something invisible lurking near. It didn't feel friendly. All of that spells danger where I'm from."

"Really. . . ." Sir Rodney backed away from Hunter and rubbed his jaw with the flat of his palm. "That's not good at all."

"No. It's not," Hunter said in a low rumble.

"We came to warn you," Sasha chimed in. "If they think we were all involved, and you know for a fact that we were not, it could kick off a war."

"Then we need to investigate," Sir Rodney said quickly. "They already think it was Cerridwen, and she is innocent."

Sasha cut a glance toward Hunter. "Well . . . maybe we can do a little digging on everyone's behalf. Do the Vampires know you've allied with the queen?"

Sir Rodney frowned. "What makes you believe

that I've allied with Cerridwen?" He drew himself up and sent an accusatory gaze around the room toward his staff.

Sasha shrugged. "Just making the assumption because you've already concluded that she's innocent, even though the Vamps beg to differ. Plus, knowing your chivalry, one can only assume that you won't allow her to come under attack if you strongly believe she's done no harm."

"Aye," Sir Rodney said, visibly relaxing and causing the rest of his staff to breathe again. "You see why I say that you are more than adequate, Hunter. With a mate as gorgeous as she is sharp, how can a man have a care in the world?"

"My worry," Hunter said slowly, "is that tonight there will be blood and we have a very small window of opportunity to find out who actually attacked them and then the more difficult task will be to get credible word to them."

"What if that invisible thing that lurked around our cabin was some sort of succubus or incubus trying to gather intel for the Vamps during the day?" Sasha looked from Sir Rodney to Hunter. "It felt seriously dark. I don't know what it was, but I do know that it was watching us and we hadn't felt anything like that for the whole time we were up in New Hampshire."

"The fact that it saw us up in New Hampshire is possibly the only thing that might keep the Vampires from believing that the wolf federations were involved in their grave lettings . . . but to be safe, you might want to tell your local Fae populations to batten down the hatches." Hunter stared at Sir Rodney. "That is just wisdom, and I would do so before nightfall."

Sir Rodney glanced at Garth and Rupert. "Send out a call back to the Sidhe to our local Fae. They are right."

Garth and Rupert bowed and withdrew from the room, their eyes offering a silent thanks to Sasha and Hunter.

"Even though this isn't your fight," Sir Rodney said, his tone now more subdued, "and you most likely will not be blamed . . . we could use your support in helping us find out what's going on."

"In for a penny, in for a pound," Sasha said as they made their way toward the NAS.

"I don't like it," Hunter said. "Even though we're sworn allies of Rodney's, all of this feels like an ambush."

"I know. But I've got to warn Madison. If these guys start gunslinging magick in the middle of the streets again, then we've gotta do something to protect the human population there." Sasha blew out a long breath as they approached the guard shack on foot. "First order of business, though, is to move my team to the best and closest military facility."

"Agreed."

Digging in her back jeans pocket, Sasha produced her wallet and ID for the young soldier in the guard shack. "We need to get an escort to Colonel Madison's office to meet with him on an urgent matter."

"Is he expecting you, ma'am?" The young guard studied her ID and then looked at Hunter with a steely glare until he produced his wallet and showed his contractor ID.

"No," Sasha said with a weary sigh, "but he will definitely want to see us."

"I should be glad to see you, Captain," Colonel Madison said, standing behind his polished walnut desk. "But when you show up on my doorstep unannounced and with urgent news, I'm never sure if I should immediately start loading a sidearm or call Washington."

"Maybe both, sir," she said, feeling an odd sense of comfort that he'd greeted her by her former rank, totally ignoring her retired status.

The colonel nodded at Hunter and extended a handshake in Hunter's direction. It was another first, and she watched Hunter step forward seeming a little taken off guard by the unusually warm gesture.

"Please, have a seat," Colonel Madison said, motioning toward the two leather chairs in front of his desk. "What's the sit-rep?"

Sasha and Hunter sat, but Hunter simply looked at her to do the explaining. "All right," she said, blowing out a long breath. "We've received intel that the Vampires have experienced daylight grave invasions, making them additionally paranoid and aggressive. They believe that the Fae are the culprits, even though the Fae claim that they had nothing to do with it—and the wolves are innocent bystanders, simply old allies of the Fae. But we have reason to believe that there will be retaliation in the near future from the Vampires, which could spill over into the local human population. I may also need to temporarily put my team out here at the Naval Air Station to keep them out of harm's way."

Colonel Madison's walnut-hued complexion turned ashen as he stared at Sasha. "Then what can we do? If we start blowing away Vamps, they'll come after innocents for sure." Panic was evident in the colonel's eyes as he searched for answers.

"That's why this is only an advisory update," Sasha said, glancing between the colonel and Hunter. "If we can investigate quickly and get word to the Vampires that the Fae were not involved in this, then it might make them hold off for a little while. The one thing I am sure of is they know humans weren't so crazy as to go busting into vamp graves . . . or at least let's hope not."

"If they had been, they'd be dead already," Hunter said in a blasé tone. "Humans are easy to track from their sweat scent and any adrenaline in their bloodstream. So if it was a bunch of wannabe Vampire hunters or idiot college kids on a dare, that would have been addressed with the first grave that got hit. Therefore, if humans stay out of the way, then they won't be in immediate peril."

"So, what do we do—declare martial law again and make people stay indoors at night?" Colonel

Madison looked from Hunter to Sasha and then stood, unfolding his athletic six-foot-three body from the chair to begin pacing. "If we do that, it'll start a panic. If we do that, all the media and crazies that are still down here trying to corroborate the existence of supernaturals will stay and it'll undo all of the public sanitization we accomplished after the last debacle. I'd have to contact the Joint Chiefs to get clearance to do that, and right now all we have is speculation."

Sasha and Hunter stood. "I realize that, sir," she said, stepping away from the desk. "We'll stay in close communication, but we wanted you to know."

Hunter nodded. "Our goal is to investigate, get word to the Vamps, and try to keep human civilians out of harm's way."

"Thank you," Colonel Madison said, looking at both of them. "But just to be on the safe side, we'll get more boots on the ground with anti-Vamp weaponry in the highly populated areas, with orders to protect civilians and clear the streets of pedestrians in the event of open warfare."

CHAPTER 7

"That went well," Sasha said in a sarcastic tone as they walked into a shadow on the base. "I think the man ages five to ten years every time he sees us."

"He didn't look well at all when we left, but there was no other way but to deliver the facts."

"Yeah, but remember when we met him? He wasn't gray at all. Now he's really salt-and-pepper."

Hunter shrugged. "It could be worse. It could have all fallen out from the shock or he could be on the verge of howling at a full moon. Remember, he was passed over and left alive by a demon-infected Were."

Sasha just shook her head as they walked deeper into the misty shadow path. "One day I'll have to deliver that cheerful tidbit of information to the man over a beer."

A slow smile crept into Hunter's expression and it lifted her spirits. It was the first time she'd seen him smile since they'd woken up and started the day.

"Okay, you're the master tracker," she said as

they came out of a shadow cast by a huge shade tree behind the team house. "How do we find something invisible that cruised us, and more important, how do we gather new information from a Vampire crime scene that's already been thoroughly trampled through by the Vampires?"

Hunter shrugged. "Why don't we ask them?"

Sasha placed both hands on her hips. "Be serious."

"I am being serious."

She looked at Hunter hard, but then her attitude softened as he nonchalantly began walking toward the front of the house. "That is genius."

Hunter turned and looked at her for a moment. Everything about him seemed calm, and he spoke as though his suggestion were the most rational thing in the world.

"If one has nothing to hide, Sasha, then it stands to reason that one can go in as a neutral party and simply state the facts—we heard there were crimes committed against the Vampire Cartel. That is a fact. Peace in the region is in every group's best interest. That is also undeniable truth. We do not support any group being attacked without cause, even if they are our allies. Very simply, the way of the wolf. We also have reason to believe the Fae whether the good Seelie or the bad Unseelie were not involved, even though we cannot prove it at this time. Also a fact. We can offer to help investigate as neutral parties, especially if it can avert the unnecessary waste of resources and lives. Humans caught in the cross fire are expensive collateral damage and could bring in the human military, which is already panicked and prone to extremes. That is in no one's best interest. The Vampires know this, even if they don't admit it to us. They can reject the concept of us investigating, but the question will linger long enough to maybe buy us enough time to learn more."

"And you just came up with this out of thin air?" Sasha folded her arms, amazed.

"No. I'd been thinking about it all along . . . ever since whatever I'd chased eluded me back at the cabin."

"But you never said anything."

Again he shrugged. "I don't speak until I've fully formulated my opinion or theories."

She tried not to smile and only narrowed her gaze. For the sake of peace she'd let the quiet dig slide. " 'Nuff said."

"Okay, this is freaky," Clarissa whispered, pressing her nose to the porch window.

Bradley rang the doorbell again. "This is the fifth psychic's tarot house we've been to and nobody's home? Is there a psychic convention in California or something that we didn't hear about?"

"Not likely, and if there was, I would have heard about it."

Bradley looked at her. "Yeah, but then why didn't you pick up on this resource outage?"

"I don't know," Clarissa said quietly. "I should have felt it, especially if all the area psychics were panicked enough to leave town or go underground.

Something is really wrong with this picture." She turned away from the window and stared at Bradley. "Better stated, something really big and really bad is about to go down. That doesn't require telepathy to figure out."

"Just come home, Son," Doc said, and then glanced around the empty lab. "We'll figure out a way to make this all work."

"You aren't disappointed?" Crow Shadow's question lingered between the two men like a third party on the cell phone with them.

"I wish we could have talked about all of this before it happened," Doc said, carefully choosing his words. "But now that it is what it is, we have to figure out the best way to bring Jennifer and the baby into the pack."

"I thought you'd be a little more welcoming, *Dad,* since you've been through this yourself."

Doc released a long breath and coaxed patience into his tone. "I am, as you young people like to say, being real. If she freaks out and ultimately cannot handle what she learns, she becomes a security risk to the entire North American clan. If she stays and a war breaks out—something that could be in the offing and too sensitive to get into detail about over the telephone—your new bride could be severely injured or worse, if our location is discovered. So don't read my hesitancy in congratulating you as some form of prejudice. Frankly, because I've lived through this, I'm worried. I also know that's what's going to be a concern for Silver Hawk and the other elders. What's more is, I worry about the future. I worry that my grandchild may come out with the same disability I have—the inability to shape-shift into his or her wolf. Then that child will know the pain that I've known all my life. That, Son, will break my heart."

"I'm sorry, Pop," Crow Shadow said in a subdued tone. "You didn't deserve that earlier crack. . . . I've been thinking about everything you said, too. Maybe that's why I'm stressing."

"Just come home," Doc replied, and then stood to go to the door. He could feel Sasha near. "You fly your ass in well before nightfall, and if you can't do that you and Jennifer and Bear get to hallowed ground and stay there until morning, even if you've gotta go find a church mission or a shelter and spend the night. You hear me?"

"Is it that bad . . . what's actually going on?"

"Yes, it's that bad," Doc replied, now looking out the window at Sasha and Hunter as they rounded the house. "And God only knows what's going on. But trust me, whatever it is, it isn't good."

Even though she and Hunter could have easily entered the house through a shadow, Sasha rang the bell. There was no need to accidentally get shot if nerves were jumpy. But thankfully the nausea had subsided.

Doc opened the door before she could draw her hand away from the bell. "Good to see you. The world has gone crazy in the last twenty-four hours."

He pulled Sasha into a hug and reached around her back to clasp Hunter's hand. "And I'm really glad to see you."

"Likewise," Hunter said, ushering the three-some into the house. "We could all use a dose of your wisdom at a time like this."

"Fresh out," Doc said, shaking his head. "Silver Hawk is on his way. Bear and Crow are coming in from Vegas with complications."

"I heard," Sasha said, jamming her hands in her back jeans pockets. "Where's the rest of the team?"

Doc glanced between Sasha and Hunter. "Clarissa and Bradley went to try to pick up intel from any psychics in the area, and no dice. Everyone they tried and had previous contacts with was gone. It's like all of the New Orleans tarot houses and palm readers simply skipped town. Winters went with Woods and Fisher to try to see if they could get any info from the graveyards, but based on the last call I got from them, everything was cleaned up and locked up tight as though there'd never been a grave invasion."

"Figures," Sasha said, beginning to pace. "The Vamps are really private and will handle it with their own brand of justice." She stopped walking and stared at Doc. "Which is why I want you all to hunker down at NAS. I've already made arrangements with Colonel Madison for you guys to go there just like the old days when we were part of the Paranormal Containment Unit—and if I had enough time, I'd be sure you guys went back to

NORAD . . . but there's not enough time for that today. But tomorrow, first light, you guys are—"

"Whoa, whoa," Doc said, gesturing with his hands. "Our job is to work as a team to avert any human catastrophes as a result of paranormal activity. So how do you expect us to make that happen sitting in Denver?"

"I'm thinking selfishly," Sasha said in a quiet tone. "I'm thinking like a civilian, and I want our families out of the hot zone. I admit it."

"And I agree with her," Hunter said, lifting his chin. "If I could coax Sasha to go to Denver with you and get her to stay at that huge underground human facility until all of this was sorted out, I would. But you and I both know Sasha well enough to know she won't do that." Hunter gave her a pointed look with a sad half smile. "So, the best I can do is support her decision to try to keep her family out of harm's way. Her family is my family; her people are my people."

"You've discussed all of this with Silver Hawk?" Doc looked between Sasha and Hunter again.

"No," Hunter admitted. "But when he arrives, I will."

"I see the two months away from the team did you both well . . . as far as strengthening the mate bond," Doc said, sounding slightly peeved. "You've clearly already made up your minds."

"We have." Sasha walked over to her father and hugged him. "I don't know why, but something about this feels more . . . I don't know . . . more dangerous than before, and I just want all of you away from it."

Doc held her tightly and released a weary sigh. "And me and Silver Hawk want to make sure that the two people we love most in this world survive. We're both old wolves. You hold the future of the pack, of the clan, of the way of the North American Shadow Wolf. Beyond all of that, you're still my only daughter."

Sasha and Hunter stepped out of a shadow behind the Blood Oasis club. For a moment they said nothing as they sized up the seemingly deserted building. The instant the sun went down the establishment would spring to life—or into living death, as the case may be. But they weren't so foolish as to believe that the premier Vampire blood club in the area was vacant. There would be lower-level Vampires in the building as security forces, as well as human guards. The question was how did one leave a message for the club owners by day without breaching security and risking getting one's head blown off?

Turning to Hunter, she searched his troubled expression for an answer. "Thanks for having my back with Doc," she said, and then glanced at the building. "Entrance strategy?"

"I meant what I'd said. I wish you weren't here right now, Sasha . . . with all my soul I wish you weren't."

The tone of his voice and the level of quiet

urgency it contained stunned her. They'd been through so many battles together and had experienced so many near misses, but she couldn't recall ever hearing outright fear in Hunter's voice until now.

"Baby, what's wrong?" She touched his arm and was surprised that he pulled her against his stone-cut chest in a protective stance and then nuzzled her hair as his gaze swept the terrain.

"I don't know," he murmured. "All I am sure of is that every sense within me registers a threat to you. I want you gone, Sasha. After we go in here and speak to the Vampire Cartel's human helpers, I don't want you on the hunt with me when the sun goes down. Not this time. Don't ask me why, because I haven't one logical reason to give you. It's just my gut. Go to NAS. Please."

She looked up and cradled his cheek with one palm. "I've never, ever heard you sound like this, Hunter . . . but you know that I can't leave you and just go sit at NAS waiting for word. I'll lose my mind."

He briefly closed his eyes and then nodded. "I already knew the answer, but I had to at least try." Glancing around, he motioned with his chin toward a long shadow by the door. "Take cover there. I'll try to raise a human from the interior and hopefully we'll get one to deliver a message."

Grudgingly she agreed and stood near the shadow while Hunter banged on the door.

"We come in peace!" Hunter called out. "The

North American Shadow Clan needs to speak to your leadership."

Within seconds the sound of a click made her and Hunter dive for the long shadow. Just as Hunter pulled his legs into it a pump shotgun blast shattered a small side window. Moving swiftly, they came out of the shadow inside the club's foyer. Hunter had the human shooter in a headlock as Sasha stripped him of his weapon. She spun on a rustle behind her and pointed dead aim at a shadow.

"Drop it. We came in peace," she said, quickly cocking the pump for another blast. "We've got an important message for your bosses."

"Tell the man to walk out slowly with his weapon above his head or he'll be wolf carrion when the Vampires find his body tonight," Hunter growled, allowing the security guard he held to see his canines beginning to extend in his peripheral vision.

"Come out, man!" the security guard finally yelled. "They said they came in peace. Just wanna deliver a message, all right."

After a few tense minutes three guards came out. Each held his weapon at an angle away from Sasha and Hunter but had not disarmed.

"Listen," Sasha said, training the shotgun on the guard who seemed to be their leader. "We heard through the grapevine that some Vampire graves got opened to daylight. We had nothing to do with it. We also heard that your bosses think the Fae were involved—the Unseelie, to be exact. We don't know the full story yet, but our main concern is that war doesn't break out in the streets of New Orleans in a way that could cause a lot of human casualties."

"If you know who we work for, then you know that retaliation is gonna happen," the burly lead guard said, flexing his muscles beneath his black T-shirt. "If you're not involved, then we suggest that you lay low until it's all over."

"Bad move under a bad moon," Hunter said, thrusting the guard he held away from him. He waited until the frightened guard ran over to the others and took cover. "If the Vampires attack the Fae and find out they were wrong, there will be a hundred-year war. You know that; they know it. Therefore, we need you to get a message to your bosses the moment they wake up."

The lead guard cracked a cynical smile. "It doesn't matter what I know or think. I just follow orders. That's how I stay alive."

"Tell them that the wolves are in a rare position to be neutral third parties—that we will be their noses to the ground by day and we'll try to find whatever evidence we can, because the Fae swear they haven't done this." Sasha lowered her weapon and stared at the lead man. "If you don't deliver the message and it's later found out that the leadership from the North American Shadow Wolf Federation came to you to offer a potential negotiation, how long do you think you'll live?"

Hunter smiled. "I may be wrong, but the way I have always heard it, Vampires hate anyone jacking with their negotiations. We are putting a firm offer on the table. We'd like to hear their counteroffer." He backed away holding up both hands in front of his chest. "That is all we came for, no more, no less."

A slow hiss made both Sasha and Hunter turn toward the sound. It was coming from a darkened alcove deep within the club. Two red glowing eyes blinked slowly and then were gone.

"They heard you," the lead guard said. "Now get the fuck outta here!"

CHAPTER 8

"That so did not go well," Sasha said, trudging along the sidewalk. "Now what?"

Hunter stopped and looked off into the distance. "There's got to be some place to start. What are we missing, Sasha?"

"The graveyards and desecrated mausoleums maybe?"

Hunter shrugged. "Couldn't hurt, but what'll be left after the Vampires just did their search and, according to Doc, Woods, Fisher, and Winters, had nothing to report?"

Sasha landed a hand on Hunter's broad back as they continued walking. "I don't know, but I'm hoping the human factor will kick in."

He gave her a puzzled glance and she motioned with her chin toward the homeless milling the streets.

"Humans are creatures of habit. Somebody saw something. Graveyards are a great place to rest and hide when you have nowhere else to go. We just have to hope that any eyewitnesses got out of Dodge with their lives when this all went down during the daylight hours and we can find at least one person with some info."

If it wasn't for Winters's genius on the computer, it could have taken days to find Monroe Bonaventure's grave. New Orleans was a complex series of elaborate aboveground cemeteries. There were just some things, like narrowing down options, that technology easily solved.

"This doesn't look like a place that a homeless person might wander in and sleep during the day without a hassle, Sasha." Hunter glanced around at the well-manicured rolling lawns and detailed landscaping.

"Yeah, I know," Sasha said in a dejected tone. "But a place like this would have groundskeepers and some kind of security to shoo out any vagrants, though." She glanced up, noting the pitch of the sun, and then began jogging. "The administration house should still be open."

As they ran side by side along the paths, she tried to memorize every detail of the cemetery that housed a seriously old Vampire, one strong enough to become a sixth viceroy. What would have made Monroe fear his own mansion and come back to his actual grave? He should have had a well-protected lair and not been forced to go to ground. The older ones rarely did that, only keeping dirt from their original burial site to give them extra power. None of it made sense. But one thing she was sure of, someone at the administration house had to be clued in. Monroe Bonaventure would not have come here without human daytime security. Who was not on the job today would be as important as who was.

Sasha stopped in front of the building and glanced at Hunter. "I want to know who was on shift when the mausoleum was desecrated, and who called out sick today."

"We are thinking as one," he said, loping up the large white steps of what looked like an old plantation house.

She rang the patron's bell and then slowly opened one side of the huge white double doors. Although sunshine brightly lit the interior and the entire place gleamed with lemon-scented furniture polish, an eerie feeling settled into Sasha's bones.

"May I help you?" a heavyset older woman wearing a floral print dress asked. "I am Mrs. Vance, administrator for Golden Estates."

"Yes, ma'am," Sasha replied, using her most polite voice. "We are here to find out what happened to our late relative's grave. . . . We understand from family sources that someone vandalized it yesterday and we've arrived as soon as we could."

The woman raised her eyebrows over the tops of her half-glasses. "You are, uhm, Monroe Bonaventure's relatives?"

"Yes, ma'am," Sasha said, trying not to smile. She dropped her voice and whispered, leaning in. "A lot of family doesn't want it known and we respect that, but family is family and when we heard of what happened here we just wanted to see what we could do to make it right."

"We promise to leave quickly, ma'am," Hunter said, needling the distressed woman. "If we can find out a little more—enough to report back to the family."

Mrs. Vance cleared her throat and nodded, seeming relieved. "Well, yes . . . yes, of course. It was all such a nasty business, but we've replaced the locks and have done what we can to repair any disturbed masonry. Some people are just so sacrilegious and have no respect for the dead."

"Terrible," Sasha said, dramatically placing a hand over her heart. "But could we speak to the groundskeeper who was actually here when the discovery was made?"

"He was so upset that he called out sick after the incident. Poor Mr. Romero has been with us for years and he gave a brief statement to the sheriff and then took ill." The administrator lowered her voice and looked around. "Some around here are very superstitious, and desecrating a grave is considered bad luck. We may well have to go to lengths to coax him back here to work after something like this. But if you'd like to see the progress of the repairs, I can give you the plot coordinates so you can look for yourselves. We can have someone take you out there, if you'd like?"

"Thank you so much," Sasha said, eyeing the building through the large picture window behind the administrator where groundskeepers seemed to be gathered.

"Then please have a seat."

Sasha and Hunter crossed the room and waited as Mrs. Vance made the call. They kept their voices to a low murmur to be sure their conversation couldn't be overheard.

"Romero has to have a locker or something in the groundskeepers' house, wouldn't you think?"

Hunter nodded and spoke in a low, barely audible rumble: "I also don't think one very old man would be the security force for a powerful Vamp. I'm getting weird vibes from this lady, and all the groundskeepers walking toward the building seem like they could double for Marines."

"I feel you," Sasha said, watching as groundskeepers suddenly flanked the building. "Maybe I need to go to the ladies' room and you should walk me, huh?"

Hunter nodded. "Excuse me, ma'am. My wife is a little overwrought by all of this. Would there be a ladies' room where she can splash water on her face?"

Mrs. Vance offered Hunter a tight smile. "Why, yes, of course, poor thing. Just down the hall to your left."

"Come on, honey," Hunter said, lifting Sasha from her chair by the elbow for dramatic effect. "Let's put some water on your face and then we can go see your late cousin's grave, twice removed."

The pair walked down the hall and calmly took the corner and then bolted. Thankfully, the massive plantation-style home was replete with shadows. They slipped into the nearest one cast by the ladies' room entrance and came out inside the groundskeepers' shed and then both stared at each other.

The scent of day-old human blood assaulted their noses. Quickly moving from locker to locker and trying to keep an eye on the windows, Hunter yanked locks off the doors with a quick turn of the wrist while Sasha rifled through the contents.

"Ten bucks says Romero is a dead man," Sasha muttered as she came upon his locker and Hunter yanked it open.

"I'll raise you five," Hunter said, showing her sawed-off shotguns that he'd retrieved from several lockers, along with boxes of silver shells. "If he was on shift when it all happened, either whoever did it killed him or his fellow grave guards did for messing up . . . or maybe the Vamps did."

Sasha held his olive green uniform shirt against her nose for a moment and then looked up at Hunter. "Adrenaline is all in his sweat. This man was freaked out."

"We need to move," Hunter said, his attention jerking toward the door. "Like now!"

The shack door burst open; Sasha and Hunter were gone.

"They came in here!" a grave guard yelled. "We didn't leave all this shit out."

Another grabbed a shotgun. "Comb the grounds; find them. I'm not getting my heart ripped out for nobody. You saw what happened to Romero."

Hands reached for weapons and shells. Boots

thudded against the wooden floor. Sasha held the uniform in her grip tightly, invisibly waiting in the shadows with Hunter until the shack cleared. She dug in the pockets as something crackled within the fabric she clutched. A long rolled-up partial snakeskin fell into her palm and she unfurled it, showing it to Hunter with a puzzled gaze.

"What the hell . . ."

"You owe me fifteen bucks," Hunter said, and then stepped out of the shadow that hid them. "Romero is dead. But what he had in his pocket isn't from an ordinary snake. It smells of sulfur."

"But why would his shirt and boots and work items still be here with this in it?" Sasha continued peering at the strange, translucent skin.

"He was human. If you are going to kill a human that has a day job and pays taxes, you've gotta cover it up, right?"

"Right." Sasha sniffed the skin. "So you'd undress the victim and stash his gear and make it look like he just left work, upset, like it was another day at the job, before you offed him."

"And if you were working in a hurry, you might not notice some evidence he'd collected at the scene." Hunter paused. "Also, what better place to stash a body but in the graveyard, where there are thousands of graves?"

She looked at Hunter. "Yeah, especially if you were trying to blame the breach all on one man to save your asses from the vamps." She spun around in a circle. "Damn. All we've got to go on is a snakeskin, which might just be a talisman that has nothing to do with what Romero saw, and a funky shirt. This sucks. But maybe it's something we can take to the lab and have Clarissa or Bradley do more research on."

"Agreed. Let's get out of here. Both Vamps and their human helpers have obviously ruined the investigation scene, and have even put the mausoleum back together."

"But . . ." Sasha looked around the shadowy locker room. "Dammit. Sunset will be in just a couple of hours and we've literally run around all day and have accomplished nothing."

"Not true," Hunter said, guiding her into a shadow. "We've put an offer on the table for the Vampires to consider—"

"Or laugh at."

"And we've alerted the human military . . . and we've called in our family to a safe base." Hunter smoothed her hair back from her face as they stood in the sanctuary of the shadow path mist. "Sometimes, Captain, a good retreat is the most logical strategy at the moment."

"Can you identify this as a talisman or a ward . . . or even tell what kind of snake this is from?" Sasha held out the skin to Clarissa and Bradley and then gently laid it down on the long lab table while the rest of the team gathered around.

"Where did you get something like this, Sasha?" Clarissa said, backing away from it as Bradley leaned in closer, inspecting the partial skin with a large magnifying glass.

"It doesn't have the markings of any regional snake I know." Bradley looked up. "What I mean is, the scale pattern is uncommon; look at the depressions in the—"

"Don't touch it," Clarissa said, grabbing his arm. "Nobody touch it."

"We got it from one of the grave guards' shirt—a guy we presume is dead," Hunter said, his gaze fixed on Clarissa.

"We think this guy either had it on him as some kinda juju or maybe collected it at the scene, but obviously never got to tell anybody who cared to hear about it." Sasha looked from Hunter to Clarissa. "You're freaking me out, 'Rissa."

Doc moved around the table, keeping his hands back but peering at the specimen closely. "Whatever it is, it came from a huge snake. This is only a partial, but if you extrapolate the size of the scales . . . man."

"You give me a diameter and I can run a model to size the thing," Winters said, heading toward his temporary computer bay. "I wish we'd had a little more time to get set up here at the NAS, but if you guys are tracking giant snakes, then I'm all for the move of being on a military base."

Woods pounded Fisher's fist. "Dude, just tell me and Fish how big that sucker is and we'll be sure to get artillery that can handle it."

"Dude," Fisher said, shaking his head. "I love this job, but remind me to tell you over a beer how much I hate this job."

"It's not from a normal snake," Clarissa said, her blond lashes beginning to flutter.

"The size alone says it's not normal!" Winters called out as his fingers flew across the keyboard.

"No," she said quietly. "This came from something that resides in Hell."

"Okay, now I'm officially freaked out," Winters said as he stopped typing.

"You're sure?" Sasha rounded the table and held Clarissa by her shoulders.

Clarissa nodded. "The energy off it is so dark and so thick that I almost can't breathe."

"That's enough," Bradley said, quickly setting down the magnifying glass and going to Clarissa. "She'd been here before and I swore that I would never allow her to get caught up in a dark divination that could jeopardize her life."

"Come out of the trance, Clarissa," Sasha said, beginning to panic as Clarissa swooned.

Doc was immediately at her side and for several minutes team members took turns calling Clarissa's name, shaking her, slapping her cheeks, until she finally came around.

"Get that thing out of here," Bradley said. His face was flushed and his expression was stricken as Hunter carefully lifted up the offending snakeskin and slipped it back into the uniform pocket.

"We need to take this to the Vampires—after we record it in the United Council of Entities Hall of Records," Hunter said. "Sir Rodney and Queen Cerridwen also need to know about this."

"Good looking out," Sasha said, and then stared

at Doc. "See if Silver Hawk can hurry here to seal this area with a shaman's prayer. If me and Hunter just bird-dogged something that came up from Hell, who knows what's gonna happen come sundown."

They stood in the depths of the Louisiana bayou with a full Fae retinue at their sides. Swamp sounds of frogs and crickets went still as the ancient council hall rose from the mud, disturbing gators and other slithering things that moved in the black water. Then they waited for the old crone who presided over all matters as a neutral party to exit the columns and come down the steps. It was a painfully slow process to watch her shuffle along the wet marble with her huge black book of records under her arthritic arm.

She stopped at the bottom step and glared at those who'd called her before the sunset, seeming genuinely perturbed at the breach of protocol.

"Who dares call a session before the moon has arisen?" she croaked, sending an accusatory glare around the group.

"We do—the North American Shadow Wolf Federation," Hunter said, and then motioned with his chin to the book under her arm. "We have evidence that could avert a war, if it is heeded."

"Speak!" the crone yelled out, and then flung the black book into the air.

The book hovered between her and the group and then opened to a blank page, allowing a raven-feathered quill pen to escape its pages with a squeal.

"I am a Shadow Wolf, with full silver aura," Hunter announced. "Therefore, my testimony requires no blood strike from your pen of truth."

"Agreed," the crone said, now seeming more curious than annoyed. "Continue."

"Our allies have been accused of opening Vampire graves to daylight, but they claim that they are innocent. We, the North American Shadow Wolf Federation, went to the Vampires today—to the Blood Oasis—to offer them our assistance in finding out who could have done this. The Southeast Asian Werewolf Federation is a neutral party and is uninvolved at this juncture. Then we went to the scene of the last crime, to the cemetery that once held Monroe Bonaventure, Sixth Viceroy of Cartel Elder Vlad Tempesh."

Hunter held out the snakeskin for the crone to examine before he continued on. "We found this in the Vampire human helper's uniform at Golden Estates, Mr. Romero, who is now deceased and was killed by his own men, we presume. This is all we have at the onset of our investigation, but we are asking the UCE court for more time to investigate before the Vampires are given free rein to retaliate. At this juncture, we need a go-between to keep the peace and to keep the business of the supernatural community beyond the eyes of the already-panicked human population. Open warfare serves no purpose."

"Aye," Sir Rodney said, "especially since we are innocent."

"So they all say," the crone muttered. "But if you

are found guilty of the serious offense of opening Vampire graves to daylight without warrant, there will be no mercy this court can offer. You are aware of the might and reputation of your adversaries."

"That we are," Queen Cerridwen said, lifting her chin. "But this evidence is strange. I have been blamed because the locks were shattered by instant freezing . . . yet what has a serpent skin from Hell to do with my so-called handiwork? Something untoward is amiss."

Grumbles of Fae soldiers' assent filtered throughout the dense foliage and even Garth seemed puzzled as the crone fingered the skin and then held it out for the pen and book to inspect.

"This is a rare artifact, something no human should have had access to—at least not one living." The crone calmly folded the skin up and placed it under the last page of the hovering book. "Let it be entered into the record that the wolves tracked a very interesting bit of evidence that requires much further investigation. I personally haven't seen the skin of an Erinyes wreath in more than a thousand years."

Sasha gave Hunter a quizzical look as the Fae collectively released an audible gasp.

"What's an Erinyes wreath?" Sasha stared at the crone and then her gaze ricocheted around to look at the others.

"It came from a type of group of demons also known as the Furies," Garth said in a hushed tone. "They are kindred to the Gorgons, but countless in number."

"Cousins. The Gorgons have hair made of serpents and turn an onlooker to stone, but the Erinyes have serpent wreaths in their hair . . . bat wings and avenge the anger of the dead," the crone remarked casually, beginning to walk back up the palatial council stairs. She called the book with a snap of her fingers. "One generally does not see those sharing graves or victims with Vampires. Yes, all of this is very curious. You may have a case indeed."

CHAPTER 9

"Okay, WTF?" Sasha walked in an agitated circle as the UCE building sank back down into the swamp and disappeared. "Furies, Erinyes—what's any of that got to do with the Unseelie or with Vampires?"

"WTF?" Queen Cerridwen asked, looking toward Sir Rodney for clarity.

"A colloquial human expression," Sir Rodney replied, smiling, "one that is a bit off-color, but warranted given the circumstances."

"How can you even joke at a time like this? Erinyes may be involved?" Queen Cerridwen paced away. "Do you know how dangerous those entities are? Surely I have done nothing to provoke them."

"Of course not," Sir Rodney said, dismissing the concept with a nonchalant wave of his hand. "But I am smiling because that means there is a shadow of doubt regarding your guilt that the Vampires must take into consideration. The Fae are not the only suspects in this travesty, and our wolf allies have found out something that should give everyone pause."

"Let us hope so," Hunter muttered as he looked up at the waning sun through the heavy canopy of trees. "We have perhaps a half hour of daylight remaining, and it is my strong suggestion that we all take cover until we hear that the Vampires accept a truce during our investigation."

"Couldn't agree more." Sasha whipped out her cell phone and began dialing with all eyes on her. "I'm going to leave a message at the Blood Oasis," she said, waiting for the call to connect to voice mail. As soon as it did, she began speaking. "This is Sasha Trudeau with an urgent message for Elder Vlad. Tell him we found an Erinyes wreath serpent skin at the site of Monroe Bonaventure's mausoleum today and he can check with the grave guards at Golden Estates. They know we were there, since they tried to kill us—just saying. We've also entered the find into the hall of records up here at UCE, so before they blow—"

A Fae archer's scream stopped Sasha's words mid-sentence. The entire group pivoted quickly just in time to see a muscular stone-hued gargoyle rip open the man's chest cavity, spilling vital organs and entrails. Garth pulled out his wand from his robe sleeve in unison with Queen Cerridwen, each respectively sending blasts of white hot light and ice as they ran for cover.

Chaos reigned high in the branches. Fae archers attempted to ward off the gargoyle onslaught with silver-tipped arrows, alternately ducking and then crouching to fire. But the sky darkened with an incalculable number of beasts. Sir Rodney was a blur of Fae motion, leaping into the battle high in the branches, blade drawn to protect his men, and sending up sparkling shield pulses to ward off the aerial attack.

For a few seconds, Sasha and Hunter could only look up at the battle taking place above their heads high in the trees. Then several beasts narrowed their red glowing gazes on Sasha and Hunter, spread their leathery wings, screeched, and dive-bombed toward them with vicious talons outstretched.

In less than the time it took to blink, Sasha and Hunter transformed out of their human forms and into their wolves to leave their clothes pooled on the ground. Oddly, the gargoyles stopped their aerial offensive mid-air and simply screeched at both snarling wolves, then turned to fly off to attack the retreating Fae.

Bounding toward a fallen archer drawn between two gargoyles, the pair of wolves rushed in trying to save him. But it was too late. The moment the hissing creatures saw Sasha and Hunter, they flew off in different directions, ripping the archer in two.

Gore pelted the ground from the air. Sasha's pristine silver coat became matted with blood splatter raining down from the trees as the gargoyles decimated the archers. Hunter moved in and out of the shadows with Sasha like black lightning, his onyx coat wet with Fae blood, their mission to cover Sir Rodney, Garth, and Queen Cerridwen while trees fell from Fae monarch blasts.

Then suddenly the gargoyles pulled back, lifting the darkness from the bayou to allow in the light of the full moon. Five platinum blond Vampire sentries touched down silently, protected by translucent dark energy shields. Their long, flowing tresses lifted off their shoulders from a supernatural source as static fury coursed down their arms and along their billowing black leather coats. Then one dark-haired female Vampire baring fangs slid out of the folds of nothingness to stand by the lead male.

"A message!" the lead Vampire shouted. "Know me as Caleb, the destroyer! I have been sent to deliver word from Elder Vlad."

It was a standoff; the Fae monarchs and Garth held wands at the ready. What was left of the Fae archers took aim at the six Vampires in the clearing. Sasha and Hunter lowered their heads, poised for an attack lunge. The silence was deafening as they waited for the Vampires to speak.

"We have no fight with you, wolves," the female Vampire said, cautiously watching Sasha and Hunter. "That is why our gargoyles pulled back. But if you continue to fight with the Fae, we will take that as an invitation to war."

"Sixty Unseelie Fae have been slaughtered!" Caleb shouted between his fangs, and then tossed the head of one of Queen Cerridwen's guard gnomes to her feet. "Ten for every Vampire viceroy you subjected to daylight invasion until I deliver you to Elder Vlad, dead or alive, milady. Your choice."

"Never!" Sir Rodney shouted, his fingertips beginning to dangerously spark. "We have new evidence entered into the hall of records, and you will owe my queen fifty-four Vampire heads for the archers of the Seelie clans that were unnecessarily slaughtered tonight!"

Caleb hissed and then spit on the ground. " 'Tis truth and a shame that your men were unnecessarily butchered, but that is on your head, however. Were you not allied with *your queen* and had you allowed her to meet justice for her offenses, Seelie Fae lives could have been saved." Caleb turned to the female Vampire at his side. "What say you, Mara? It seems that the Fae have joined forces now and one side is just as culpable as the other, yes? Frankly, I can no longer tell them apart; can you?"

"No, Caleb," Mara said with an angry glare. "The Seelie monarch said 'my queen.' How cozy, how familial . . . how very, very stupid in a time of war and retribution."

Garth cut a worried glance toward Sir Rodney and then the wolves.

"Seems your elderly advisor also finds this folly. Dismay is written all over his wrinkled face. Shame that you have not heeded his counsel," Caleb said with an evil smirk. "No matter. Be ye foolish or wise, sixty Fae will die per night until Elder Vlad is satisfied with his request for *your queen.* We are done for this evening, as we have met our nightly toll from your legions."

"Then tell Elder Vlad this, messenger," Sir Rodney said, boldly walking forward. "The Seelie had no hand in violating his viceroys' graves, nor did the Unseelie. The wolves had no hand in that affair whatsoever, as you know, and I will not involve them as anything more than investigators. We will uncover the truth. We have found evidence of Erinyes at Bonaventure's tomb—"

"Games and falsehoods that any good wizard could produce from a coven's shelves," Mara sneered, staring at Queen Cerridwen. "That is not evidence; it is *a pity* if it is the best you can do."

"My best is beyond your comprehension," Queen Cerridwen said with eerie calm, making the female Vampire back up as ice crusted the ground beneath her feet. "For the price of sixty innocent Fae, there will be blood."

"Make sure you carry our full and allied Fae message back to your cartel!" Sir Rodney shouted. "Vlad is the fool, a madman foaming at the fangs, if he is to believe that we will allow the Fae to be subjected to torment and death without retaliation. There will be no grave deep enough or a night dark enough to hide him from the Fae onslaught that will leave his ancient bones bleached by the sun! Give him that message, faithful dog!"

"Oh, I shall," Caleb said in a dangerous murmur. Then they were gone.

Sasha and Hunter shifted back into their human forms and slowly walked to find their clothes. What was there to say? War had just been declared. The Vampires didn't want to hear jack about possible secondary sources. The Fae were so outraged by the loss of lives tonight that they were beyond reason. Now that the Vampires understood that the Seelie and Unseelie were going to stand as a united front, that meant all the Fae establishments in the center of New Orleans—ones that were blindly frequented by human tourists and locals— would be under attack. And as stubborn as Sir Rodney was once he got a righteous Scottish bee in his bonnet, there'd be no closing a place down for the cause of fear, even if it meant human lives were at risk.

Hunter tossed Sasha her jeans and top, finding their clothing pile first. They said nothing as they dressed and simply listened to the Fae as they gathered their dead and injured.

"We need to help them get to the Sidhe and then warn our people," Hunter said in a flat tone.

Sasha simply nodded without looking at him and then stooped down to tie her boots.

"Oh . . . my . . . God . . ." Clarissa stared at Sasha hang jawed as both Sasha and Hunter filled in the team.

"That's why I need to know everything you can tell me about what a frickin' Erinys is," Sasha said, sending her gaze from Bradley to Winters and then Clarissa. "We need to understand why one would be in a graveyard opening vamp tombs, how they come out, when they come out—"

"How to kill them," Winters added in, staring at his computer screen as he did a database search. "Just sayin'."

"Right. You took the words right out of my mouth, Winters." Sasha looked at Doc and Silver Hawk. "If there's a way to barrier these Erinyes things and gargoyles from establishments in the same way we can keep vamps out with a prayer circle, that would help here as well as at the Fair Lady tavern in town or at Finnegan's Wake, and Dugan's Bed and Breakfast."

Hunter's grandfather nodded and his expression remained calm, set in the leathery wrinkles of his face. Two long silver braids hung down his chest over his plaid flannel shirt and he breathed in slowly and exhaled slowly, as though in a semi-meditative state.

"Daughter, I have already gone to the four corners of this military facility to say chants and send prayers up to the Great Spirit that the plague of war will pass us by, and it seems that my prayers were answered. The wolf clans have been absolved of any violence. But I will make prayers in the daytime for our Fae friends and to protect humans that visit their sites from harm. This will take time, though. They have many businesses and shops. How long do we have before the next Vampire onslaught?"

"We may have, at most, twenty-four hours until the next bloodletting," Hunter said, locking gazes with his grandfather.

"I can accomplish that with Doc," Silver Hawk

replied, gaining a nod of agreement from Sasha's father.

"But Bear Shadow and Crow Shadow should be with you, Grandfather, to protect you as you are sealing a building in prayer. The gargoyles are not bound to the darkness and at dusk they attacked. We have seen what they can do."

"I have advised Bear Shadow and Crow Shadow not to travel here yet by human aircraft," Silver Hawk said quietly. "Especially not Crow Shadow, who now has a human mate who cannot enter the shadow realms. I am an old alpha with shaman sight and can easily navigate the shadow paths. You and Sasha are clan alphas and have the protective amber and silver amulets to keep you from accidentally entering a demon portal while in the realm between worlds. It is best that only a few of our people come here to investigate and that we remain as neutral as possible so that we can learn the truth."

"We can cover them," Woods said. "Me and Fisher may just be so-called familiars, with a little wolf in our DNA, and can't shift or whatever, but we are Delta Force trained and can handle a mean M16, an RPG launcher, and ain't bad on mortars. So if some gargoyle mofos want some action while Silver Hawk is praying around buildings with Doc, we can bring it."

"Much obliged, Lieutenant. It would sure make me feel better to know you and Fish were out there in a Jeep covering our clan elders," Sasha said, dragging her fingers through her hair.

"Roger that. Consider it done," Fisher said, giving Sasha a nod.

"Okay, so whatcha got, Winters?" Sasha walked over to Winters's computer propelled by nervous energy.

"Wikipedia says—"

"Please," Bradley muttered, and then stood to go to the crate of books he'd brought to their temporary lab at NAS. "They are chthonic entities, Greek demons of the underworld. 'The Erinyes' means, quite literally 'the angry ones.'" He flipped open a page in a thick, dusty tome and began reading, "'The Furies are the same creatures, but the Roman version.'"

Looking up, Bradley held the group captive with his minilecture. "They are without number, but the three prominent ones that come to the fore in literature are Tisiphone—who punishes crimes of murder. Her name translates to 'Avenging Murder.' Then there's Megaera, or 'Grudging,' and Alecto, 'The Unceasing.' They go after those who have sworn a false oath, if they have been called. To call them requires a ritual sacrifice, a live victim, that must be placed in a megaron—a sunken chamber—where they rip the sacrifice to shreds and eat it alive. "

"Great, Brads." Sasha blew a damp curl up off her blood-splattered forehead, wanting a shower in the worst way. "So, we've possibly got an avenging, grudge-holding, unceasing crew of very angry demon bitches in the mix to contend with—ya gotta love it."

"If we can figure out which one was called or, better yet, who called it, maybe we can find out who's targeting our local Vampire population." Doc looked around the group and let his gaze settle on Clarissa. "Between you, me, and Silver Hawk, we ought to be able to do some sort of divination."

"No," Sasha said before Bradley could open his mouth to protest. "The Vampires always lie, so they could have sworn a false oath that pissed anybody off from an average tarot card reader to the Devil himself. Until we know how far and deep this goes, I don't want anybody trying to do a divination on a creature that is some kind of avenging demon, all right."

"Sheesh," Winters muttered. "You don't have to tell us twice."

"But that's probably why the Vampires didn't want to hear our findings. They damn well must know what one of these creatures is, and may simply believe Queen Cerridwen conjured it up from the depths."

Sasha stared at Hunter's dirty face, loving him even more for the way his shrewd mind worked. "Which has to be why they want her brought to Elder Vlad, preferably alive. Now that I think about it, their gargoyles didn't seem to be trying to kill her out in the swamp. They just circled her and Rodney like birds of prey, swooping and diving, making them hunker down while they slaughtered their soldiers. They didn't even go after me, you, or Garth."

Hunter nodded. "It is all very curious."

"Yeah, well, it certainly makes sense why all the local psychics went into hiding. If the Vampires are looking for human diviners, those with a soul who can connect with one of these things and figure out who called it up, I'd take down my shingle for a couple weeks, too—at least until all of this blows over." Bradley glanced at Silver Hawk. "So, can you add some extraspecial barriers around Clarissa . . . just in case?"

"It is done, now that I understand the enemy we face." Silver Hawk folded his arms over his chest and closed his eyes.

"What say we go check out the local black-magic covens?" Sasha said, looking at Hunter. "They may be shady, but they are human and the Vampires must have gone to them, right?"

Hunter rubbed his jaw and frowned. "Yes, so why would the normal psychics go into hiding, then?"

"Yeah, true." Sasha let out a hard breath and slumped against the wall. "Shit."

"When you debriefed us, didn't you say that the locks were frozen and then shattered, which is how whoever got into the crypts to open them?" Winters glanced between Sasha and Hunter. "Seems real coincidental to me."

"Yeah," Hunter said, now giving Winters his full attention along with everyone else in the room.

"Well, the use of cold is in the purview of the Unseelie," Winters pressed on, pulling up an Excel spreadsheet that he was using to track the facts, "and if the Unseelie were involved, wouldn't they have the spell-casting know-how to cover their tracks to human divinations? Like, I'm just sayin', they'd know that the first thing a pissed-off Vampire cartel would do would be try to get a black coven or a really strong diviner to figure out who called up some Erinyes on them, right? And, if you ask me, it really does look fishy that both the lock was freeze-busted and then evidence of this avenging demon was out there . . . around the same time a human body got buried in the graveyard. . . . Ahem, let us not forget Mr. Romero."

"You are indeed a boy wonder," Sasha said, pushing off the wall she'd been leaning against. "Because let's face it, the Unseelie could break into the tomb, but a seriously old and powerful Vampire is no slouch in the strength department. One might be able to bust open a crypt door, but it's quite another thing to be able to physically or even magically drag a superstrong Vamp out into the sun without Unseelie causalities."

"It would have to be a team effort of several Unseelie working in unison to have that much combined power to overthrow the death struggle of a viceroy," Hunter said, walking off to stare out the window. "Or it would take the strength of an Unseelie monarch." He rubbed the nape of his neck and then turned back to stare at Sasha. "Which is why all things point back to Cerridwen, who had both opportunity and motive, unless some rogue Unseelie Fae simply opened the tomb and then . . ."

"The avenging demon busted in there and dragged the viceroy out." Sasha shook her head. "Damn, that's cold, but that's exactly how I'd do it to save my side from collateral damage."

"But let's say, for the sake of argument, that it wasn't Queen Cerridwen," Doc said, his worried gaze roaming to each face in the group. "Then what Unseelie would benefit from Vampire wars? Why would they try to bring down the House of Hecate, because this is where all of this could have been going, if Sir Rodney would have turned her away at the castle?"

"And an educated bet was that Sir Rodney would have turned her away," Sasha said flatly. "Only somebody maybe didn't expect him to be such a romantic."

"Ah, the X factor," Bradley said with a half smile. "Quantity unknown."

"But that leads us right back to square one. Full circle and no cigar, folks." Sasha began hunting along the choices of artillery that Woods and Fisher had spread out on the table. "Maybe it's time to have a conversation with the queen about what her succession plan is if she were to meet a sudden demise. That could tell us a lot." Sasha picked up a small handheld Uzi and fit in its magazine with a click.

"Before anything, I need to let Shogun know what's happening." Hunter rubbed the nape of his neck, becoming agitated. "I have to warn my brother, but he never told me where he was staying."

Sasha checked both safeties on her weapon and

then looked up at Hunter. "Don't howl. The Vamps might take that as a rallying call to arms from the wolves and get any lone wolf out there accidentally ambushed. But I know who might know."

Hunter gave her a puzzled look and simply cocked his head with a question in his eyes.

"Amy Chen's parents have a store near Xavier. She lives with her parents," Sasha said calmly. "If anyone has his cell number, it would be her."

"Good answer," Hunter said, moving straight toward the door, but Sasha flat-palmed his chest with one hand and simply shook her head.

"Don't freak the Chens out, man. You're covered in Fae blood splatter and gargoyle gook. Why don't you take five and give in to a shower—I'm just sayin'."

CHAPTER 10

A quick hot shower, a change of clothes—courtesy Colonel Madison's order to two MPs to get Sasha and Hunter uniforms—and she was good to go. Sasha fingered her engagement ring that she'd threaded onto the silver chain that held her amulet while she waited for Hunter in the Jeep. Back in the bayou, one shape-shift and she'd almost lost it. The silver amulet always seemed to hang right and to fall in place just so when she'd transform, but even that was a battle hazard. Now she thoroughly understood why wolves didn't wear the traditional American demarcation of being unavailable. One thing for sure, though: She was tired of living like a nomad.

Somewhere along the way from New Hampshire to the NAS she'd lost her duffel bag. She was pretty sure that she and Hunter had dropped their belongings at Sir Rodney's sidhe, since that was the first stop. But between all the shadow hopping, location changes, and then a shape-shift, she couldn't be a hundred percent certain where she'd left anything. And that was the problem. They were always on the move. Nomads.

Her goldfish, Fred, had died months ago, due to either lack of care or overfeeding by Mrs. Baker. Sasha shuddered to think about how her brother was going to cope with a baby on the way. How did Shadow Wolves rear children anyway, or was it just that her life as the pack's female alpha and enforcer mated to the pack's supreme alpha male was the thing that made her life so insane? Did wolves do the suburbs, soccer practice for kids, or Little League? Sheesh.

The more she thought about it, when was the last time she'd even been in her own apartment? It was tidy, IKEA furnished, but it wasn't *home*. Hunter had his bachelor's cabin out in the Uncompahgre, and they'd created a love nest in a cabin up in New Hampshire. But where was *base camp* going to be? The French Quarter? It was one more thing that she and Hunter never talked about; life would just get crazy and then they'd up and shift and run. Then celebrate. And not a lot of talking got involved in the celebration. Howling, yes. Talking, no. Right now, for some reason, she had questions. About a hundred of them.

Sasha stared at the diamond-heavy ring that dangled at the end of the silver chain looped around her neck. New dog tags for sure. Her brother had gotten married. Hunter was talking about getting married. Shogun was planning on getting married. Bradley and Clarissa were gonna probably cave any day now.

"You okay?"

Sasha almost leaped out of the Jeep and then closed her eyes and allowed her body to slump. "Don't do that, jeez."

"Walking light is just force of habit," Hunter said, looking concerned as he jumped into the driver's seat and gunned the engine. "I guess with gargoyles flying I should have announced myself sooner. Sorry."

"It's cool," she said, glad that Hunter mistook her jumpiness as mission related. Once he'd mentioned gargoyles, the other thoughts that had been tugging at her faded into the background of her mind. "I think you were right to want to take the Jeep. No sense in freaking out the Chens by stepping out of a shadow in their store."

"I was also hoping that it might be a good opportunity for you to have a brief word with Amy." Hunter glanced at Sasha from the corner of his eye as they pulled up to a military exit checkpoint. "I sort of promised Shogun you would, even though we have other pressing matters. This is important to my brother."

Sasha nodded and handed the clipboard to the guard shack MP, saying nothing until they had clearance. "Okay," she said, once they were well past the barricade.

Hunter glanced at her again. "Just 'okay'?"

Sasha shrugged. "Yeah. Like, Oooo. Kaaay. What?"

"Usually there's much more than 'okay.' " He held up a hand and smiled when she drew a breath.

"I'm okay with 'okay' as long as you're okay with 'okay.' I just didn't know if it was okay—but I'm pissed or okay—cool. Sometimes I don't speak she-Shadow and I wanted to be sure I wasn't in the doghouse."

"You're not in the doghouse," she said, finally cracking a smile. "It's just, what do you guys want me to say to this young woman? In fact," she said, turning around in her seat to fully face Hunter. "What does any woman say to another woman about something like this?"

"Okay," he said, giving her quick glimpses between trying to keep his eyes on the road. "This is what I meant by are you okay with this. My gut is never wrong; my wolf is always right. You're—"

"Twisted up, Hunter." Sasha sat back and ran her fingers through her damp hair. "Amy loves the ground that man walks on. To her, he's *a freakin' deity.* I mean, Hunter, she sees him as the knight in shining armor, the man who saved her from demons! He was gentle, and patient, and met her family. His ferocious nature only came out to protect and serve her, to save her life. Then he delivered her to a magical castle and nursed her back to health, and brought her home to her parents, who wept at her return. Then he goes with her to China and meets all her relatives . . . and sends gifts and receives her like royalty—because he is. Then you guys concoct a plan in the woods, mind you, while I'm not there, and I have to be the one to tell this poor girl there's no Santa Claus?"

"Sasha, I—"

"No, let me finish," she said, feeling her face become warmer and warmer the more she thought about it. "This is much worse than the whole Santa Claus analogy, which doesn't even *begin* to do it justice. No, Hunter, you guys owe me big-time for this because I have to tell some virginal young bride-to-be that her fiancé gets really, really horny when there's a full moon out and needs to go break-your-back primal, so, sorry, he'll cheat."

"Oh, man, Sasha, my brother really does love her, even though he has a Werewolf compulsion that Shadows don't own. You make it sound so . . ."

"Real? The word 'real' comes to mind, Hunter." She folded her arms over her chest but kept looking straight ahead as he drove faster. "Upper and lower canines presented, eyes glowing gold, and this dude will be howling on his wedding night and then need a half a side of raw beef to come down or go into priapism. Or he'll have to be in a Werewolf brothel every twenty-eight days when the moon goes full."

"Damn . . . ," Hunter muttered. "I know, but you make it sound so . . ."

"Not one affair, not one little indiscretion that maybe a marriage counselor can fix," Sasha railed on without missing a beat.

"But it's a biological issue—a . . . a . . . disability." Hunter glanced at Sasha and then looked straight ahead. "Baby . . . he's a Werewolf, for crying out loud."

"I'm not arguing his pedigree; I'm just stating

the facts that I have to convey to a normal human chick who is crazy in love."

"Well, I know Shogun loves her, too," Hunter said with triumph in his voice.

"Did you hear what I said?" Sasha turned in her seat and waited until Hunter glanced at her. "The operative words are 'crazy in love.' It's the kind of thing that gets a man poisoned at his own dinner table or stabbed to death in his sleep. He may be a Werewolf, but she's a woman, so hey."

"You think she'd go there?" Hunter quickly turned and looked at Sasha, who casually shrugged and turned away to stare out of the window.

"You never know what a person will do. I don't think she'll leave him, no matter what he says. And he's not going to be able to fix this. We are talking about a pattern, Hunter. A lifestyle or whatever. Call it what you want to, but it's gonna be brutal, emotionally, on the bride. So, unless that fragile lotus flower of a girl can land on her feet after a hard wolf toss or take a running body slam on a hard rollover—"

"Okay, okay, we owe you," Hunter said, gripping the wheel.

"Oh, maaaan, what am I going to tell that poor girl?" Sasha let her head drop into her hands. "Now that supernaturals are coming out of the closet, there should be a new instructional-video industry that springs up for human education."

"Now that would beat chasing gargoyles and Vampires at night," Hunter said, swallowing a smile.

Sasha slapped his arm and then they both laughed.

"Be serious, Hunter."

"I am being serious. . . . I'm not shy."

"You are incorrigible."

Hunter waggled his eyebrows as he turned into the Chens' block. "You don't know the half of it. Moon's up. I'm showered. Hungry. The subject matter is—"

"Get out of the Jeep, man," Sasha said, shoving Hunter's arm.

"It all begins with wolf play, an aggressive push, a bite, and—"

"You are so getting on my nerves," she said, trying not to laugh, and then leaped out of the vehicle.

As Hunter turned off the engine, she listened, trying not to smile at his low, subsonic chuckles. He was right on her heels.

Walking away from him quickly, she rang the bell to the apartment that was above the now-locked storefront. This detour made no sense. But she knew Hunter well enough to know that, he was trying to tidy up loose ends before potentially going into battle. That whole honor and my-pledge-is-my-bond thing sounded good on paper but was sometimes a royal pain in the ass. Like now, when they had much more important things to deal with. Besides, this was Hunter's pledge, not hers, but he'd gotten her all mixed up in the whole convoluted mess!

"Hi," she said, waving through the window at Amy with her best pasted-on smile. Sasha tried not to fidget as Amy managed the locks and opened the door.

But rather than invite them in, Amy rushed out of the house, grabbing Sasha by an arm.

"I am so glad you and Shogun's brother are here. We must hurry."

Sasha stumbled forward, amazed at the strength the petite girl suddenly wielded. "Okay, okay, but what's going on?"

"I'll explain as we drive," Amy said. "Is that your Jeep?"

"Yes," Hunter replied, frowning, rounding the vehicle, and opening the door.

"You have brought weapons?" Amy asked, quickly climbing in.

Sasha slammed the door as Hunter piled in behind the steering wheel. "Okay, now you're scaring me. What's going on?"

Amy held her head in her hands. "I can still see with Lady Jung Suk's eyes. When Shogun's demon Were Leopard aunt possessed my body, even though you killed her, some of her powers stayed with me. I wasn't sure of it until the moon rose and Shogun sensed a presence while we were out in the park. He was trying to explain something to me about our marriage and then he stopped speaking and stood." Amy looked up at Hunter and Sasha with tear-filled eyes. "I saw it, too," she added in a quiet tone. "It was clear, like water moving past us. He brought me home and said to stay there and be safe . . . and not to tell my parents. I did as he'd asked. But then he left to draw it away from us."

"Do you know where my brother went?" Hunter said, gunning the engine and careening away from the curb.

"At first I wasn't sure, because he never told me. Then as I sat in the kitchen trying to have some tea to calm down . . . I stared into my cup, thinking, and I saw." Amy looked between Sasha and Hunter. "It's the new house you have built your business in over in the French Quarter. He went to a shed there."

"Weapons," Sasha said, glancing at Hunter. "We have heavier artillery there than a normal gun shop and it's closer and has easier access than the Naval Air Station or the base."

"No doubt he saw what we saw in New Hampshire," Hunter replied in a low rumble. "Let's just hope we're not too late."

"Has the call to arms gone out?" Sir Rodney walked back and forth along the windowed wall of his war room, looking out of the leaded beveled glass with his hands clasped behind his back.

"Sent spell-protected by way of the cauldrons of Forte Inverness to every Seelie Fae magick advisor of the nobles throughout England, Scotland, Wales, and Ireland—and all of those present here in the Americas." Garth looked at his fellow advisors, waiting on the rail-thin Rupert to set down food and drink for the monarchs. Garth's suspicious gaze fell upon Queen Cerridwen. "And, Your Majesty, should we send a missive to your northern stronghold so that you may deploy some of *your* resources, as well?"

Queen Cerridwen gave Garth an icy glare but responded with cool regard. "Trust me, dear Garth, the moment the first Unseelie head rolled, my resources were fully deployed—and my people are already aware that we are allied with the Seelie on this. The greater question is, are your people equally aware of this union?"

Hunter stopped short as he turned off the engine. "Amy shouldn't be here, if Shogun has cornered prey."

"Damn," Sasha muttered, and then turned around to stare at Amy. "Half of me wants to tell you to wait here; the other half of me knows that's how the innocent always gets killed in a horror movie."

"Then that settles it: I'm going with you guys," Amy said, nervously glancing between Hunter and Sasha.

"All right, but stay on our heels just in case," Sasha said, pulling a handheld Uzi out from under the tarp on the backseat.

Hunter had already begun walking toward the house, stuffing a Glock 9mm in his waistband. Sasha hung back with Amy, visually casing the house for signs of a struggle or forced entry while Hunter issued a low, quiet howl to summon Shogun so that they didn't startle him.

Signaling with two fingers that they should move

forward around the back, Hunter ducked low under the windows and hustled down the side yard. After a few seconds, Sasha and Amy mimicked his steps and then waited. The back door was ajar. The shed door was open and the guts of the alarm system were a jumble of spaghetti wire.

"Shogun!" Hunter called out, leaning against the wall next to the door frame and then opening the door with a quick side kick.

"Brother?" Shogun called out.

Sasha and Hunter slumped with relief.

"Shogun, I was worried!" Amy shouted, and bolted past Sasha and Hunter.

Hunter closed his eyes and banged the back of his head against the wall. "My brother will never forgive us for this, you know that, right?"

Sasha nodded and placed the safety on her weapon. "Yeah. But what can you do?"

Hunter stood at the back door as Sasha trudged up the steps. By the time they got into the darkened house, Amy was hugging Shogun in the middle of the kitchen floor.

"I was so worried," she murmured, burying her face against Shogun's neck. But he looked over the top of her head at Hunter and then Sasha with an accusatory glare.

"Did she tell you I was chasing something unseen and dangerous?" Shogun held Amy protectively for a moment and then stepped away from her to confront Hunter.

"Yes, Brother."

"Then why the hell is she here!"

Stepping between the potential combatants, Sasha intervened. "Because I was trying to talk to Amy and she began telling us about the invisible entity while driving—and there was no time to double back."

It was a stretch, but Sasha watched Shogun pace away from Hunter and rub the nape of his neck.

"My apologies," Shogun finally said, trying to coax away his distended upper and lower canines, albeit his eyes still glowed gold in the darkness.

"Blame it on the moon, man," Hunter said, trying to appear casual, but Sasha noticed that the muscles in his shoulders had bulked in preparation for a wolf fight.

Quiet strangled the room for a few moments and then Shogun suddenly looked at Sasha and spoke with unexpected candor.

"Did you and Amy have a chance to speak?"

"Uh . . ." Sasha dragged her fingers through her hair.

"Yes," Amy said quickly. "Of course."

"And you're still here?" Shogun stared at Amy for a few moments and then walked deeper into the kitchen's shadows beyond the light of the moon.

"Why wouldn't I be? I love you." Amy walked toward the darkness, but Shogun held up both hands.

"Don't," he murmured. "What Sasha told you is true. Go home to your parents' house, especially tonight."

"Come on," Sasha said quietly, guilt lacerating her soul. She so wished she'd had a chance to speak to Amy, but like everything else in her life, things had happened too quickly. "I'll take you back while Hunter and Shogun go after that thing that cruised you. I can catch up with them later by jumping the shadows."

Amy shook her head no and continued advancing on Shogun. But there was something in her walk, something in the attitude that seemed to possess her entire body that put the three wolves in the room on high alert.

"I want to hunt it with you," Amy said in a slightly deeper voice than normal. "I want to help you kill it." She stopped in a pool of moonlight and stretched like a lazy feline would stretch in the sun.

Hunter and Sasha backed up, glancing at Shogun for a sign of what he wanted to do. But Shogun quickly sidestepped Amy, looking at them for answers they didn't have.

"Amy," Sasha said quickly. "When we talked, you said you've been feeling a lot of the old things you felt when Lady Jung Suk was in your body, right?" Sasha looked at Shogun, hoping he'd catch her cues.

"Yes," Amy said, closing her eyes and rubbing her arms as though to warm herself. "And I could see with her telepathy tonight. I never could do that before."

"Are you cold?" Shogun asked, and then turned quickly to Sasha and Hunter. "The entity that once inhabited her was a snow leopard, used to the Tibetan climate. Maybe—"

"I'm not cold or possessed," Amy said with a sultry chuckle. "Every full moon since Lady Jung Suk temporarily entered my body, whatever was left after you killed her seemed to get a little stronger . . . and I said nothing because it frightened me so. First it was just an amazing rush of energy. Then the next moon left me with clarity like I've never known—keen senses. Now, I really can't say what is happening to me." Amy opened her eyes and her once-dark irises were a deep, shimmering gold like that of an Amur big cat.

"That's not supposed to happen!" Shogun said, rounding Amy to stand by Sasha and Hunter. He glanced at them both. "Is it?"

Amy tilted her head, questioning.

"Your eyes . . . ," Sasha murmured in awe.

"What about them?" Amy looked from one face to another.

"She cannot go home to her parents like this," Hunter said, keeping his distance.

"Definitely not," Shogun said, racing between the counter and the door arch while rubbing the nape of his neck. "She also cannot be left alone. Who knows what she might do? And this might have been caused by whatever I was chasing—"

"*We* were chasing, Brother." Hunter held Shogun's gaze. "It cruised Sasha and me up at the cabin in New Hampshire. Sasha and I went after it, but it also got away. Something that elusive is potentially demon in nature. Your aunt was infected. . . . We don't know how bad a situation this could truly be, man."

"You all speak of me as though I'm not here in the room with you," Amy said in a too-calm tone.

The three wolves kept their eyes on her as she moved around the kitchen.

"I'm hungry. Very hungry." Amy opened the refrigerator door and then slammed it shut. "There's nothing here. I have to go out and hunt."

"Not a good idea," Shogun said carefully. "I will hunt for you and bring you back something—"

"Raw," Amy said, slowly licking her bottom lip as she captured Shogun's gaze and held it.

Shogun swallowed hard. "Absolutely."

"Brother . . . be advised, she could be infected." Hunter turned and placed a palm in the center of Shogun's chest. "You need more information."

"Maybe we should bring her to the Sidhe, where they have, uhm, facilities and a full magick team . . . and maybe Silver Hawk can come, too, so he can divine whether or not she's been infected?" Sasha looked between Hunter and Shogun. "But she's gotta be quarantined in case . . . the less desirable aspects of Lady Jung Suk are also with her."

"All right," Amy said calmly with a dangerous smile. "I like the castle. But I don't think anything is wrong with me beyond wishing that I was alone with Shogun right now."

CHAPTER 11

Amy bolted from the Jeep almost before Hunter had turned off the engine. He'd driven the vehicle as far as it could go off road, following a narrow gravel trail that terminated in mud and underbrush. Shogun was out like a shot behind her, leaving Hunter and Sasha no choice but to grab the weapons that had been stashed in the vehicle and make a mad dash to follow them.

Thankfully, Amy stopped at a quarter mile, bent over, and began panting. Shogun skidded to a halt beside her but then whirled on Hunter and Sasha when he saw them bringing up the rear with their guns drawn.

"You will not shoot her like she's some animal!"

"Whoa, whoa," Sasha said, tilting her weapon up in a defensive position and holding it so that her finger was nowhere near a trigger. "This is for the bad guys. The demons out there or Vamps, remember?"

Hunter nodded but only slowly tilted his weapon away from Amy.

"All right, then don't forget that Amy is not a demon or a Vamp. She's just going through a first moon," Shogun argued, beginning to pace between Amy and a nearby tree. "Who among us hasn't experienced that first rush?"

"I'm sorry I ran," Amy said, starting to hyperventilate. "I feel like I'm burning up. I needed air." She blotted her damp forehead with the back of her arm. "I feel like I'm suffocating."

Hunter approached Shogun cautiously. "Stand downwind from her," he said quietly. "You cannot watch her go through this while in your wolf. You must keep your head and stay in your human, if you're going to help her through this."

Shogun nodded and stepped back but watched Amy with tears in his eyes as she began to shred her clothes.

"She's beginning to change, Shogun." Sasha bit her lip and looked away for a moment to steady her emotions. "It's not a normal transformation like one of us born into our wolf. She's going into her Were form but turning like a person bitten . . . and virally infected."

"No!" Shogun shouted, clasping his skull between his palms. "Give her a chance. See if it's full-blown. Doc has meds. Silver Hawk has chants!" He spun on Hunter. "How many times have you and I looked down the barrel of a gun when everyone thought we were lost to the virus?"

Hunter held up a hand to stay Sasha's clear shot. "We will wait. We will watch. But if it becomes inevitable . . . Brother, we will do what we must so that your conscience can be clear."

"If you murder her and I allow it, my conscience will never be clear, nor will my soul rest."

Amy's wail broke the standoff, jerking everyone's attention toward her rapidly changing form. Standing before them half-nude and shuddering, she tore off her shoes and jeans, shredding the fabric of her bra and panties, and then dropped to the ground in agony. Shogun rushed forward, but Hunter caught him by the arm.

"For the sake of your entire pack, your clan, your federation, you cannot."

A feral scream made Shogun close his eyes. "But she's in such agony."

"And you and I both know that's not how we shift when healthy."

Shogun's furtive gaze searched Hunter's eyes for a moment before he turned back again to witness what none of them could look away from any longer. Amy's once-ivory skin was becoming mottled and stretched as her spine elongated with her wails. Limbs distended and her skeleton painfully rearranged itself, cracking and splintering, intensifying her shrieks.

"Merciful Jesus, let me shoot her now, Shogun!" Sasha yelled, walking closer with her gun cocked.

"No!" Shogun shouted. "I have undergone a hard transition and I am not a demon! Sasha, remember you vouched for me once when I looked like this!"

He spun around to look at Hunter. "You, Brother, went against my own men when they were ready to give up on me. Until we have evidence of an attempted attack or the blood test results back from Doc Holland, then we wait."

Sasha pulled back her weapon and wiped her forehead on the back of her wrist as Amy's jaw cracked and rearranged itself. She stared at the pain-riddled creature on the ground that had human skin and a leopard's body until her vision blurred with tears.

"This is inhumane to leave her like this," Sasha whispered, and then dabbed at her eyes. "She's in so much pain."

Suddenly Amy's convulsive transformation stopped. She lay eerily still and not breathing, with her eyes open—gorgeous, glassy cat eyes that were a deep golden hue refracting the moonlight. Sasha covered her mouth as Shogun wrested himself away from Hunter with a sob and knelt beside Amy, not touching her but allowing his trembling fingers to hover just inches above her skin. Then just as quickly as she'd stopped breathing she suddenly gasped in a huge inhale and her mottled skin gave way to a pristine white coat dappled with beautiful snow-leopard rosettes.

In a soundless cat growl that caught the moonlight against her massive fangs, Amy sprang up, took one look at Shogun as though to taunt him to a chase, and took off.

"Stay in your human!" Hunter shouted as his

brother leaped up from the ground and began running after Amy.

Sasha and Hunter were right behind Shogun, clearing bramble and fallen logs, rocks, and swamp debris. Trees became a blur. Thick night air whipped Sasha's face. The graceful feline they chased was a majestic sight to behold. Soon it became clear that Amy wasn't fleeing; she was hunting. The scent of a small herd stung Sasha's nose. Adrenaline coursed through her system. Her wolf was near. She could feel Hunter's and Shogun's wolves straining to break free to hunt under the moon. Five o'clock shadow covered their jawlines. Sweat slicked their arms and created deep Vs in their T-shirts as sinew worked beneath fabric and skin. Their wolves wanted out in the worst way. So did Sasha's. But now was not the time.

Pack instinct kicked in the moment they saw the herd. Deer scattered; one doe looked up a second or two later than the others. She was marked by fate.

Shogun broke off from his pursuit of Amy to flush the prey toward her. Sasha and Hunter cornered the flank and sent the frenzied creature back to Amy when the doe bolted left. Although Amy missed the initial tackle it soon became clear that she was enjoying the chase as much as she wanted to bring down her first kill. She'd let the doe evade her, only to catch the deer a hundred yards later in one of the most elegant takedowns Sasha had ever witnessed.

Wolves had power, but the big cats had style.

Sasha slowed, panting, watching as Amy's body elongated from a masterful bound to tackle a creature three times her size and weight to the ground, then delivered a bone-crushing bite to the doe's windpipe.

Sasha, Hunter, and Shogun skidded to a halt as the snow leopard they'd chased looked up from her kill victorious and possessive. Amy gave them a bloody feline growl while hunkered down over the still-twitching doe.

"She's absolutely breathtaking," Shogun murmured.

Amy stood and dragged the doe deeper into the underbrush and then with one powerful jump took her high up into a tree with her. Glowering down at them, she positioned her kill and began eating.

"You might want to give her some space until she's done," Sasha said softly. "Cultural differences. We're wolves. We hunt in packs and eat in packs. Lions are the only big cats I know of that work as a team and share their kill. Leopards are solitary. Get any closer and she might take extreme offense and think you're trying to steal her dinner from her."

Shogun turned and looked at Sasha. "Yes . . . wise. I had forgotten." His voice held an awed, far-off quality as his line of vision drifted back to Amy. "But I now see why my uncle left the pack and walked away from his governance to live his life in exile in Tibet. Who could blame him for being seduced by the grandeur of the snow leopard?"

"Stay in your human," Hunter repeated in a low rumble. "Amy is too far away from hers now to know who you are and will not react well to your wolf."

There was nothing to do but wait and listen. A full hour passed while Amy gorged herself. The sound of flesh ripping, sinew tearing, and cartilage and bones cracking reminded Sasha just how powerful her future sister-in-law actually was. It also kept Sasha aware of just how strong Lady Jung Suk had been—strong enough to leave some of her DNA in Amy Chen's body after a temporary possession. The question was, however, was it demon-infected DNA or something they all could live with? And how much control would Amy be able to exercise over her big cat? Would Amy be able to think through her transformations in the future and would they always be so brutal?

Sasha said a little prayer as she watched Amy eat. She was indeed a majestic creature, just as she was a wonderful gem of a human being. Yet the dichotomy between Amy the pretty young woman and Amy the snow leopard devouring a doe in the moonlight was startling. It was obvious that Hunter was just as conflicted and was struggling with the possibility of having to make a very hard decision.

But there was something about Amy and the devotion that Shogun had for her that made Sasha violate every bit of soldier logic within her. Had it been anyone but Amy, Sasha would have pulled the trigger the second she saw Amy begin a hard transformation.

That was just it, though. Sasha couldn't. She didn't. She wouldn't. And that worried her.

Amy's movement in the tree branches above made everyone on the ground leave their private thoughts to see what their reluctant charge would do. Stretching, Amy came in close to the trunk, studied her options, and leaped down to the ground, slowly stalking Shogun. Before anyone could react she had slipped into her human form so smoothly that Sasha drew in a quiet gasp.

Bloody, sated, naked, Amy spoke to Shogun in a soft voice that had a sultry undercurrent within it.

"I just needed to eat. I was hungry." Amy's eyes still shimmered in the moonlight as she slowly approached him.

"I will never let that happen again," he murmured. "I will always feed you, just as I will always hunt for you."

Standing an arm's length away, Amy reached out, but to hold up her hand. "I know now that you would even die for me, but I could never allow such a terrible thing."

"Friend, not foe!"

Sasha pivoted quickly with the others to look up at Fae archers who had dropped down into the trees surrounding them. Before anyone could speak, a horrific chain of events unfolded in slow motion before their eyes. A diligent Fae soldier caught sight of Amy covered in blood and standing within arm's-length distance of their wolf ally, Shogun. When she turned to look at the archers, moonlight caught in her eyes and glinted off her retracting fangs. A bloodied half-eaten doe was draped over a huge tree limb oozing gore.

At the same time Sasha, Hunter, and Shogun drew in a breath to shout, "No!" the archer released his silver-tipped arrow. Shogun yanked Amy behind him and the arrow thrust him backward, pinning Shogun to a tree through his shoulder. Amy was momentarily trapped between Shogun's body and the huge tree. Pandemonium broke out as Sasha and Hunter shouted for the archers to hold their fire.

Archers dropped down from tree limbs and surrounded them. Shogun's yells of agony echoed throughout the night. In one powerful move he snapped the protruding arrow off at its base, releasing another cry of agony as he lurched his body forward to free himself and Amy from the tree.

Blood ran from Shogun's shoulder like a river. The wound sizzled and popped in angry hisses from the invasion of silver within his Werewolf body. Amy caught him as he slumped forward, pressing her palm against the gushing wound in a futile attempt to staunch the heavy bleeding.

Hunter caught Shogun under his good arm and shouted for Amy to back up, while Sasha stood in front of Amy to shield her body from the archers.

"We thought she was attacking," the shooter said, glancing around at his fellow archers. "I d'not know she was friend—she seemed to be foe. My deepest regrets, on my mother's soul. This was the last outcome anyone wanted."

The lead archer tossed Sasha a hunter's cloak,

and she quickly caught it and then surrounded Amy with it.

"She isn't feral . . . not yet anyway. She was just reaching out to him in tenderness." Sasha walked a path back and forth. "There's no time to explain it all. We've gotta get this man in to your magick advisors stat to see if they have an antidote to silver burn before he goes into shock."

"Done," the lead archer said, motioning for several archers to run ahead and send word to prepare the sidhe for incoming wounded.

Another bloodcurdling wail from Shogun made everyone around him cringe.

"Let's move, people!" Hunter shouted as Shogun began to convulse.

Sasha body-blocked Amy and went to Shogun's wounded side. Half-dragging, half-lifting Shogun on the side of his body that she held, Sasha spoke to Amy in bursts: "You can't touch him again. Look at your hands."

"I didn't mean to infect him. I just caught him, wanted to stop the bleeding!"

"We know," Sasha panted, and then almost fell when the full weight of Shogun's body suddenly dropped on one side.

Hunter caught him and lifted him over his shoulder, but the sight of Shogun passing out was clearly too much for Amy to bear. She ran at the somber Fae archers, screaming at them in frustration.

"I will never forgive you for this if he dies!"

Sasha grabbed Amy by both arms and spun her around to face her. "It was a horrible, horrible accident. But killing someone won't bring Shogun back. Right now, we need all of your focus and prayers on making sure Shogun doesn't die. That means all of your cooperation to not create another problem for the sidhe to have to address while they're trying to heal him. Shogun getting help right now is more important than your righteous indignation."

"I swear it was an accident, milady," the leader of the Fae archers said gently. "Shogun is a friend. A warrior whom we've fought with and respect. No one ever meant for something like this to 'appen."

Amy swallowed hard and turned her face away, seeking Sasha's shoulder. Sasha petted Amy's hair but looked at the guilt-laden expressions on the archers' faces. "We know."

CHAPTER 12

They hadn't been in battle, weren't directly engaged in a war, and yet here they were again trudging to Sir Rodney's castle with the bloody and the wounded. Sasha was so disgusted she could spit. Shogun was passed out and being carried by Hunter and a Fae archer; the arrow wouldn't kill him, but Amy's panicked attempts to stop the bleeding might. Yet, who could have blamed the poor woman?

All of it had happened within the blink of an eye, when taut nerves and full-moon rapid reflexes had kicked in. Shogun got shot, broke the arrow off. Aghast, Amy covered the gushing wound with hands already bloodied from her previous kill. Now Sasha's future brother and sister-in-law had to spend the night in a sidhe dungeon waiting on blood tests and surgeons. Plus Sasha and Hunter needed to get hosed down, too. Both of them were splattered with Shogun's blood, and the short carry to the gates of the sidhe had left them drenched in it.

Sir Rodney met them at the gates with Garth and Queen Cerridwen. "Are you injured beyond Shogun?" Sir Rodney called out, rushing in closer.

"No," Hunter shouted back, "but my grandfather must hurry! This man is in pain and going into shock. He knows the medicine of the wolf packs to deal with silver burn."

"We've got a silver-shock antidote here," Garth said, running alongside Shogun's body as his men accepted it from Hunter. "Once we became allies, we retooled our infirmary."

"Good looking out," Hunter said, falling back. "But his fiancée also needs a bath . . . and quarantine in comfortable environs, even if it must be behind silver bars for a few hours."

"Just until Silver Hawk gets here with Doc's results," Sasha said in a reassuring tone. "It's a precaution for him now more than ever."

Sasha waited until Amy nodded and then rushed away to catch up with Shogun while Garth's men transferred him to a livery. Before Sasha crossed into the magick density there was something basic that had to be done. She had to communicate with her team.

Placing the cell call to her squad and the NAS, Sasha punched in the connection with bloodied fingers. The moment the call connected, she relayed everything to Doc in one long run-on sentence.

"We're on it," Doc replied quickly. "We're sending Silver Hawk back your way with not only his medicine bag but some serum."

"How bad is it, Doc?" Hunter said, speaking into the phone over Sasha's shoulder.

"I won't know for a coupla hours." Doc let out a harried breath. "Step outside that magick citadel and call me back—I'll have word then, all right?"

"You and the team lay low," she said. "Be careful. I love you."

Sasha looked up at Sir Rodney. "Sometimes this is just faster than a Fae missive, no offense."

"None taken."

She hated this and could tell Hunter did, too. Seeing both Amy and Shogun behind bars in separate cells wore on every fiber of Sasha's being. But to the Fae's credit, they'd transformed each cell into a modified bedchamber, replete with a privacy screen. At least Shogun wasn't in agony anymore—at least not from the wound in his shoulder, which had been patched up and was beginning to heal. But there was no measuring the personal agony he was experiencing as he sat, freshly bathed, over a nearly raw steak and sullenly ate so that his body could regenerate. He and Amy couldn't even touch fingers through the bars because the bars were silver coated and they were Weres.

Clean clothes and a bath hadn't made Sasha feel clean or much better. The entire business of separating Amy and Shogun sucked.

"We'll be back," Sasha said as gently as possible. "The moment Silver Hawk comes and Doc gives us word, this confinement will be over."

Shogun nodded but didn't look up as she went to Amy's cell and clasped the bars.

"It's all so unfair," Amy said in a fragile voice, and then wiped at two big tears that rolled down her freshly soaped cheeks. "Why can't we Weres touch silver? Why can't I come to the bars and clasp them like you . . . or go in and out of the shadows so that I can be with my fiancé? Why does the moon make us lose all self-control, but you are a wolf, too, like my Shogun, and are able to keep your human much closer? I don't understand what they think will happen! Why are we caged? The Fae shot him and he was no threat. Why would they do that?"

"Because they were aiming for you, and I would take a hundred arrows that one should never mark you."

Amy bit her lip and pressed her hands against the wall that separated them and for a few moments Shogun just closed his eyes and breathed in her scent.

"You bathed in lavender," he murmured.

"Yes . . . they said it was calming." Amy's voice became a soft purr. "But knowing you will be all right is what helped."

"In a few hours it will be midnight . . . and the pull you feel now is only a fraction of the power within that gets released at the apex of the eve. If we are infected, there will be no control." Shogun looked up from his plate and stared at Hunter. "I will answer your other questions for you, sweet Amy. Visit with me in voice, since we cannot touch. It will give us something to focus on, something to keep us close to our human side while we endure this torture. My brother and his mate cannot even fathom how we feel. . . . They are Shadow Wolves; we are Werewolves. There is a difference."

Shogun left Hunter's gaze and began to slowly cut his steak. It was the most dignified dismissal Sasha had ever witnessed. The alpha clan leader of the Southeast Asian Werewolf Federation had spoken. Sasha pulled away from the bars feeling the sting of Shogun's words. She could tell by Hunter's lowered gaze that he did, too. But what else was there to do?

They turned and left the dungeons, escorted back to the main castle's war room by three burly palace guards. Nine more hung back, keeping their gazes lowered. Guilt stained their faces as they moved to lock the outer dungeon doors and then take up their watch posts.

But the question that haunted Sasha was how could they find out who called the Erinyes? Was that what was stalking the wolf leadership? The bizarre thing was, however, something had cruised them and simply spied on them without harming them. That wasn't like any demon attack she'd ever heard of. Most times when a demon happened upon you it was going in for the possession or the kill. Whatever this was seemed like it was just curious or gathering data. No matter what its purpose, the whole thing was unnerving.

With no immediate leads at their disposal, the

only person to cross-examine would be the queen. Sasha released a soft sigh as she and Hunter entered the war room. The last thing she felt like dealing with was another pissed-off lover.

"How is he?" Sir Rodney said, pouring a stein of ale all around. He stood as Sasha approached the table, and took a seat with Hunter after she did. "This is all such a nasty business."

"My brother is probably going to be all right physically," Hunter said, and then rubbed the nape of his neck. "If he is not infected and the girl is not infected, he will be a happy man. If not, I might as well go down there and put a silver bullet between his eyes. He will never be the same again if Amy Chen has to be put down."

"I don't understand this thing that has happened," Queen Cerridwen said quickly. "Lady Jung Suk was a demon—she made a pact with that traitor from my court, Kiagehul, to become invisible and to be able to possess that poor girl. Therefore, when she was summarily executed, everything of her should have gone away." Queen Cerridwen stood and paced and then set her cold blue gaze on Garth. "If you cannot redress that butchered spell, then I will have my top advisors leave the safety of their haven to come help our strong allies."

"Now milady is usurping your advisors with her own?" Garth said, narrowing his gaze. "'Tis a dangerous thing indeed, milord."

"'Tis a dangerous thing to speak so rashly before my queen, Garth. Do not forget your place."

Sir Rodney took a slow sip of his ale and stared at Garth over the lip of his stein.

Garth simply nodded and stood back from the table. But the brief volley of angry words gave Sasha the in to the conversation she'd dreaded.

"If there was a breach in loyalty . . . treason, then could it be possible that someone in your court who has not been routed out yet might be interested in your demise?" Sasha leaned forward, studying the queen's intense composure. "No blame against you, but they did plot an overthrow before. The last time it was Sir Rodney's. Could it be that someone from the Unseelie Court is trying to implicate you in Vampire attacks to cause a costly war . . . then they could double back and strike their own deal with the Vampires—selling you and Sir Rodney out, now that you're allies?"

"Completely Machiavellian and completely possible, were it not for the fact that Rodney and I have swept our courts with the most insidious round of spells we could muster. Truth spells and oath sealers that would wither a liar right before our very eyes. All of our most trusted advisors were subjected to this. Our inner circles are squeaky clean." Queen Cerridwen lifted her porcelain chin and drew up her fragile features. "That is the first thing I thought, too. I like how you think."

Sasha released a quiet breath of relief. The last thing she wanted to do at the moment was offend Sir Rodney's latest lady love. This day and night had already been eventful enough.

"Even Kiagehul's kith and kin have been inter-rogated and bewitched," Sir Rodney said, lifting his stein. "The Fae are ruthless when betrayed, as well ye know. This time we left no stone unturned."

"No offense, but the Vampires are equally ruth-less when violated," Hunter said evenly. "I hope that you have barricaded your establishments for the onslaught due tomorrow night."

A sly half smile appeared on Sir Rodney's face and he shared a glance with Queen Cerridwen. "On the morrow, my wolf friend, the Vampires will wish they had never beheaded a single Fae. Our establishments are bespelled, readied for the at-tacks. We have imported the best magick slingers from the old country—London, the Bonnie Isles, Wales, and my beloved Scotland. They have sent their executioners from Romania and Transyl-vania and the old Czech Republic, and so forth. They tipped their hand with the gargoyle on-slaught. Our advisors have scryed into the caul-dron pools to learn of this, using the skin of one of their captured beasts. They will rue the day they have come to tangle with the House of Shannon of Inverness!"

"Okay . . ." Sasha said carefully. "But there's also a human population in the center of New Orleans where the French Quarter is—where a lot of your establishments are and where the Vampire blood clubs are located."

"We are aware of this problem, but sometimes in war there are sacrifices," Queen Cerridwen said. "We have done our best to use methods that will minimize human casualties. . . . Our forces are poised to strike and then draw the fight into the bayou, but we cannot guarantee that there will be no loss of human life."

Sasha rubbed her palms down her face and leaned on the round table on her elbows. "I understand, and given the circumstances, if it were the wolf federations under attack, we would have to employ the same methods. But this thing with the Erinyes is sticking in my craw."

"And mine," Hunter said, suddenly standing and beginning to pace. "What was it that came to spy on me, Sasha, Shogun, and Amy, but didn't attack?" He turned suddenly, searching all the faces in the room. "The Erinyes are demons, yes? They are Furies; rage is what propels them. So why would they just come as invisible beings and stare at us?"

"That's what we can't figure out," Sasha added. "It's as though whoever raised these things said, 'Go check on the wolves in the area, but don't attack yet.' We're being monitored in a very weird way."

"Erinyes redress the fury of the dead. If you are not being attacked, then whoever raised those entities must not have seen the wolves as culpable of whatever crime or offense they feel had been committed." Garth looked at Sir Rodney. "Which would certainly rule out the theory we'd been working on that Kiagehul somehow left a back-door spell that would avenge him upon his death, so that those that had wronged him would be beset by Erinyes. The wolves were the ones that hunted him down and dragged him to court. The wolves helped us collect the implements to break his nasty spells on the House of Shannon."

"Right. That's why none of this makes sense." Sasha sat back in her chair and took a sip of her ale. "We've been wracking our brains on this, trying to figure it out from every possible angle. The Vampires have any number of groups that could be pissed off at them. But there's only a few that can actually raise demons, have a human soul, and deal with the element of cold like the Fae. . . . I mean, no dark coven is a match for your Fae sweeps, and I doubt one would try to go against them, no matter what the Vampires promised."

Hunter looked up at the moon. "My grandfather should be near by now, and Doc should have an answer." He glanced back at Sasha. "Perhaps once he has communed with my brother, we can go into the shadow lands with him and walk near the demon doors for answers?"

Both Shogun and Amy looked up in unison as the dungeon doors opened. This time no guards came in with Hunter and Sasha, only Silver Hawk wearing his ceremonial garb.

"What is the meaning of this?" Shogun said in a quiet, lethal tone, standing slowly, his eyes filled with rage. "You have come to murder us in our cells with a shaman as witness! Will that make you both sleep better at night?"

"You promised!" Amy shouted, and then rushed the bars, forgetting about the silver and burning her hands. "At least open the cells and let us die together!"

"No one will die," Hunter said, presenting the keys. "We came to beg your pardon and ask your forgiveness that precautions had to be met. My grandfather came in ceremonial robes to marry you here and now if you want, so that, Shogun, your one request—to not dishonor Amy—could be met. We owed you that . . . and if you would still like, we will also stand with you at your more formal ceremony."

Amy held out her hands, trembling as Silver Hawk first opened her door and then placed a balm from his medicine bag on her palms.

"Child," he said in his ancient, wise voice. "A beautiful bride in a gossamer gown must be able to touch the face of her beloved without pain. Trust me and allow me to heal you."

Hunter opened Shogun's door and was met with a warm hug.

"Thank you, Brother. . . . Forgive my harsh words."

"No apology required. If I thought you were going to kill my mate, my reaction would have been no less."

"You know the Fae," Sasha said with a warm smile. "They have wronged you with an errant arrow and have rolled out the red carpet to try to make things right. There's a suite for you upstairs filled with the best of everything. Be happy."

Shogun left Hunter's side and went to Sasha but looked over his shoulder. "May I?"

Hunter nodded. "Yes . . . because you are settled."

"I am settled," Shogun said, and then drew Sasha into an embrace. "Thank you, sister."

She nodded and released him, glad that the butterflies had gone, glad that there was no twinge of what-if in his eyes or her gut, even under the full moon. Their eyes met and he gave her a brief nod that contained a wistful sadness merged with understanding as he left her side and found Amy in her cell. Patiently waiting until Silver Hawk had removed his hands from Amy's injured palms Shogun went to her and then drew her into his arms.

Their kiss was slow and questioning, building in ardor as Shogun's fingers threaded through Amy's silken river of onyx hair. Silver Hawk lowered his gaze and stepped away. Two Fae guards opened the dungeon door as Hunter, Sasha, and his grandfather moved toward it, blocking the eager guards from entering.

"They are prepared for the ceremony upstairs," a guard said brightly. "Glad that all is well. So, we stand at the ready to escort the bride and groom to a much cozier stay. Our Fae hospitality is legendary."

"That it is," Sasha said with a smile, walking past the guards without looking back.

"But what of the ceremony and the feast?" The second guard glanced back at the slowly closing door.

Hunter and Silver Hawk shared a look as the outer dungeon door slammed shut. He landed a thick hand on the confused man's shoulder. "Maybe in the morning. I'm sure Sir Rodney will definitely understand."

CHAPTER 13

"If World War Three wasn't about to go down tomorrow night, I'd say all's well that ends well. True love abounds in the sidhe and several very evil Vampire viceroys had a date with the sun that they probably deserved anyway . . . hey." Sasha kept walking up the steep, winding staircase that led to the main castle hall. Why couldn't life just be uncomplicated for once?

Hunter gave Sasha a sidelong glance as they reached a landing. "Were it only that easy."

"Yeah, I know. Who am I fooling?" Sasha released a hard sigh and kept pushing forward. Her body was exhausted, but she knew sleep would be impossible with all of the issues racing through her mind. "It would have been great to see if maybe Amy could go into trance and give us any insight as a supernatural seer, but fat chance of that happening tonight. I can't blame her, but damn. We've gotta find a way to figure out what opened Pandora's box with the Erinyes and how to send them back before this Vamp war really gets further out of hand."

"Sometimes just being still, daughter, is the hardest thing to do. But the answer is within the stillness. We sometimes learn that in the shadows."

Sasha looked over her shoulder at Silver Hawk and gave him a smile, even though what he'd said made her want to scream. Right now her nerves couldn't take an ancient parable. Right now her brain could not begin to process cryptic statements. But she loved the old man way too much and respected him far too much to respond with more than a simple nod. Still, she was sure he knew what she'd been thinking by the sly half smile he'd unsuccessfully tried to swallow.

"Don't worry, Sasha," Hunter said as they reached the guarded door. "Grandfather makes me insane, too, when he starts talking in old Ute riddles."

"I will leave you," Silver Hawk replied, unfazed. "Get some rest. Tomorrow will be eventful. I feel it in my bones."

Two guards at the top of the stairs banged on the heavy oak door to have it unlocked from the outside and then moved to let them pass. Another castle guard stepped forward with a huge key ring in his hand and a question in his eyes.

"Milord . . . where are the betrothed?" The guard looked first to Silver Hawk, who was the eldest in the small retinue of three.

Silver Hawk chuckled softly. "They have married

wolf-style in your dungeon, and should be allowed their privacy."

The Fae guard frowned, clearly not understanding. "Ah, you are a cleric amongst the wolves. A leader of your kind, then so be it. I shall inform Sir Rodney . . . but he will be wondering about all the food and drink."

"I think Sir Rodney will be okay with just allowing the party to go on regardless," Sasha said with a smile. "Maybe in an hour or two you guys can send down some grub . . . but I'd sorta wait until the couple asked for it before just barging in on them, you know what I mean?"

"Indeed!" the guard replied with a bow. "We Fae do love a festive event, and if our guests are happy we are happier."

"I assure you," Hunter said, giving Sasha a wink, "my brother and his new wife are very happy."

"Then it is settled," the guard said, striding away. "Fare thee well. I shall inform Sir Rodney."

"The food and drink will not go to waste," Sir Garth said, coming out of nowhere and startling Sasha, Hunter, and Silver Hawk. "Please follow me. We don't have much time."

Shogun's kiss began with a gentle tasting of her mouth, the delicate probing of his tongue. Amy could almost feel Shogun breathe her in and allow her scent to flow over his palate before he'd swallowed it. She'd been the one to deepen the exchange, hungrily suckling his tongue and giving in to the insane warmth of his embrace.

His wide, hot palms splayed across her back as she arched against him, needing every inch of her skin to come in contact with his. Clothes were in the way. Fabric taunted her raw nerve endings; she wanted it off of her, off of him. Yet he was still handling her as though she were a fragile object made of glass. She could feel him holding back, keeping the wolf within him at bay, even after knowing what she had within her.

Before she could stop herself her nails scored his back, shredding the silk shirt the Fae had given him, drawing blood—she didn't have to see it; she could smell it. The pungent scent hung in the air as she pulled back from their kiss and stared at him.

"I'm sorry," she murmured, her voice now thick and weighted with desire as her fingers gently played over his wounds. "I didn't know my hands would do that. . . . I . . ."

Amy's words trailed off as she stared into Shogun's dark brown eyes, watching them slowly become lit from within. Anticipation swept through her, stoking her need. A split second gave way to a lightning-fast response and her windpipe was being gently held by sharp upper and lower canines. All she could do was breathe. The threat was implicit. The threat was exhilarating.

Searing palms lifted her, separating the flesh of her buttocks, straining the thin gauze gown, straining her patience, while his powerful jaws remained locked over her trachea. Arms around the crown of his head and the nape of his neck, she kept her eyes closed as he moved her across the floor, still holding her tightly in an act of pure wolf possession. He had her by the throat, had claimed her body as his territory. Short panting bursts of breath were her agreement to submit. It all happened in the jag of fractured seconds that awakened Were instinct within her core.

Species didn't matter. He was male; she was female. Her body spilled its need for him, wetting her thighs, wetting his belly as he carried her, the scent straining his reason as he put her down hard on the small bed and blanketed her. Trembling, she couldn't speak as he pulled back and stared at her, crouching above her. She studied the question in his eyes, then answered it, tearing away the remnants of his shirt, and then traced the ridges of his chest and his nipples, finally reaching around to gently touch where she had raked him, only to feel the wounds already beginning to heal.

A gentle nudge with the side of his jaw pushed her to lie back. Capturing her hands within his, he swept her knuckles with a passionate kiss and then stared at her hands in awe.

"So delicate and yet so dangerous," he murmured, turning her palms over and kissing the centers of them.

She withdrew her hands from his, ashamed at how she'd accidentally hurt him, but her protest died under the press of his lips. Colors swirled behind her eyelids. His warmth erased all doubt as his fingers threaded through her hair and then found the edge of her dress. But pure shock made her eyes fly open the instant the fabric ripped.

His kiss deepened as her dress tore away from her body in a steady drone until it was halved. She watched him as he stared down at her, first drinking in her soul from her eyes and then giving himself permission to take in her nudity as though devouring her.

Yearning for his touch, she arched her body up to meet his but was rebuffed by a forceful kiss against her abdomen as he drew away.

"I'll hurt you like this," he murmured, and then shook his head.

Her palm cradled his cheek. "And I will heal. . . . Do what you must, but never let there be others."

"How did . . ."

Amy placed a finger to Shogun's lips. "I can see with my third eye. I may be a virgin, but I am not blind . . . and whatever Lady Jung Suk left me when her spirit fled my body, it was not naïveté." She allowed her gaze to linger on Shogun's handsome face and then slowly rove down his sinewy physique. "And I should thank her for that," Amy whispered.

Taking Shogun's hands within hers, Amy placed them against her breasts and then dropped her head back with a breathy moan. The long-awaited sensation pebbled her arms with gooseflesh and made her reach for him, pulling at him, not sure how to stop the ache of passion within her.

An assault of textures set her skin on fire and

she cried out as his full, smooth lips brushed over her tight nipples, then torso, followed by the trembling touch of his calloused hands. Everything he did deepened the ache and deepened the arch in her back. The dry heat of his touch gave way to the wet heat of his tongue as he laved her nipples, trailing kisses beneath the petite swell of her breasts, and across her belly. New beard shadowed his jaw and prickled her inner thighs, making her crave his mouth even more.

Her breaths had become ragged and her hands had become fists as his tongue sent spirals of pleasure through her until she dug the crown of her head into the pillows. Her voice was now a cross between female and feline, zigzagging between shrill cries of ecstasy and low, mewling purrs of profound release. No man had ever had access to her body like this, and certainly none of her self-pleasuring had produced climaxes as soul wrenching.

He'd opened her with his tongue, suckling her bud, French-kissing her swollen lips, now his finger played at the sensitive opening of her flower. It was too much to bear. She had to get away from him just to catch her breath.

In one lithe move, she slipped from his grasp, closed her legs, and balled herself up tightly at the top of the bed, panting. When she opened her eyes, his golden stare hunted her. He said nothing, just slowly wiped the slickness from his mouth with the back of his hand, breathing her in. It was such a sensual act that it sent a tremor of renewed heat through her. She watched his nostrils flare, watched the slow blink of his eyes, and then she quietly uncurled herself and moved onto her hands and knees before him.

"I wanted this to be different for you," he said in a deep murmur, then closed his eyes and turned his face away. "Special . . . not here but in a beautiful suite . . . after a ceremony that would honor both you and your parents."

"I am with you and that makes it special. I am yours alone, and that makes it beautiful. That you risked your life for me not long ago is the greatest honor you could have given me and my parents."

She saw his breath hitch and something feral within her snapped. Seconds stretched as she lunged forward, pounced, and flipped him onto his back. It was his turn to have his throat in her jaws while she hurriedly ripped away the heavy fabric of his pants and spent buttons. He didn't struggle, simply breathed, waiting for her to pull back and release his windpipe. She looked down at him, knowing half of his legs were still trapped by his pants. A single tear slid down his cheek. Her hand went over his heart and it felt like it was beating a path out of his chest. He bit his lower lip as he stared into her eyes. She understood agony. He'd just taught her the definition.

Straddling him slowly, she felt for his member, not taking her eyes away from his. Vein-corded heat filled her hand; his gasp as she touched him made her briefly close her eyes. By blind touch she studied the pattern of what would soon enter her. Each palm stroke along his wet, need-slicked length helped her memorize it, stopped his breath, and caused her opening to contract. Her fingers slid over the groove of the bulbous head, and she wondered how the two organs would fit, the disparity was so great, but desire won out.

Instinct told her she needed his girth to staunch the ache. Lowering herself down, she fit him against the entrance of her flower and then took a deep breath.

He quickly held her arms. "Not all at once," he said, breathing hard. "You'll tear and I'll lose control like that. . . . There's another way. You must let me guide you and move slowly."

"You'll lose control?" she murmured in a husky whisper.

He nodded, trying to shift her off him to change positions, but she shook her head and let him know just how strong she really was.

"Then lose control, Husband," she said quietly, staring at him, and suddenly sat down hard to fully take him in.

His wail of pleasure drowned out her wail of pain. He arched hard as though an electric current had shot through his body, and she moved against him with frenzied purpose. In a hard roll they were on the floor. In seconds he'd kicked out of his pants and pulled her beneath him. Her hair was in his fist and his kiss swallowed her cries. Her punches against his sides and back to get him to stop thrusting slowly converted to a grasping hold as her legs anchored around his waist.

Pleasure melted away pain. The burning at her rim quieted as the deep ache within her canal ripened, then blossomed on her throaty moan. His hand slid beneath her waist and his angle shifted. Her eyes crossed beneath her lids as he found a sweet spot deep within her.

Tearing his mouth from hers, his head dropped back as she scored his chest. Her hands sought his hair, her mouth hungering for his, chasing the sensation, chasing the thunderous orgasm unfurling within them. . . . Then it roared to life on a spontaneous convulsion, one vertebra-cracking explosion that left them both a crumpled heap on the floor.

She couldn't open her eyes as pleasure tore through her. The only thing that grounded her was wrapping her fists in his long, silken black hair.

"Are you all right?" he rasped, cradling her body away from the damp dungeon stones.

She simply nodded. "No other women. I am Were and I am your wife."

"No other women," he whispered, burying his wet face against her neck. "The ancestors have answered my prayers."

Garth stopped at a stone door that was ajar, put a finger to his lips, and slipped beyond it. Sasha, Hunter, and Silver Hawk followed quickly, entering the dark cavern relying on night vision that the elderly Gnome apparently didn't need. It was clear by the quickness of his steps that Garth knew every nook and crevice of the tunnel by heart. Things skittered; beetles and slimy things took cover at the invasion. But the group of three kept pace behind Garth until he cleared away a large stone by the wave of his wand and then moved back a hang of bramble with his arm.

"Does your human contraption work here, milady?" Garth asked, looking at Sasha. "We are outside the magic barriers. This section of the fortress is merely the craft of camouflage."

"Contraption? You mean my cell phone?"

"Yes, that thing that allows you to talk to your human soldiers."

Sasha pulled her cell phone out of her pocket. Within seconds it began vibrating. She gave Hunter and Silver Hawk a glance, and then returned her focus to Garth.

"I'm assuming you know what this is all about?"

Garth nodded. "Our reinforcements are coming in from across the waters—riding Dragons. Your humans will be at risk if they try to fly their planes and use weapons against them. Our home allies 'ave combined their magic and come through the Fae Stonehenge portals. The human soldiers may not understand and it could cost them their lives; more important, it could tip off the Vampires."

"Oh, shit!" Sasha looked at her BlackBerry. Colonel Madison had left a series of urgent messages that were blocked while she was inside the magic barriers of the castle. Walking in a circle,

Sasha connected to the return call. He didn't even wait to hear her voice.

"Trudeau, where the hell have you been?"

Sasha held the phone away from her ear. "Long story, sir, but your radar may show—"

"Something insane coming in hot over Lake Pontchartrain!"

"Aye, it would make sense that the Scots would lead by invoking the lake power of Loch Ness," Garth said, quietly conferring with Silver Hawk.

"What? Who are you talking to?" Colonel Madison yelled.

"Friendlies who are aware of the situation, sir. I'm on my way." Sasha looked at their pack shaman. "Silver Hawk, can you stay here at the sidhe with Garth while Hunter and I head to NAS? We need you both to try to make contact with the Dragon squads to ask for tolerance while we negotiate with the Air Force to try to get them to stand down."

She and Hunter didn't wait for the old men to nod. They were in and out of a shadow, and in the war room with Colonel Madison, stepping out of a darkened corner so quickly that they almost got shot.

"Jesus H. Christ, Trudeau—I still can't get used to seeing you two do that." Colonel Madison motioned for the men in the room to stand down.

"The radar is going nuts, sir," a radar engineer said as Sasha neared his screens. "I think these guys are jamming. I set up one-minute tells and initially there was just a huge blob of fast-moving activity, then it looked like it exploded into all these smaller blips headed for New Orleans."

"We've scrambled jets—"

"No, no, no," Sasha said quickly. "Call them back!"

"That blob," Hunter said, pointing to the screen, "is where a full European Dragon-rider Fae strike force is coming in from Scotland, England, probably the Netherlands, Ireland, wherever the Seelie strongholds are."

"The Joint Chiefs will need an explanation." Colonel Madison's attention ricocheted between Sasha, Hunter, and the radar screens. "I'm in command of the Paranormal Containment Unit, but the commander of NAS is responsible for anything unauthorized coming into our airspace."

"Then get that commander on the phone and tell him that not only will his men be in peril if they don't stand down, but it's also likely that a couple of billion dollars of aviation equipment could get fried out of the sky if they don't heed your advice." Sasha turned back to the screen, watching fighter jets close in on the scattered targets.

"Get me Commander Davis on the line," Colonel Madison barked to his men. As soon as the line connected, he wasted no time with formalities, filling in his Air Force colleague quickly.

"We had to scramble F-16s, Madison, until we had a confirm that this was supernatural and not a foreign hostile," Commander Davis argued. "But Dragons, are you shittin' me?"

"Roger that. Get your men out of the air."

"But if Dragons are headed toward New Orleans, our job is to protect the U.S. from any—"

"Get your men out of the sky, man!" Colonel Madison yelled, and then put Commander Davis on speakerphone.

"Tell your men to open a channel," Sasha said, walking around the table. "By now they ought to have a visual. They are gonna be freaked out and will need you to talk them down and give the order to come back to base."

"Who's speaking?"

"Captain Sasha Trudeau," Sasha said, without thinking, and then amended her title. "Recently retired, and on retainer with the PCU under Colonel Madison—special project of the POTUS and the Joint Chiefs."

The room was silent as a disgruntled noise filtered through the speakerphone.

"Open a channel," Commander Davis finally said to his men. "I want them to rendezvous back to base. Tell them to fall back."

But as soon as the channel opened, the frenzied voices of men in the air filled the speaker:

"There's fire everywhere! I've never seen anything like it, sir!"

"Something's got my plane from beneath! I'm in a hard roll and can't shake it, can't eject—there's something on top of my bird, sir. I'm going down!"

"I've got a visual, but I can't fucking believe what I'm seeing, sir!"

"Tell them not to fire! Pull back!" Sasha shouted. "Tell them to stop pursuit!"

Sasha and Hunter stared at the screens. The fighter jets were inside what looked like an asteroid belt of fast-moving screen blips.

Gun reports from aircraft-mounted machine guns and explosions filled the speaker as men's screams made Sasha close her eyes.

"Call them back," she said firmly, and then leaned into the speaker. "This is not our war, call those men back."

"What do you mean, this isn't our war!" Commander Davis shouted. "I've just lost two pilots and—"

"Then save ten more and call them back!" Colonel Madison yelled. "If it is paranormal, and it is, I have the authority!"

"Fall back," Colonel Davis grudgingly said after a moment. "Head back to base."

No one spoke as they listened to the retreat. Sasha prayed that it wouldn't be too late. Once a Dragon squadron sensed an attack, they'd go after the offenders until the last Dragon was in the air. But the eerie quiet and then hearing the base protocols to land planes finally made her release her breath. Obviously the Dragons had bigger fish to fry.

"I'm sorry for your loss," Hunter said to Sasha, and then looked at Colonel Madison.

Colonel Madison kicked over an empty chair. "A damned waste. It didn't have to happen." He turned toward the speaker and yelled, "It didn't have to happen!"

CHAPTER 14

Damage control was already under way as Sasha and Hunter walked down the long corridor to her team's temporary offices. The media spin would be that two fighter pilots crashed when they collided during a night training mission—hence all the fire and explosions. The ammo wasn't supposed to be live; some poor grunt made a mistake. Sasha raked her fingers through her hair. When was it going to end?

Hunter held her elbow just as they got to the door. "It wasn't your fault. It wasn't their fault. It was tragic—no more, no less."

She nodded, glad to be able to look into his intense brown eyes. There was a level of calm there that she required now. A steadiness that she couldn't wrap words around but that mattered very deeply.

"Thank you," she said in a quiet voice, still numb from watching two human beings die for no good reason. She stroked Hunter's cheek with her knuckles. "There was a time when it was all so simple. A Dragon terrorized a village for a bit, and then some hero came along and slayed it. A demon-infected Werewolf might ravage a country town, until the locals got up enough nerve to go hunt it down with pitchforks and torches, and behead it." She smiled, loving the way she'd coaxed a smile out of hiding on his somber face. "Then there was always that one really over-the-top Vampire viceroy, who got staked in broad daylight after the locals got tired of him bleeding out their daughters. What happened to simple, Hunter?"

"Technology killed it," he said, giving her a hug. "Seems like everything is moving faster . . . problems are bigger. Before, one brave knight could solve it all and go down in history for a century or two until the next monster reared its ugly head."

"You're making fun of me." She kissed his neck quickly and then pulled back.

He nodded and smiled. "Yes. I am. It was never as simple as was recorded in legend."

"I know." As her smile faded she touched his cheek again and reached for the door.

"But I wish it was, Sasha." He held her arm. "For you . . . I so wish it was."

"For you, too," she whispered, and then turned back to the door and opened it. There was no time to preserve their private moment.

Her team members were on their feet the second they saw her enter the lab.

"Good to see you, Cap. To say it's been a madhouse around here is an understatement." Winters shook his head and looked up from the screens.

"Good to see you, too, Hunter. But, seriously, I think we lost a coupla jets, even though I can't confirm it. They got all need-to-know-basis on me and wouldn't let any of us into the situation room without you."

"Do you know what's going on?" Woods asked, pacing between Winters's computers and Clarissa's medical testing equipment.

"You know we're locked and loaded, but who can fight what we can't see—especially if the brass is keeping us in the dark, ya know?" Fisher pounded Woods's fist as he passed him.

"There have been some awful losses," Clarissa said, hugging herself. "I can feel it."

"Was it the Erinyes?" Bradley asked, his worried gaze falling on Sasha and Hunter and remaining there.

"Okay, okay, people, here's what's up," Sasha said, moving to the center of the room. "The Seelie are really pissed at having lost sixty innocent members of their community to an outright butchering by the Vampires. So they sent in for reinforcements from Europe. Real cowboys—the Dragon-riding kind."

"Holy molie," Winters said, slapping his forehead.

"Are you serious?" Woods just stared at Sasha for a moment and then shook his head. "Don't answer that."

"I wish I wasn't." Sasha gave Hunter a sidelong glance. "The Fae opened up some kind of magick transport portal or whatever over Lake Pontchartrain tonight to bring their guys in before dawn."

"Needless to say, it's going to get hectic come the dawn." Hunter glanced around the room. "There will be blood. The two pilots that went down tonight foolishly fired on a Dragon squadron that was in the air. That squadron took the action as an invitation to war. Probably the only reason the rest of the pilots weren't wiped out was because Sasha had the foresight to know how the Air Force would respond and asked Garth and Silver Hawk to try to open a channel of telepathic communication with the Seelie."

"Is the government aware of the fact that World War Three is about to happen over the residential district of New Orleans tomorrow morning?" Bradley wiped his palms down his face.

"Just sayin' . . ." Winters looked around the group. "Because if they came in over the lake, and are hunting highfalutin' Vampires, they won't find them in the graveyards anymore. Just a hunch."

"Right," Sasha said in a weary tone. "After losing top viceroys, other VIP Vamps have most likely gone underground beneath their mansions."

"Then there's the clubs," Winters said, ticking off possibilities on his fingers. "The casinos. Any Vampire holdings in the region."

"Which means if the Fae destroy Vamp establishments, or any fronts that also cater to humans, they will go after the Finnegan's Wake bar, The Fair Lady, Dugan's Bed and Breakfast, the list is endless." Bradley's eyes were wide behind his horn-rimmed glasses. "This could get insane."

"Correct," Sasha said. "Which is why we have

to find out what the Erinyes connection is and try to prove to the Vamps that this wasn't the Fae. Problem is, at this juncture, the Fae are poised for retaliation."

"We could do a séance and call one of them up," Bradley hedged, and then looked around the group.

"Dude, are you nuts?" Winters was out of his chair and had bolted across the room. "Call up a demon? Be serious!"

"It can be done," Bradley said with more resolve. "Then you send it back."

"And do what?' Winters dragged his fingers through his hair. "Ask it why it's pissed off?"

"Precisely," Bradley replied. "It's a last-ditch effort, and we're definitely running out of time."

"Okay, let's keep that as an ace in the hole, Brads," Sasha said in a skeptical tone. "Because from what I heard about demons, when you bring one up and get it to do something, you seriously owe it—and generally it wants a human sacrifice."

"Right . . . ," Clarissa said slowly. "But wasn't that part of the deal that got very messy with the Vamps?"

The room became still as all eyes focused on Clarissa.

"Baron Geoff Montague made a deal with Queen Cerridwen's court member Kiagehul," Sasha said slowly. "That Vampire rat bastard Montague cut a deal with a turncoat Unseelie, Kiagehul . . . who used Lady Jung Suk—a Were Leopard—to do their dirty work."

"Lady Jung Suk had vengeance in her heart against her nephew, Shogun, and was willing to become disembodied to temporarily possess poor Amy," Clarissa said, walking toward Sasha. "Wasn't the deal supposed to be that Amy's soul would be lost, thrust out of her body and given to the demons, and Lady Jung Suk would take over the poor young woman's body?"

"Yes," Hunter said in a faraway tone. "But during the battle in the bayou, the girl never died. We cast the demon spirit out of her . . . and from what we learned tonight, many of the Were traits were left in Amy . . . much to my brother's good fortune."

"So the demons got played twice," Sasha said, grabbing Clarissa by both arms. "First by whatever spell and promise had to be made to them by whatever Lady Jung Suk and Kiagehul cooked up . . . and then by whatever part the Vampires played in trying to use that demon essence of Lady Jung Suk to make the wolves go to war."

"And not only didn't it work, but they got non-human deaths—or sacrifices, for lack of a better term." Bradley looked around the room. "Nobody who died owned a soul."

"Elder Vlad suicided his own man," Fisher said quickly. "Damn, this is gonna make me start smoking."

"Yes. Right in open UCE court," Hunter said. "Baron Montague's story was found wanting, Elder Vlad was furious, and he butchered his own man right on the spot."

"Just like Queen Cerridwen literally iced that crazy bastard Kiagehul." Sasha shook her head. "And we trapped and offed Lady Jung Suk in the bayou."

"But they all had outstanding affairs with the demons," Bradley said. "The 'they' being the Unseelie Fae, via Kiagehul, and the Vampires—unwittingly so, via the late Baron Geoff Montague."

"Yeah, but what about that other crazy bastard, Russell Conway?" Woods glanced around the team and pushed off the desk he'd been leaning against. "Seriously. Like didn't he come to town dragging a demon, too?"

"He did, but that was a personal deal forged years ago. He was to give that demon his human soul when he died, and he did. Case closed," Bradley said, folding his arms.

"And it took a squad of Marines, a garrison of Fae, and a bunch of wolf enforcers to put Conway out of his misery, too. . . . Sheesh." Sasha glanced around the team again. "Where's Doc?"

"Looooong story," Winters said. "Crow came to town, needed to talk to Doc. They went for a walk on the base. Bear Shadow escorted Crow Shadow's new wife back to the Uncompahgre, because Crow said it wasn't about not doing their job. But to be sure Jen was gonna be all right, Bear had to get her tucked in with the she-Shadows, or you know, they might not accept her . . . which could be messy, if tempers flared."

"Okay," Sasha said in a clipped tone, dropping the subject at that. She didn't want to even think about her brother's pregnant wife possibly being pack-rejected during a potential time of war. Part of her understood, but part of her was annoyed beyond words. If Crow Shadow had just listened to her and stayed in Vegas with Bear Shadow, far away from the pack, until things blew over . . .

"They are warriors and pack enforcers, Sasha," Hunter said in a quiet tone. "They could no more stay out of the battle than you or I could."

She knew that, but it only mildly helped stem her annoyance. More than anything, it just added one more group of people to worry about, more lives that could be lost, and more potential tragedy that could wreak havoc on everyone's emotions.

"We've definitely narrowed things down, then," Bradley said, breaking the tense silence. "The serpent-like demon that overtook Conway isn't in the same category as the Erinyes."

Grateful for the return of focus, Sasha paced to the lab table and sat down hard on a tall metal stool. "Okay, so, if we put two and two together, and I'm no demonologist or anything, but it looks like the Erinyes are now playing both groups that conjured them up against each other. That's just my layman's take. You've got the vamps that owe them and the Unseelie that owe them . . . and both the Vamps and the Unseelie were trying to make the wolves go to war."

"Exactly," Bradley quipped, and opened a big, black textbook on the lab table beside Sasha. "So, they are making the Vampires and the Unseelie suffer the fate of the spell they'd been conjured to perform—since the Vampires and Unseelie essentially used the demons to perform said tasks, but the demons were not paid for their services."

"Ergo why the Erinyes are involved," Sasha said in an exhausted tone as she closed her eyes and waved her hand in the air as though conducting an orchestra.

"Yes, precisely," Bradley said, reading over the tops of his glasses.

"But wait," Winters said, frowning. "I thought the Vamps and the Unseelie dude were the ones who didn't pay up ... so these righteous vengeance demons wouldn't be trying to avenge Baron Montague or Kiagehul."

"Out of the mouths of babes come words of wisdom," Clarissa murmured.

Bradley glanced at Clarissa and nodded. "The dead that was righteous, I guess, as demons probably would see it, and who was escorted to Hell under protest was Lady Jung Suk. She gave up her body—for an evil cause, true, but she did. She was supposed to get a new body out of the deal, and she didn't. And basically went down—and since she'd probably given away her soul years ago for whatever . . ."

"If I know Shogun's aunt, she'd negotiate with the Devil and find a contractual loophole in eternal damnation." Hunter returned his attention to Sasha. "Which is why it will be imperative to keep Amy and her family safe until this is over."

"Maaaan. . . ." Sasha jumped off her stool. There

were just too many loose ends to tie up and something was bound to fall through the cracks.

"Look, I know how you feel, Pop, but I didn't mean for it to happen like this." Crow Shadow walked away from Doc Holland and sat on the desk that was on the opposite side of the room.

"No, Son," Doc said in a quiet, stern voice. "You *don't* know how I feel."

The two men stared at each other until Crow Shadow looked away.

"I have lived the trauma of being a human with a wolf trapped inside me, never knowing why. My own father walked away from my mother and left her to go insane—"

"And that's why I couldn't leave Jennifer!"

"I'm on your side," Doc said, losing patience. "You don't have to raise your voice to make me understand. If I had known your mother was pregnant with you, I would have never left her side. And knowing your mother, she would have killed me if I'd tried."

"I know you all didn't get along, but damn, Pop . . . you didn't have to go there about my mother. She is still my moms."

Doc nodded, but his expression held no apology. "It wouldn't have been personal. It was about the survival of the fittest. Your mother didn't want to be put out of the pack or have her reputation tarnished for falling for a half-breed like me. But as much as she hated that the child she carried was a quarter human, she couldn't make the decision to terminate you." Doc looked away toward the window. "I guess just like my poor mother couldn't, no matter how my father treated her. So, there you have it."

"I don't understand what you're saying, man. There you have it?"

"Yes," Doc said calmly. "There you have it. My father walked, your mother hid, and they were both full-blooded Shadow Wolves. Now you've come back to the pack dragging a full-blooded human wife thinking that everyone at home is gonna be singing 'Kumbaya' and will treat your baby— *my grandchild*—like a full-blooded Shadow Wolf."

Doc used the silence to make his point and gave Crow Shadow his back to consider as he slowly walked to the window to stare at the moon. "I'm getting too old for this bullshit. I wish it would be right for you, Son. Wish I could make heartache and prejudice just disappear, just like I wished I could save your sister, Sasha, from all she had to endure. But I'm just a man. An imperfect being. I'll always love you. So will your sister and, I suspect, her husband and team. . . . But the Shadows are creatures of staunch tradition. I don't even know if Silver Hawk will be able to get them to welcome you and Jennifer with open arms."

Getting to the Chens was priority one. Sasha and Hunter raced through the dense shadow land mist but began to slow down as the cavern became darker and darker and the indisputable smell of sulfur stung their noses.

"I don't understand," Sasha whispered, taking her sidearm out of the holster.

"Something's definitely not right," Hunter said in a low tone, his gaze scanning the barren terrain.

Suddenly a ragged splinter of pitch-black darkness ripped open before them and a howling wind blew them backward. They hit the ground with a thud, stomachs and chests exposed to the onslaught of gargoyles pouring out of the disturbed border. Covering their faces and curling up into tight balls to protect vital organs, Sasha and Hunter hunkered down as leathery wings and scaly legs bumped and pushed past them in what seemed like an aerial stampede.

Although reflex made her want to fire on the beasts, gut hunch told her that they were focused on getting out of the demon doors, through the shadow lands, and out into the night. Their flight pattern seemed disoriented. As they battered and bumped her and Hunter's bodies, the one question that continued to assault her mind was, why didn't they attack? Gargoyles were the pit bulls of the old-world Vamps. She and Hunter were fresh meat. And what the hell were these things doing coming through protected shadow lands?

The answer came quicker than she'd expected. Just as the last of the flying stampede exited through the shadows, three huge demons leaped out of the tear between worlds.

Mesmerized, Sasha lifted her head, but Hunter pressed her face down quickly and turned his away.

"Don't look at them," he warned through his teeth. "This is not our fight."

He could feel their eerie presence pass over her; their cold, massive bodies sent a shudder through her as she squeezed her eyes tightly shut. But curiosity made her peep at their retreating forms.

Massive talons had replaced what should have been human feet. Their legs were covered in scales, and muscular spaded tails bullwhipped the air behind them. Serpents hissed and struck out from the thorny crowns they wore, and their muscular blue-gray arms terminated in vicious claws. Their backs were a sinewy network of corded tissue that worked in unison to move huge bat wings to lift them in flight.

The moment they were gone, the sulfur cleared and the black rip that hung in the air sealed.

"Twenty bucks say the Vampires called the gargoyles," Sasha said, slowly lifting her head and placing her gun back in its holster.

"I'll raise you ten that anything called up by the Vampires is no longer welcome to use the demon tunnels," Hunter said, dusting himself off and pulling Sasha to her feet.

CHAPTER 15

She needed to be at three places at once, but Hunter wasn't hearing anything about splitting up and each doing a part of the mission solo. They had to get Amy's parents back to the Sidhe, and also get word to the Sidhe to try to get Sir Rodney's forces to stand down. But there was also the not too likely chance of getting word to Elder Vlad without a fight—and even if they did, him standing down just on a my-word-is-my-bond code of honor scenario was insane. Still, they had to try.

"I don't get it," Sasha said, thoroughly agitated. "This is what we do—combat. We've been in a hundred brawls before. What's different about this one, Hunter? You are on me like you're my freakin' shadow, and we need to fan out to accomplish everything we've gotta do."

"I *am* your shadow," he said, not looking at her as he stepped down harder on the gas pedal.

"Ha, ha, very funny," she said, and then looked out the window. "We can't keep asking for Jeeps from the base, either, and not bringing them back.

There's a pattern here that's not gonna go over well with the brass."

"The shadow lands are too dangerous at present. Amy Chen's parents cannot physically withstand the distortion, because they are human. Do you have another alternative I should explore?"

She hated it when he got snippy. "No . . . but we could have saved time by—"

"We've discussed that option and I told you my reservations."

Oh, so now he was gonna try to pull the badass male alpha wolf thing on her and put more bass in his voice than was necessary? Sasha rolled her eyes. Pulease.

"And what if I just went to Amy's house alone?" Sasha folded her arms, not liking his tone.

"I would have followed you to be sure you were safe."

His response was so bland, so calm, that she wanted to scream.

"I do not want to fight, Sasha. I just want to deliver the humans to the Sidhe and avoid a war. I should not have to become locked in a confrontation with you now, simply because I seek peace."

Sasha blew a stray wisp of hair up off her forehead. Oh, brother . . . now her man had become the Zen master!

"May I come in, Mrs. Chen?"

The older woman stared out through the cracked door, keeping the chain lock firmly latched. She could not place the man's face, but things inside her head told her that he was a friend of her daughter's. His face was handsome, his eyes strange and crystal blue . . . his hair long, flowing blond so fair that it was almost white.

"Again, I ask for an invitation. May I come in, please, Mrs. Chen?"

She cracked the door open a little wider. "Ah . . . Well . . ."

"No!" Mr. Chen shouted. "We do not know you!" He slammed the door shut and shook his wife hard. "What are you doing? Sasha Trudeau is on the telephone and says there are people trying to abduct our Amy again. It is like the trouble before."

"Heads-up," Sasha said, bailing out of the Jeep. "Vamps!"

Hunter swerved the vehicle to a stop and rushed up the storefront stairs. "Mr. and Mrs. Chen, are you all right? It's Hunter!"

Sasha swept the alley and then took a running leap to catch a fire escape grate to propel herself up to the rooftop. A boot kick to her jaw sent her sprawling backward. She answered the affront with a hail of silver shells. But the quick-moving flash of white hair and black coat eluded her. She watched him jump buildings, grab a fire escape, and swing to a landing on the ground. Their eyes met. He gave her a toothy smile and then headed toward the house.

A pump shotgun blast met him in the doorway, giving Sasha just enough time to drop down behind the injured Vampire and cock the hammer on her weapon. In a flash he was gone. Hunter spun and gave the shotgun back to Mr. Chen.

"That only slowed him down. It was just a regular shell, not hallowed-earth packed or silver." Hunter nodded toward the Jeep. "C'mon. We don't have much time. They'll be back."

"Why does this keep happening? What have we done?" Mrs. Chen cried as they hurried down the steps.

"They don't want you; they want your daughter. Some really, really bad men want her dead," Sasha said, pushing the older couple into the car. "And we don't want that to happen."

"But why?" Mr. Chen said, leaning forward. "We don't understand. We are simple people. Honest people."

Sasha couldn't answer; there just wasn't time. A thud on the roof rocked the vehicle and she renewed a clip, then shot skyward while Hunter careened away from the curb. No matter how fast Hunter was driving, the Vamp kept its footing and moved with grace, avoiding every shell. Frustration tore at Sasha, making her fling open the Jeep door and flip herself onto the roof before the Vampire could reach through the compromised metal to yank out the Chens.

Instead of the platinum blond male vamp, a dark-eyed female terror stood before Sasha baring fangs. Wind from the hurtling vehicle and supernatural energy lifted the Vampire's black coat and suddenly two razor-sharp daggers slid into her palms. She smiled at Sasha and then slashed forward the second Sasha lifted her weapon and fired. A burning, stinging pain shot up Sasha's forearm. Fuck. She was cut.

The Vampire's smile widened. "Just give them to us and you'll live, wolf."

"Sorry. Can't do that, bitch." Sasha lunged and the Vampire tumbled over her, now standing at the front of the vehicle with Sasha crouched on the roof above where the Chens sat in the backseat beneath her.

"This is no business of yours, wolf!"

In a split second, Hunter's hand crashed through the roof and grasped the Vampire by her left leg. The Vampire screeched and yanked to get away while the Jeep perilously swerved.

"Oh, but it is," Sasha said, holding on, and quickly unloaded two slugs in the center of the Vampire's forehead.

Burning ash immediately covered the top of the vehicle and Sasha hunkered down as soot and debris flew over her. At the intersection, Hunter slowed down and Sasha jumped off the roof and got back into the vehicle.

She looked at Hunter's bloodied fist. "Thanks. . . . You need to have Garth or Silver Hawk take a look at that."

Hunter grabbed her arm and turned it over, looking at the deep slash. "And you."

"Yeah. She got me."

"I smelled it . . . the blood. If we didn't have

human passengers I would have come up there
and ripped her worthless throat out."

"Now the wolves are officially involved!" Elder
Vlad paced away from the long onyx table in his
dining room and waved for his servants to take
away the nude dead woman littering the furniture.
"That is a good thing, given the recent develop-
ments. But the one thing I have yet to understand is
how you have allowed them to destroy my Mara?
Is this what you have come to grovel at my feet to
explain?"

"Yes," Caleb said through a labored breath, holding his injured chest. Black blood oozed through his
fingers as he clung to the ravaged flesh destroyed by
a close-range shotgun shell. "But I must feed, Your
Excellency."

"And so you shall," Elder Vlad said, slitting his
wrist over a golden goblet. He watched Caleb lick
his lips and stared at the trembling hand that reached
for the goblet, somewhat amused. "Where are the
Chens?"

"Still with the wolves that escaped, Master."
Caleb dropped to one knee, weakening by the moment as the pool of black blood around him widened
on the cold stone floor.

"And you were not able to do such a small task
for me alone?"

"I came directly here once I was injured . . . but
not before telling Mara. We work as a team."

"And you left her to be incinerated by the
most troublesome pair of wolves in our region!"

Elder Vlad flung the goblet away to the stone floor. "All you had to do was collect Amy Chen's parents—two weak humans—and bring them to me! To avoid more Vampire losses I needed them tonight! Do you understand that there is no negotiating with demons once they are owed and feel betrayed?"

"Yes, Your Grace," Caleb stammered, beginning to wheeze. "But the wolves were an added complication."

"Added complication?" Elder Vlad swept away from Caleb, trembling with rage. "You have *no idea* about what it means to endure a so-called added complication! Will Elder Kozlov understand that we were in error? That our initial assessment of the situation was incorrect and that we unnecessarily baited the Fae into a global confrontation—all because you and Mara were sure that this was an attack by the Unseelie but were wrong? Will our Transylvanian Council understand that we overlooked demons on a vendetta—demons whom we owe? No, Caleb, *that* is a complication of the highest order . . . and all that I'd asked was that you rectify the situation that you created, and you couldn't even do that."

Caleb gasped and lay down prostrate on the floor in his own blood and began to weep as he dragged his body toward Elder Vlad's feet. "I will make this right. I swear to you . . . I will make amends."

"What shall I do with you? This isn't even my debt, technically, but with Erinyes there is no such thing as a technicality. They only understand absolutes. Such as it is, demons do not understand fine points, shades of gray, or compromise. Nor does Elder Kozlov, whose reputation precedes him in zero tolerance for error. The demons were promised the pristine soul of the Chen girl. Period. Or they will exact the price of retribution in that which Baron Geoff Montague sought their services for. The toll of not paying the demons what they're due is the total destruction of this region's Vampire and Unseelie population—just as the baron had colluded to wipe out the Seelie Fae and the wolf federations with that little slug Kiage-hul. It is all very simple, not that complicated at all. Bring me the Chen girl."

Caleb grasped Elder Vlad's ankles and pressed his blue lips to Vlad's boots. "Just allow me to regenerate and I will make this right."

Elder Vlad kicked him away. "Drink your fill from the floor like the pitiful dog you have become. Why is it so hard to find good help these days?"

"Okay . . . this is going to be a really delicate dance we've gotta do," Sasha said in a private whisper. She came in closer to Hunter as she looked over her shoulder at the Chens.

"I know. They are already frightened out of their minds. Plus, they probably now believe their daughter is marrying someone from the Korean mafia, or something equally insane."

"And marrying a Werewolf is better?"

Hunter stared at Sasha for a moment. "How can you make jokes at a time like this?"

"I'm just saying." Sasha let out a long breath. "Okay, I'm sorry. But it keeps me from just losing it altogether. Battlefield humor. Learned it while in the Service and it's a hard habit to shake."

"We have to split up."

Sasha just looked at Hunter.

"I know, I know," he said. "But I've got to get to my brother and Amy while the Fae roll out the red carpet for the couple's parents. We can have the wedding, feed Amy's parents, get them nice and re-laxed . . . you know, distract them so they don't have a heart attack."

"Sooooo . . . I get to stay with these very freaked-out people in the castle and make up all the ex-planations while you go tell Shogun and his wife to get ready."

"Right."

"And this is the better end of the deal how, Hunter?"

"You'll know better what to say to these humans. . . . You do damage control and diplomacy far better than I do—and you were the one who helped them think this was just an oasis before . . . a small village in the bayou. A little yeast that helped the bread rise is what you told me before. I cannot lie. . . . You . . . have a more dexterous way with words, Sasha."

"Watch it," she said, pointing at him within the inches between them. "Calling me a good liar does not win you brownie points, mister."

Hunter glanced over his shoulder at the Chens, who were huddled in a tight, frightened hug only ten feet away. "You know what I meant. . . ."

"You owe me, big-time, buddy," Sasha said as the Fae guards came to collect them. "And later I'm cashing in on that for all the points that's worth."

Hunter waggled his eyebrows. "I'm banking on it."

Ditching the Chens in a comfortable suite with food and wine was not as easy as she thought it might be. Amy's parents now had questions, like 3 million of them, all delivered in rapid-fire broken English. The sumptuous environs of the sidhe now were being equated to a drug dealer's hacienda— and the Chens swore that they'd somehow been abducted through the swamp across the border to Mexico.

Rupert, Sir Rodney's trusted valet, stood at the door confused, trying to read Sasha's eye signals and facial expressions. But the man was clueless. He didn't understand what the Chens were babbling about or why the more hospitality was thrust on them, the more Amy's mother cried and father protested.

"You need to give these people something to relax," Sasha finally whispered, stepping in close to Rupert. "But I doubt they'll drink or eat anything you offer. It's a matter of principle. They are very honest people who are completely freaked out."

"I would imagine," Rupert finally said in a dignified murmur, peering over Sasha's shoulder and dispassionately watching Mr. Chen try to comfort his near-faint wife. "They did, after all, have a run-in with Vampires. Unpleasant sort, especially for red-blood bleeders."

"Exactly," Sasha said, trying to bridge the human–Fae cultural divide. "They don't understand any of this and can't tell a Vampire castle from a Sidhe stronghold . . . so can you just make them chill out so I can go get my arm healed? I also need to talk to Sir Rodney, stat."

"Are we prisoners, then!" Mr. Chen demanded, clearly upset by the private exchange taking place between Sasha and Rupert at the suite door. "You have hidden my daughter and are holding her hostage?"

"No," Sasha said in a weary tone. "Don't you remember before, we were the good guys? We saved you and called you and told you what was going on."

Mrs. Chen nodded and blew her nose on one of the linen table napkins her husband had given her. "Then, you are still the police? The side of good?"

"Yes, ma'am," Sasha said, giving Rupert the nod to hit the Chens with a little Fairy dust. "Your daughter saw something that she probably shouldn't have. Uh, she can ID bad guys. We thought we got all the bad guys before, but we didn't. They now want to make sure she isn't a witness. But all these good people here are on your side. They are even going to a lot of trouble to make sure her wedding day is perfect . . . and, uh, that you all are safe. It's a part of our new uhmmm . . . Homeland Security witness protection program." Oh, brother . . . maybe Hunter was right. She'd dumped the whole can of yeast in this loaf!

"And you will keep us safe?" Mr. Chen said, wringing his hands. "And what of my store and friends?"

"We'll make sure that whatever you lose, the people who caused your problems will pay that back." Sasha squared her shoulders. If there was any truth to what she'd just said, this was it. The Vampires were so gonna pay this nice family back for all the trauma and drama they'd experienced.

Sasha stared at Mr. Chen and lifted her chin, then cleared her throat, forcing authority into her voice. "So let the store stay closed for a week or two . . . and uhm, once this nasty business is all over, you'll be able to go back to your old life."

"And my daughter is safe?"

Sasha nodded. "Right now, she's in good hands."

"Shogun!" Hunter called out. "Brother!" He listened carefully, cringed, and kept his eyes averted. He so did not want to be standing at what had become his brother's wolf den door at a time like this. It was humiliating. Even the guards gave him broad smiles from where they played cards in the next room. When there was no answer, the guards shrugged and went back to their game.

"My timing is not good, Brother, but I would not . . . disturb you . . . unless it was urgent." Hunter waited and kept his gaze to the floor. Finally, after a moment he heard rustling sounds but still didn't look up.

"Hunter?"

A wash of relief ran through Hunter. The last thing he wanted to have to do was go inside the cell to get Shogun's attention. "Yes . . . my apologies. But there's been a bit of a complication."

"How so!"

Hunter closed his eyes. The angry wolf had entered his brother's voice and Hunter couldn't blame him a bit.

"Vampires attacked Amy's parents' home and—"

A female shriek rent the air and within seconds the inside dungeon door flew open. Amy stood before Hunter disheveled and wearing only a sheet. Shogun was right behind her wrapped in a duvet.

"But we got to them in time," Hunter said calmly.

Amy melted against Shogun's body as he lifted Hunter's fist, inspecting it.

"You did battle for my parents-in-law?"

"Of course," Hunter said, staring at his brother. "I told you, your family is my family. Amy is now my sister, just as she is Sasha's sister. Also know that Sasha took a Vampire blade to her forearm, as well. But we are whole."

Shogun nodded. "It seems that I am again in your debt. Forgive my irritable tone just now."

"When it comes to family, there is no debt. When it comes to one's wolf, no apology is needed."

Hunter extended his left hand and arm to Shogun for an awkward warriors' handshake.

"You need to get that looked at," Shogun said, glancing at Hunter's right fist.

Amy touched Shogun's chest and then turned to look at Hunter. "My thanks are not worthy of your sacrifice . . . but please, tell me, how are my parents? Where are they?"

"Right now they are in the castle. . . . I have no idea what truths Sasha had to bend in order to get them to calm down. But I am sure that she used all of her human diplomacy, and perhaps even some Fae assistance, to help them relax. However, I suggest that you move to a better suite . . . maybe arrange to be married in the castle after all. The details I have left in Sasha's capable hands."

Amy buried her face against Shogun's chest. "My parents are here. They cannot see me like this—I'll die!"

Garth sat across from Sasha in the medicine room watching Silver Hawk perform an ancient Shadow Wolf healing. "We have a different way," Garth said, openly intrigued that the laying on of hands could knit skin and torn muscle. "Our healing is branded with centuries-old magick."

Silver Hawk nodded. "Asking the plants for their nutrients before using them—out of respect for the part they will play, observing Mother Nature's rules out of respect for her natural earth laws— asking the Great Spirit to guide my hands out of respect for Divine Intervention . . . asking the cells within Sasha's body to listen to my energy and to heal, out of respect for the interconnectedness of all things living . . . it is all miraculous and centuries old, therefore magic, too . . . yes?"

"Yes, my friend, you are wise." Garth gave Silver Hawk a little bow from where he sat on a toadstool across the room.

Silver Hawk smiled and briefly looked up from the task at the old wizard Gnome. "Words often get in the way. Magick, magic, healing, faith, belief, medicine. The objective is the same: that her arm heals. If it does, then what does it matter what we call it by name?"

Garth smiled as the wound on Sasha's forearm slowly sealed. "This is what I like most about the Shadow Wolves: You see all things as being a part of the whole. You do not split things up and say, 'Because you are this sliver of life, you do not belong.' That is truly the magick; it is knowing that we are all connected. We are all of The One."

"That is the missing element that the darkness does not see. They are blind and angry and use hate to create great divides." Silver Hawk nodded and then removed the poultice from Sasha's arm. "You must eat and then rest, daughter. By the dawn you will be as good as new."

"Thank you, grandfather, but I don't think I can rest," Sasha said, leaning forward to kiss Silver Hawk's weathered brown cheek. "Like I told you, the Vampires tried to abduct Amy Chen's parents, which can only mean that they *know* they owe the Erinyes. Once Hunter comes down here and gets his fist healed, we've gotta send a message to the Vamps that we're on to their game."

"Eat, first," Garth said. "I will bring Sir Rodney into the Roundtable Room with Queen Cerridwen. They need to hear what your investigation has uncovered. They also need to understand that we now know why the Erinyes are attacking the Vampires and using Unseelie methods to do so in order to create war."

Garth stood and smiled a wicked little smile. "No need to trouble yourselves about delivering a message to the Vampires. We will send them a Fae message that they will not soon forget. Ah, Elder Vlad, you have finally been had. He has killed sixty Fae and then learned that he has been rash. That will not sit well with his hierarchy, I'm sure . . . and all the more reason he must appease the demons, very discreetly. He cannot just come out and admit that he has ordered our countrymen killed with no sure evidence. Nor can he admit that he must give the demons what they seek before another sunrise or there will be more Vampire tombs raided."

"But as messed up as this whole situation is, doesn't that make you feel a little better about Queen Cerridwen?" Sasha said, standing.

Garth shrugged. "Only marginally. She's still quite the icy bitch, for my tastes."

CHAPTER 16

"Darling, you are cooling our guests' hot meal," Sir Rodney said, and then nodded to Garth to tap on the table with his wand to break up the ice that was creeping toward Sasha, Hunter, and Silver Hawk.

"But Rodney, this is an outrage!" Queen Cerridwen swept away from the round table and every footfall sent wide concentric circles of frost across the floor.

Nonplussed, the wolves kept eating, needing the rare steak to replenish them after the respective battle injuries sustained and the healings performed.

"Now, my dear, I know this is infuriating, but save the frozen daggers for the Vampires," Sir Rodney said calmly, taking a liberal sip of his Fae ale.

"What! Save it for the Vampires?" Queen Cerridwen shouted, sputtering tiny snowflakes as she waved her arms about. "I will . . . I will . . ."

"Send them a very cold missive, milady?" Garth stared at the queen.

Nervous servers hastened to Hunter's side, insistent on giving him more baby carrots, peas, mashed potatoes, and gravy, despite the fact that all he'd said he wanted was the meat on his plate. Silver Hawk just smiled and gave Sasha a sidelong glance.

"You'd do well not to tempt me with sarcasm, old wizard, especially when icicles dance at my fingertips just now."

"At your own risk, my friend," Sir Rodney said, slowly standing to stretch. "Our queen is in ill temper after hearing the wolves' report, or has that fact escaped you?"

"I own up to no sarcasm, sire." Garth looked at Queen Cerridwen with an open, earnest gaze. "I am quite serious. We need to send the Vampires a missive tonight, but they cannot read our silver-sent messages. The queen, who has been the most savaged by their attacks, with the loss of sixty of her countrymen, compared to a few of our guards that valiantly fought them off in the bayou, should inform them of our displeasure and awareness of their ruse."

"Quite so?" Queen Cerridwen narrowed her gaze on Garth, searching his expression for fraud. "You are serious."

"I am, my queen. I owe you an apology. I judged you from the past out of deep loyalty and love for my king." Garth bowed toward her and then stood straight, lifting his chin. "If we combine forces, what we send should cast daylight in the midst of their night."

"Oh . . . I see. . . ." Queen Cerridwen returned to the round table and waited for a chair to pull itself back so she could sit. Hunter and Silver Hawk stood and Sir Rodney waited until she sat down. "Thank you, Garth. I should like to repair any unpleasantness that fell hard between us."

"As you so wish, milady."

"Good, then it is settled," Sir Rodney said, sitting down with Hunter and Silver Hawk while Garth remained near them with his hands clasped within the sleeves of his robe. "There are a few points of order."

Sir Rodney glanced around the massive circular table and waited for everyone's full attention. "First, the testimony of the Shadow Wolves must be added into the records of the United Council of Entities. Garth, send a Fae missive to them with the blood signatures of the leaders of the North American Shadow Wolf Federation on it. We shall make it known that the wife of Hunter's brother, also our Southeast Asian Werewolf Federation ally, came under attack to satisfy an old demon debt by those who'd already been put to death by Vlad's very hand for treason. This debt should have been satisfied by the Vampire Cartel in some other way, and even the young woman's parents were attacked—he attempted to abduct them as hostages. The felonies involved in this are numerous. In any event, all of that spurious behavior, my friends, is a clear act of war."

Hunter sat back from the table and laid down his fork. "That's right. I had forgotten how this really should be understood in the greater context. An attack on Amy and her parents is an attack on the House of Shogun, the house of my brother, thus an attack on the House of the North American Shadows. . . ."

Stunned, Sasha held her fork mid-air dripping au jus. "Which means that no matter how the Southeast Asian Werewolf Federation may feel about the internal politics involved with Shogun marrying Amy Chen, this is still an act of war upon the House of Chen-Kwon." She looked at Hunter and then Silver Hawk. "We need to tell Shogun to get a missive to his people overseas and any people he has here in the states to tell them that he's safe, Amy and her parents are safe, but that Vampires came after them."

Garth nodded. "Perhaps our queen could assist in our international communications needs by helping to get the word to the Werewolves in a non-silver method?"

"Consider it done, Garth." Queen Cerridwen gave him a respectful return nod from where she sat.

"Thus, I believe a marriage would be prudent tonight, before the missives are launched," Silver Hawk remarked calmly, and then went back to his plate. "We will need a valid marriage to add additional credibility to our claims."

"But when the attacks actually happened, my brother and Amy were not yet—"

Silver Hawk waved away Hunter's statement with his fork. "They were betrothed, with an imminent wedding. This is the element of surprise. The Vampires had no way of knowing how important that young lady or her family is to our collective families." He looked around the table. "The answer is always in the stillness, in the shadows. Just as you saw the truth in the shadow lands, my son. You saw the Erinyes chase the gargoyles out of the demon realms because they'd been called by the Vampires. And the love of your brother for Amy Chen was in the shadows, a secret that none of the Vampires knew until it is now too late."

"This indeed gives us leverage," Queen Cerridwen said, making a tent in front of her mouth with her fingers. "They will rue the day they started this war . . . and by us entering the charges that involve Amy into the record, the Vampire Council of Old would be well advised not to have all of the Unseelie, all of the Seelie, and both factions of wolves hunting their lairs by day."

Sasha smiled and gave Queen Cerridwen a wink. "It would truly be a foolish move on their part to persist. But, more importantly, this will hopefully give Amy and her family a little respite from being constantly hunted by Vampires who need to make a deal right with some demons."

"Yes," Sir Rodney said, landing a firm hand on Hunter's shoulder. "Your brother needs to know that his new bride will be protected going forward. That is precisely why I also want to call the bluff of old Vlad by asking that the crone of the UCE court call up the demon Erinyes as witness of his debt to them. . . . This way, none of us have to call a demon or owe a demon, the crone is certainly used to all of the machinations that go along with that, and I'm sure the Erinyes would be more than willing to share their displeasure with any and all who would listen."

"Brilliant," Sasha said through a mouthful of steak. She swallowed it quickly, feeling much improved, and then wiped her mouth on her linen napkin. "But those gargoyles aren't local. I'd like to tag one of the little bastards with a message to send it running back home to wherever worldwide Vampire headquarters is. How much do you want to bet that Elder Vlad didn't tell The Most Scary that he literally bombed an Unseelie outpost for no reason?"

"And now has a dragon squadron on his ass," Hunter said, biting into a huge hunk of his steak.

"We could capture a gargoyle," Garth said slowly. "And we could tag it with an ice missive." He stared at Sasha. "That is sheer genius."

Sasha smiled. "All right, then . . . we've got a wedding to do tonight, an ice missive to get over to old Vlad, a silver Fae missive to enter into the UCE court docs, some kinda message to get to Shogun's people, courtesy of our queen, and a gargoyle to tag, all before sunrise. Piece of cake."

"Why the rush?" Amy's father asked as he stared at his wife.

"You ask too many questions, old man," she said, fixing the bow tie of his tux. "Look around at all of this expense the U.S. government is paying in this witness protection program—and not a penny to be paid by the father of the bride. Our daughter made herself a good bargain."

"But you were the one who said that our daughter shouldn't marry into these people who are strange and dangerous!"

"Shush," she hissed. "This Shogun is wealthy—we saw that from the wedding gifts he sent, *and* he is of royalty but *chooses* to do the honorable work of fighting bad men. Our friends will die of envy."

"Our friends could die of mobster bullets and so could we."

Mrs. Chen pinched her husband. "Not another word to ruin this night."

"Ow!" He shrugged away from her and whispered hotly in her ear, "The fortune-teller said that they should marry on a full moon next month! And why can't they have a good Chinese monk do the ceremony? Who is this *Indian* shaman? Does he know our ways? Is he licensed to perform legal ceremonies? This is all very rushed and very strange."

"Next month, this month, it is a full moon and look at your daughter's face." Mrs. Chen dabbed her eyes and turned away from her husband. "Look at her beneath the veil; she is so beautiful. . . . I have waited all my life for this day. And the groom, so handsome. You be quiet about Silver Hawk. This is the groom's grandfather and cleric, so he will be good enough for us."

Sasha gave Hunter the eye and Hunter smiled.

The man always looked good in a tux. Wolf hearing had helped her decipher the tense exchange between Mr. and Mrs. Chen, and Sasha knew Hunter had heard the loud whispering, too, even though it had occurred all the way across the large formal dining room. She watched as a huge red paper Dragon came to life with the drumming. Lyrical flutes and Chinese strings blended in as tiny Elves maneuvered the Dragon along the aisle. It had taken every bit of negotiating skill she owned to get the Fae to do some of the ceremony with regular labor, lest they send Amy's parents into apoplexy.

Clearly the Chens were not ready to witness real magick, so a real red Dragon was out of the question, just like a magically floating chair was. No. Regular palace guards would just have to hoist the petite bride up and carry her to Shogun the old-fashioned way while Hunter waited beside him as his good-luck man.

But Mrs. Chen was right. Her daughter was exquisite in her red silk traditional Chinese wedding gown. The handiwork of Fairies was evident to Sasha, because preparing the hall and getting Amy's hair twisted up into an elaborate basket weave pattern, replete with Chinese bridal crown, would have taken a normal salon six hours. Fairies were known for their attention to detail, and they'd spared no magick in transforming Amy's makeup, doing her manicure, bathing her in a sweet oil–infused bath, and dusting her with the most sumptuous of fragrances. They'd literally transformed the hall into a red silk paradise, and the tables behind the ceremony were laden with aromatic traditional Chinese dishes kept piping hot by Fae sleight of hand.

However, the young woman's glow was authentic and all her own. Through the red mesh veil, tears sparkled in Amy's gorgeous eyes. Her fragile beauty was breathtaking as her lotus blossom bouquet gently trembled the closer she got to Shogun. Sasha blinked quickly and looked up, fighting the moisture in her eyes. She pressed a palm to her heart for a moment and then allowed her palm to fall away from her deep crimson sheath. No two people deserved love and peace more than Amy and Shogun, and to be chosen as Amy's good-luck woman was definitely an honor. Sasha just hoped she could live up to the title.

"Are you ready, Brother?" Hunter said quietly, glancing at Shogun. Hunter smiled as Shogun simply nodded but never took his eyes off his approaching bride.

Sasha swallowed hard, wishing that she'd had the forethought to take her engagement ring off the silver chain that held her amulet to slip it onto her finger. She'd never attended a wedding in her life and hadn't expected to be so affected by this beautiful midnight ceremony under the moon.

With deep reverence she watched the couple come together and then go to Amy's parents to kneel before them and pour tea as Silver Hawk's deep rumble of words spilled out blessings upon the couple, blessings upon the ancestors, reminding all in attendance of the need for, and strength of, family. Even Queen Cerridwen moved closer to Sir Rodney as Rupert hugged himself and bit his trembling bottom lip.

Unconsciously Sasha's hand went to her ring as her gaze slid to Hunter. His steady gaze had never left her, and a silent understanding passed between them. Silver Hawk's words flowed through her soul, breaking down the last of her barriers, the last of her reservations, until suddenly she wished that Doc had been there, wished that her entire team could have seen this . . . wished that she had not wasted so much time fighting everything and everyone around her, yet there was still more fighting to do.

But not for this lovely couple, she told herself. Not for her brother. Not for her sister. Not for the honorable Chens.

"You are now husband and wife," Silver Hawk said. "Let the mate seal never be broken. Shogun, you may lift Amy's veil and kiss your bride."

CHAPTER 17

With unsteady hands, Shogun lifted Amy's veil. But before he could lean down to kiss her, the dungeon doors blew off. Screeching Erinyes nightmares billowed up from the depths of the castle, dropping dead Fae dungeon guards like bloody refuse from high above the ceremony.

"Look away!" Garth shouted. "Lest ye turn to stone." He spun around and blinded the Chens and then wielding his wand yelled out, "Mirrors!"

Erinyes flew upward and closed their eyes, screaming to avoid their own images. Mrs. Chen fainted into her blind husband's arms, and he quickly covered her body, huddled against the ground, calling out for his daughter in sheer panic. Wand blasts exploded furniture as Fae castle staff screamed and took cover while palace guards stormed the room.

"Battle stations!" Sir Rodney shouted, leaping over a table and calling a wand into his hand.

Queen Cerridwen materialized a mirrored shield

in her fist for Sir Rodney to look at and then tossed it to him. "Fight with this, milord!"

Archers instantly broke through the windows, aiming at the Erinyes who circled above the chandeliers in the vaulted ceiling. Every wolf shed their human form and Amy was now a deadly feline force.

"Return what is ours by right, Cerridwen of Hecate!" one of the Erinyes yelled, and then dove toward Amy, avoiding the queen's icy wand blast.

But the Erinyes obviously didn't expect to have to drag a Were Snow Leopard to Hell with a pack of wolves on their heels. The demon chasing Amy reached out and received a brutal rake to her face as Amy gracefully leaped behind an overturned table. Shogun caught the beast's spaded tail in his massive jaws, flipped her over, and tackled her to the ground just in time for Amy to slash in and disembowel the creature. Hunter jumped up from behind another table and ripped off the wing of another attacker coming in on an assist as Sasha scored the throat of one who made the mistake of looking over her shoulder when Silver Shadow leaped onto her back. Sir Rodney worked in tandem with Garth, blowing Erinyes away from Amy and shielding castle staff.

Both Amy and Shogun flipped out of the way of the first maimed beast's talons, and before she could get up Queen Cerridwen flash froze the Erinyes in a permafrost tomb.

"I owe you nothing!" Queen Cerridwen yelled. "You made a deal with a member of my court who was executed for treason! I gained nothing from his unsanctioned bargain with you and was none the wiser of the deal he cast!"

"Liar!" another of the Erinyes screeched, going to her dead sister in fury. She stood and pointed toward the queen. "So says the Vampire Vlad! He claims you and he had a deal and you reneged upon him. You killed your own man in open court after he killed his own in an act of loyalty to you!"

"Then let Elder Vlad bring proof of his duplicitous claims!" Queen Cerridwen shouted back, looking into a mirror as Hunter, Sasha, and Silver Hawk—now the wolf Silver Shadow—held a line around the queen, snarling.

"Be gone from my castle, demons!" Sir Rodney shouted. "You dare breach a Fae sidhe on spurious charges, your next attempt will be your last!"

"We had right to follow the trail of the Unseelie whom we bargained with into your dungeon!" the lead she-demon screeched. "We can enter anywhere there has been a bargain made between us and the damned!"

Sir Rodney and Garth gave each other a look.

"But you cannot enter again once barred by the righteous—and Kiagehul was executed by my own hand! I have joined forces with the Seelie!" Queen Cerridwen shielded her sight with her forearm as she lowered her wand toward the she-demon. "Look around, Erinyes. The proof is before your very eyes. The Unseelie and Seelie houses stand united. The wolves stand with us. If I wanted that bargain that was struck by Kiagehul with Vampire

Vlad, why am I not in his lair plotting to give you the girl you seek?"

The Erinyes passed uncertain glances between them, their red eyes blazing in the mirrors with unbridled rage.

"You best pray, ice queen, that my sister thaws out in Hell," the demon crouching above the fallen one hissed.

"Take the virgin and only give her back if this lie bears out as truth, Megaera!" another called out as the leader lifted off holding her frozen sister. "We must give the master his due!"

"There is no virgin in this room," the one identified as Megaera replied, glaring at the snow leopard. "Our payment is not only late, but the package is damaged. We will seek recompense. Know that, Unseelie!"

Just as quickly as they'd flooded the main dining hall, the Erinyes took flight in a massive dark flock of screeching anger and disappeared down the dungeon steps.

Garth immediately sealed the dungeon door. Fae staff began quickly collecting the dead. The castle became a frantic hotbed of guards and wizards rushing about. Amy transformed into her human body, grabbed up her human gown, and raced over to kneel by her distraught, blind parents. The wolves came back into their human forms and dressed slowly and silently, numbed by fury.

"How the hell did they breach my dungeon?" Sir Rodney bellowed, going over to the now-sealed door and lobbing a punch at it. "Tell me whot in 'eaven's name must we do to seal the sidhe from demon invasions, man!"

"You held Kiagehul the traitor there," Queen Cerridwen said in a dangerously low tone. "We were lucky, this time. But the demon spoke the truth—they had barrier rights to come search the location of where the last deal was obviously made . . . and it was in your dungeon, Rodney."

"And no one thought to properly seal the dirt floor to a possible demon breach?"

"We didn't realize he'd had time to spell-cast during his short internment," Garth said quietly, and bowed his head. "Silver Hawk . . . if we might avail you of your services to put down a prayer made by a righteous man."

"Gladly," Silver Hawk said in a quiet tone. "They will not get through again."

"My brother was down there with his wife," Hunter said between his teeth, pacing. "An hour earlier, Shogun would be dead and Amy would be missing."

"And where are my Griffin Dragons? Where was the aerial support!" Sir Rodney shouted, now walking in an agitated circle.

"Pure stone, sire," an injured palace guard rasped. "Broken into a thousand pieces in the courtyard where they fell the moment they stared at the beasts through the window. Killed two good men from the falling rubble."

"Aye," another guard said in disgust.

Sir Rodney closed his eyes. "On the morrow, the Vampires will know what a breached sanctuary feels like." He turned to Garth and gave him orders in a low, deadly tone: "Prepare all missives with my queen for immediate delivery. Add this to the list of offenses once you tally the dead and injured. A pox on Vlad Tempesh!"

A whimper from Amy's mother drew attention to the Chens. Amy looked up with tears streaming down her cheeks. "Is there any way to allow them to sleep and to only remember the beautiful wedding, the feast, and all that was good before it was ruined?"

"Of course, child," Garth said with tenderness in his gaze. He waved his wand and Amy's parents slumped. Two guards rushed over and lifted them as Rupert hurried behind them. "When they awaken, they will remember all that was good and having too much wine and rich food. . . . Should any memories ever invade, they will be thought to be the dreams of the overfed."

"Thank you," Amy murmured, and Shogun went to her.

"We're going to make this right. I promise you."

"Brother, if you have never heeded my words before, please heed them now—stay with your new wife. If the castle comes under siege again while Sasha and I are gone, you and Silver Hawk must be here."

Shogun gave Hunter a nod, but Sir Rodney's eye held a question.

"Surely you're not going out into the night, now, after such an attack?"

Silver Hawk captured Sir Rodney's gaze as he

stepped forward. "They must. Sasha's family and
Hunter's pack brothers are on a human military
base that is ill prepared for a supernatural onslaught."

"Get down!" Woods yelled, spraying the windows
with an M16.

Glass and wood became a hail of shrapnel. Two
Vampires bust into flames as hallowed-earth-packed
shells riddled their bodies. Crow Shadow sailed
through the second-floor window, tackling a Vampire on the ground, brutally savaging him. Fisher
pulled a pin on a grenade and lobbed it out of an
adjacent window, creating a diversion so that Crow
Shadow could get away unharmed as two more
Vamps touched down to assist their comrade.

Base sirens screamed. Pandemonium was in
full effect. Clarissa and Winters hunkered down
under a lab table as Bradley quickly created a
brick-dust circle against possible demon incursion.
Doc was pure motion, sealing the doors and vents
with holy water and prayers. MPs kicked in the
door, poised to burst into the room, but never even
got to lodge their complaints. Vampire mercenaries led by Caleb yanked the men off their feet,
snapping their necks. But the moment the Vampire
tried to enter the room, a blue-white holy water and
prayer barrier scorched his leg.

Caleb drew back with a furious howl and fas-
tened his hatred-hardened gaze on Doc Holland.
"Smoke them out! I don't care if you have to burn
down the entire base to get to these rats, do it! But

I want them alive. An exchange for the girl— Sasha Trudeau's entire family for one Amy Chen."

Instantly the Vampires disappeared and took up a position outside the windows, staring up, waiting. Fire roared into the room and soldiers, airmen, base staff, and commanding officers moved at a frenetic pace outside, yelling at the Vampires to get out of the way while desperately trying to extinguish the supernatural blaze that was impervious to human efforts.

"We've gotta bail out, Doc," Woods yelled over the din coughing, "or we're gonna burn alive!"

Bradley pulled Winters and Clarissa from beneath the lab table and headed toward the windows. Smiling Vampires waited patiently, their toothy smirks a promise of cruelty.

"If you jump," Fisher said, coughing, "I'll cover you. I'll try to scatter 'em so maybe you can get through that vamp front line to the guys on the base working the hoses."

"Then what?" Doc yelled, shielding his face from the heat with his arm. "They'll kill every man that tries to keep them away from us."

"Fish, put the rifle down before a sniper thinks you're their biggest problem!" Woods yelled, and then grabbed Clarissa's hand to pull her closer to the fresh air.

The trapped team looked up as the fire roared across the tiled ceiling.

"We've gotta go, now!" Woods said, pulling Clarissa by the waist as she doubled over, gagging from the billowing smoke.

Woods hoisted Clarissa over the window's edge with Bradley as Fisher helped Winters hang and then prepare to drop. Vampires leered up, making gestures with their hands to let Clarissa and Winters go. Several brave servicemen ran over, only to get murdered outright for their trouble. Base personnel stopped dead in their tracks for a moment. Colonel Madison leveled a revolver at the Vampire line.

"PCU! Those are supernatural hostiles! Cover those civilians with silver shells now!"

Several Vampires turned back toward the direction of Colonel Madison as Clarissa fell to the ground with Winters. Bradley bailed over the edge of the window to try to put his body between hers and certain danger as Doc came down with a thud right behind him.

Vampires rushed in, but a black blur leaped out of the shadows, savaging the Vampires that moved toward members of the team. Doc flung out a burning spray of holy water as Bradley blinded a Vamp with a fistful of hallowed earth.

"Do not shoot that wolf!" Colonel Madison yelled. "Those two men in the building are mine!"

Fisher picked up his M16 and went over the wall with Woods, shooting at airborne Vamps. The two soldiers hit the ground, and watched in horror as Vampires turned on Colonel Madison's men. The team was trapped against the wall of the burning building; Madison and his men wouldn't be able to hold off the onslaught for long. Then suddenly the moon went dark.

"Hold your fire!" Bradley called out.

Vampires scattered as white lightning bolts exploded asphalt behind them. The team flattened their bodies to the ground. Military personnel took cover, watching in awe and not sure what to fire on as huge Dragons dive-bombed out of the sky. It was as though a supernatural cavalry had arrived with what seemed like knights in medieval armor riding them and casting white light charges from the tips of strange blades.

M16s, rocket-propelled grenade launchers, Humvees, and tanks sat poised, still, while servicemen looked up and gaped. A huge fire-breathing Dragon touched down in front of the civilian team, pawing the earth and snorting, daring a Vampire to come near its protected charges.

Then just as quickly a funnel cloud opened in the center of the base yard, spewing up concrete, gravel, and asphalt with what seemed like a thousand gargoyles. Two more wolves leaped out of the shadows, one massive black beast and a slightly smaller one of exquisite silver.

"Trudeau, Hunter, over here!" Woods cried out.

The Dragon guard looked up, snorted fire, and then scorched several gargoyles as it lunged into the air. Sasha and Hunter immediately went on the offensive, attacking a downed gargoyle that was still alive before it could rejoin its funnel cloud. They gave the team a glance. Crow Shadow exited a shadow and joined them, and then the three wolves fanned out to take a protective stance in front of their family members.

Above their heads the skies were filled with an aerial dogfight that left the humans on the ground gaping. Gargoyles dive-bombed Dragon riders, attacking each Dragon ten at a time, grasping onto the massive beasts' backs, legs, and tails in an attempt to scurry up close enough to kill the Fae riders. But the Dragons scorched the incoming danger as though burning locust swarms while swatting away some with slices from their deadly tails.

Standing, and held to the Dragon by the sheer force of magick, gallant Fae riders hacked at interloping gargoyles that tormented the Foe's mounts with demon teeth and vicious claw slashes. Soon the military ground forces were able to make out sides and, with Colonel Madison's commands, sent mortar fire into clouds of gargoyles to help the dragons even the score.

But not to be outdone, the Vampires made another run at the human soldiers on the ground to stop their assists. Torn, Hunter peeled off with Woods, leaving Fisher, Sasha, and Crow Shadow to protect the team. A Vampire blur that was headed toward Madison was knocked out of the air. Both Hunter and the Vampire hit the ground with a thud. Madison's men leveled weapons, but Madison shouted, "Wait!" Hunter stood up with the Vampire's esophagus in his jaws and then leaped into a base shadow to return to Sasha's side.

Dragons roared as gargoyles screeched a retreat and headed toward the wide cavern in the middle of the base yard. Sasha looked at Hunter, and as the last gargoyle tried to dive into the pit they both jumped at it in unison, tackling the screeching, fighting-mad creature to the ground. Dragons landed. Several Fae riders dismounted and ran over to the captured demon.

"Let it go and we'll fry this bastard back to livin' hell," a Fae air commander said, pointing his sword toward it as his men shouted a collective, "Aye!"

Hunter transformed, using all the strength within him to hold the creature down and then getting help from Crow Shadow. "No," Hunter panted. "Sir Rodney wants to send one back to Transylvania with a message tagged on it."

Colonel Madison came over with his men, gingerly passing snapping dragons. "What the fuck. . . ."

"Aye," the Fae commander said, and then spit. "Oh, we'll tag the little bastard all right. Anybody need a lift back to the sidhe?"

CHAPTER 18

Total fatigue liquefied Sasha's bones. Every battle injury she'd sustained in the last twenty-four hours cried out as her body slid down into bubbles on the opposite end of the huge claw-foot tub that she and Hunter shared. Sure, Silver Hawk had sealed up gargoyle gashes, fractures, cuts, bruises, and scrapes. But her muscles and newly healed and extremely tender soft tissue whined for regenerative sleep.

She could tell Hunter felt it, too, because the poor man just laid his head back with a wince and remained very, very still in the hot herbal water.

"You okay?" she finally asked.

"Yeah," Hunter croaked, and then took in a deep breath through his nose.

"Some ride, huh?"

"I don't want to talk about it."

"I'm still a little queasy. . . . I wouldn't care if I never saw another dragon again."

"Nausea is not my issue," Hunter said with another labored breath. "The knights have special leather-reinforced gear designed for their profession. We don't."

Sasha lifted her head and stared at Hunter slack jawed. "Oh, baby . . . did you tell Silver Hawk?"

"I didn't have to."

"Did it help?"

"I suppose he healed any nerve damage or internal injuries, but it's all soft tissue down there. Need I say more?"

Sasha squinted and then sat up carefully, allowing the hot water to swish around her back. "Aw . . . man. I promise to kiss your boo-boo and make it feel better later."

"Yeah," Hunter said on a heavy exhale. "But right now, just let me quietly die a thousand deaths in the tub, alone, for a while, okay."

"'K'." Sasha slipped out of the water and then walked around to his end of the tub and placed a gentle kiss on his forehead. "I am so sorry that happened to you."

He kept his eyes closed and nodded. "I love you, too." But then he captured her arm as she moved away from him. "Are you sure you're all right?" He stared up at her and searched her face for the truth.

"Yeah, I'm okay."

He pulled her close to him and nuzzled her belly. "Promise me you'll tell me if you don't feel well."

"Yeah, sure," she said, and frowned and then bent to kiss the crown of his head. "I'm fine. I'm more worried about you, truth be told."

"The worst of it is over. . . . Dry off and get in bed. I'll join you in a bit."

"All right," she whispered, and brushed his mouth with a soft kiss.

Sasha grabbed a large, fluffy white terry cloth towel and slipped to the other side of the privacy screen. As usual, Fae hospitality knew no bounds. The bath was infused with Fae herbal healing, and just soaking in the water made her feel like she'd taken a sleeping pill. She pressed her face into the fragrant towel and was almost lulled to sleep by its warmth while still standing up.

Across the room a gleaming oval table was set in the far corner with two dome-covered silver serving trays. All she or Hunter had to do was speak the requested menu item of their wildest dreams and then lift the dome—Fae room service had no competitors in the human world. Same deal with the cleaning service. All she and Hunter had to do was drop their soiled clothes in the hamper provided and freshly laundered clothes would be there in the morning. That is, if one wanted their old clothes back, because the handcrafted armoires and bureau drawers offered the finest array of choices made out of the best cottons, linens, silks, and leathers one could ever hope for. Muddy boots went outside the door, and sometime in the bewitching hour of the night fresh-polished shoes would return, courtesy of the castle Elves.

The suite that Rupert now dubbed "their castle suite" was furnished with royalty in mind. Exquisite chaise lounges tastefully dotted the room, along with overstuffed Queen Anne chairs, a thick hooked rug, and pretty silk-covered settees near the fire. A four-posted rice bed sat alone with polished step stools beside it, the bed loaded with insanely soft pillows, a hand-embroidered goose down duvet, and sheets so soft that they felt like they were petting her.

The warm earth and moss tones of the forest that surrounded her calmed her weary mind while the call of the soft bed drew her across the room as though she were in a trance. All of her good intentions to wait up for Hunter and to check on him slowly evaporated as her body sank into the preheated warmth of the bed. Her thoughts drifted lazily between semi-conscious awareness and her knowing that her family was safe. Even Crow Shadow's new wife and Bear Shadow were collected by the Fae and brought in by Dragon escort. Just for a few hours, everyone and everything was all right. Sasha smiled as she drifted off to sleep stroking the place on her belly where Hunter had left a kiss.

The old crone screeched and held the Fae missive aloft. "Book! Fetch thee here and take a memo!" She waited until the dusty black tome hovered in the air before her and opened itself to a blank page, its mate pen poised just inches above the ancient living parchment. "There has been mischief and malfeasance afoot!" she exclaimed. "Involving all of the usual suspects. Enter this Fae missive into the official record."

* * *

Elder Kozlov snarled as his henchmen held down the screeching gargoyle and skinned it alive for his council.

"They have tortured a creature of this council, burning a declaration of war into its very body," a red-eyed Vampire hissed, extending the bloody skin out for Elder Kozlov to inspect.

"It appears the Fae wanted to get your attention, Your Eminence," one of the Council Elders said in a low, lethal tone. "They certainly have mine. This is highly unusual, even for the Fae."

Elder Kozlov flung the dripping, scaly gargoyle skin on the table and then summarily sent a black bolt toward the squealing creature to silence it. "If these charges are true . . . then, gentlemen, we have a very disturbing problem in New Orleans."

"Where is Caleb?" Elder Vlad bellowed, snatching the closest mercenary to him with a fistful of his leather coat.

"He did not come back with us, Your Grace. He said that he would search for the girl into the very dawn."

"Which is only one hour from now!" Elder Vlad flung the mercenary against the stone wall, causing the others around him to carefully back away.

"The Fae have brought in Scot Dragon riders," the crumpled soldier said.

"And Brits, and Welsh, some Irish, it seems," another amended.

"Then if we cannot find the Chen girl, take all

of New Orleans' human population hostage, if that will bring her to me!"

"Yes, Your Grace," the fallen Vampire said as he slowly stood.

Elder Vlad smoothed a palm over his bald scalp. "Leave me!"

He waited until the room was cleared and then walked over to the large fireplace mantle near his throne and closed his eyes. In his mind he could see Elder Kozlov deep within the subterranean lair in Transylvania that never knew sunlight. Elder Kozlov looked up from his council throne and made a tent with his spindly fingers before his mouth, his expression unreadable.

They have beset us with Dragon riders from Scotland to England and all small provinces in between, Your Eminence, and have decimated your gargoyle reinforcements. We may need more support.

Elder Kozlov closed his eyes. *Request denied . . . on the grounds of possible treason.* The ancient Vampire took a shuddering breath. *Explain to me about the Erinyes, Vlad.*

Caleb stumbled through the brambles, sloshing through the marshy bayou bog. Tears stung his eyes as he dropped to his knees and called out into the night, "Crone! Sanctuary, old woman!"

Slowly the UCE council building lifted out of the swamp and Caleb glanced at the dawning sky.

"Sanctuary for a testimony, I beg you!"

The doors opened and the old crone took her time to walk down the long, flat marble steps.

"What do you know of this unfinished business with the Erinyes?"

"Enough to have me tortured for a hundred years under Vlad Tempesh," Caleb said, swallowing hard.

"It will be daylight in less than an hour."

"Rather to burn and end it all than to be locked in a tomb, starving to death, going insane for a century," Caleb said quietly.

"They will surely kill you for your blood oath in the book."

Caleb shook his head sadly. "No, they won't. Death is a release, and my kind is so much more creative than that."

"Erinyes, hear me!" Megaera shouted to the numberless throngs of demons that perched on the hot crags and cliff ledges. She sent her withering gaze into the darkness, breathing in the sulfuric fumes that issued up from the bubbling lava pits. "We have bargained well and victory is at hand!"

A collective screeching cheer went up as Erinyes bumped and resettled themselves amongst the rocky inferno.

"Soon, we shall have the bodies we need to travel freely. The Dark Lord wants our legions to roam the earth, unencumbered by the demon incarceration rules set down eons ago to contain us in servitude!"

Again jubilant chaos broke out amongst the Erinyes, and Megaera turned away from the raucous crowd to tend to her fallen sister.

"Our plan worked beautifully, did it not?" Alecto stroked their injured sister's serpent-twisted hair and then gazed at Megaera.

Megaera nodded and hissed. "The Dark Lord feeds on all compromised human souls himself, as was struck in the great bargain at the dawn of time. But he has graciously given us any wills that we might claim from the supernatural world. That is a bargain indeed. We have found our carriers."

"Truly," Alecto croaked, and came nearer to the rocky ledge where their fallen sister, Tisiphone, lay. "I wish it could be the Vampires, though. Such power . . ."

"The Vampires are of no use to us, as their souls are already given over to our Master the moment they take a human life to feed."

"And their bodies go to ash and embers when killed in battle," Alecto said with a cackling laugh. "Ah, but the Fae . . ."

"Yes, the Fae are another matter entirely. Mother Nature holds their souls in her orbs of light—"

"Unless they strike a poor deal and bargain it away from her, like Kiagehul did."

Megaera nodded. "Yes . . . like Kiagehul."

"And of the wolves?"

Megaera shook her head. "Too close to human, they are not immortals but simply have longevity. Unless one turns to us, like Lady Jung Suk did, the battle for their souls falls into the realm of the great bargain. The Light and the Darkness must fight to sway it and claim it."

"But she came to us. . . . We cannot be blamed for her barter."

"Calm yourself, Alecto," Megaera crooned. "She was already dark when she came to us. The Dark Lord already had her in his records, so that upon her death he owned her. But she was wise and struck an accord for self-preservation to extend her life, even if her body was destroyed. She seduced Kiagehul and got him to call upon us to strike such a deal . . . and got him to implicate a foolish Vampire."

Alecto released a screeching laugh. "Fools. Now the Unseelie and the Vampires owe us, because they never delivered the Chen girl as a sacrifice."

Megaera smiled and wagged her gnarled talon at Alecto. "What the Vampires remain ignorant of is, the debt can easily be settled by the Vampires giving us any young virgin for Lady Jung Suk to occupy, although why she would want a virgin is beyond my comprehension."

"Or the ice queen could end it all by doing so . . . true?"

"Ah, but, Alecto . . . our ice queen has found a warm heart within her frozen chest, and her summer king will never allow the butchering of an innocent human girl. Thus, as long as the Vampires remain ignorant, they will not fulfill the sacrifice. Kiagehul was very shrewd not to tell Baron Montague of his conjurings . . . just as Lady Jung Suk did well to leave a back door open for herself in case she was betrayed by the Unseelie or the Vampire. However, we must now act quickly to put pressure on the parties to go to war, lest the Vampires learn that all we need is a sacrifice to replace Amy Chen."

"Then why not release our legions on the Unseelie before the dawn and butcher them all? We could then inhabit their bodies and go free in the morning and it would be glorious!"

"Not so simple," Megaera warned. "Although Lady Jung Suk gave us the spell that would allow us to host within the Unseelie bodies before her demise, we cannot give ourselves a sacrifice. If it were that easy the demon legions would have been freed eons ago. It requires the willing or those in our debt to cast the spells and to let the blood. But our patience has paid off. Kiagehul opened the door. . . . who knew the ice queen would reunite with her estranged ex-husband? That now gives us access to the Seelie as well. But we cannot slaughter them. It must be done by those who have an outstanding debt to us—the Vampires—or it will not be seen as a sacrifice and we will not be able to inhabit their bodies. Cerridwen will not kill for us, but the Vampires had no qualms."

The heat of Hell slowly brought Tisiphone around. The injured she-demon awoke with an agonized screech and her sisters held her down while small, ravenous Harpies bickered and shoved her disemboweled innards back into her splayed stomach cavity.

"Think of how easy it has been to send all of New Orleans' supernaturals to war," Megaera murmured, "and summon patience."

"If we cannot kill them, then yes, let them foolishly butcher themselves," Alecto hissed. "And we have the snow leopard to thank for sharing her embodiment spell."

"Let us not forget that fool Kiagehul, who opened the door and thought that he could negotiate with the likes of us."

Alecto nodded. "But what of the Chen girl?"

"She is of little consequence, a mere pawn to make the Vampires attack and to raise the ire of the Fae. Focusing on the girl also brought in the wolves as allies, increasing the Fae garrisons from far and wide so that the Vampires would use ultimate force against them. It is a beautiful plan. When it is all over, the death toll of the Fae will be counted as their *sacrifice* to us for late payment on a debt owed and we will inhabit the fallen."

The two sisters erupted into foul screeching laughter as they dug their claws into Tisiphone to continue to hold her down.

"Megaera, how long until the army of darkness is built?" Tisiphone rasped.

"We are one war away from having enough bodies for all our sisters, and then we shall gather the soulless fallen and be free to roam the earth as we so desire. All of the combatants are poised for confrontation by the next sunset. No longer will we be trapped in the pit waiting to do the bidding of those who summon us for a specific task. No . . .

my sisters. We shall inhabit the bodies of dead
Seelie and Unseelie Fae alike, and Vampires will
do our killing for us. If no blood be on our hands
and a question of pending debt to us be in the Vampires' intention while they are on the killing field,
then we will accept those deaths as payment and
the spell comes to life . . . and so will Lady Jung
Suk."

CHAPTER 19

"I don't care how many times I mull this over in my mind, something about this smells to the high heavens, Rodney." Queen Cerridwen paced across his private chamber in her nightgown and stood by the window to watch the coming dawn.

"I agree, but we must strike while the sun is to our advantage."

She closed her eyes as he came to her and allowed his warm palms to slide down her arms. Leaning into his embrace, she soaked in the heat of his chest against her back.

"Call it feminine intuition ... call it whatever you will, but I feel we must employ shrewd strategy here. We are dealing with Vampires and also demons. Bargains with them are not always clear-cut."

Sir Rodney placed a gentle kiss against her neck. "Sounds like you have intimate experience in negotiating with them, love."

She drew herself up slightly, tensing, and opened her eyes, then answered him carefully. "Yes, unfortunately ... that is true."

His thumb caressed her neck where he'd left a kiss and he spoke slowly and calmly, never raising his voice. "I know and we both know that I know." He shook his head and released her. "With all your beauty . . . and all your glamour, I can see where Vlad has riddled your body with his fangs. . . . I can feel it with my heart where he's desecrated the one sanctuary I had."

"We've both had other lovers," she whispered, neither turning around nor denying the charge.

"So true, and I think that you can hear from the tone of my voice that I care not to challenge you or your choices. . . . It's just that this one makes me very, very sad."

She spun on him, tears glittering in her eyes. "All of yours made me sad."

"The cold taketh away and the summer gives," he murmured, going to the dining table across the room. "I'm not in a contest with you this morning, my love." He poured himself a cup of tea and added cream to it, thoughtfully stirring it. "But I never took up with a Vampire against you." Sir Rodney took a slow sip from the porcelain cup and set it down very precisely and then looked at her. "I never breached your sidhe with demons sent from my ill-begotten folly. Last night took all that I owned not to allow the summer to die within me."

Cerridwen placed a trembling palm to her chest. "Oh . . . Rodney . . . I . . ."

He held up his hand and to her horror she saw tears glittering in his eyes. She watched them balance at the precipice of his thick, dark lashes. "The

Gordian knot has frayed and dawn approaches. I see clearly and have no more shield or defense against you. A woman can always fight more deadly than a man, can always cut deeper, war longer, and will always triumph after the last man stands. I am felled."

She swallowed hard as he took up his tea again with a shaky hand and brought it to his lips, then cleared his throat. "But did you not see last night why I love the humans so—why I rally to their condition? Could you not see with your own eyes how their weakness, and even their frailty, is their beauty . . . why I have instructed my Faries and Pixies, all manner of Seelie, to assist them in their firefly-like existence?" He set down his tea and held her gaze. "Cerridwen, they don't have long to live. To torture them with cruel Unseelie tricks is like pulling the wings off butterflies. To what end?"

When she didn't answer him immediately but looked away, he crossed the room in a sudden explosion, grabbing her by both arms. "To what end!"

"I don't know?" she wailed, and snatched herself away from him to hug herself. "Guilty as charged, but I have changed!"

"Did you not see that poor girl's parents? Demons in my dining hall? Dead fucking palace guards dropped like bloody confetti from the ceilings above my guests' wedding! Why, Cerridwen? Because you entered into a deal with Vampires who'd made a pact with a demon?"

He walked away from her breathing hard. "And no matter what, I still loved you. No matter what, I would not give you over to your ex-lover's rage. I would face all of Hell alone before I gave him the satisfaction of beheading you."

Sir Rodney's hands were shaking so badly when he picked up his teacup that he flung it against the stone wall with a crash. "And no matter what, I wouldn't listen to the sage advice of my closest advisors . . . nor would I ever tell that poor young woman who had her wedding night ruined by death and damnation that you were a party to her being abducted and nearly sacrificed to her husband's insane aunt." He drew a shaky breath and leveled a hard point in her direction. "Cerridwen, I swore I would never allow you to make me say these things to you, but after last night I am filled to the brim and so close to murder that it frightens me."

Sir Rodney turned and looked at Cerridwen, this time unable to stop the tears from spilling over his lashes. His voice was a hoarse murmur as he spoke: "Did you think I didn't know? Did you think I didn't wrestle with my own outrage to see you standing at the edge of my Sidhe seeking asylum after all you've done? Did you think you'd tricked me, played me like a house fiddle? No, I'm not blind or thick. It was a matter of choice to lower my drawbridge to let you in. So, no, I wouldn't abandon you at your lowest ebb, my love, because although deserved, that would be cruel . . .

and I have been called many things, even daft—
but never cruel."

"What can I do?" she whispered, stricken.

Sir Rodney shook his head. "I don't know."

For a long while she stood at the edge of the
bedchamber they'd shared just staring at him, her
heart shattering like broken glass as she looked at
the damage she'd wrought and the pain she'd
caused him, now wondering why.

"I will fix this, Rodney," she whispered.

"You cannot," he replied, and then finally sat
and dropped his head into his hands. "Come daylight, infantrymen, cavalry, and Dragon riders
will expect their monarch to lead them . . . and
one poor little girl, a woman not yet twenty years
old, and her husband, my good wolf friend, will
be hunted forever for something they didn't do."

"Do not open the graves at first light," she
said, rushing to him and going down on her knees
before him. "Rodney, I beg of you. Allow me the
chance to fix what I've wrought." She gathered
his hands within her own and looked up at him.
"The one thing they never bargained on was this.
Us." She squeezed his hands within hers, noticing
that they'd begun losing their customary warmth.
"This is not a deal, nor a marriage of conve-
nience."

He smiled a sad smile. "No, that is true. It has
never been convenient."

She swept his mouth with a brief kiss and returned his sad smile. "Never convenient, always

complex, but it was not theirs to understand. It was ours."

He touched her cool cheek and studied her panic-stricken gaze. "Some things are beyond repair, Cerridwen. . . . That is why it is ill advised to ever break them if you cherish them."

"It can be fixed!" she said, tears now streaming. "Don't say that!"

"How?" he asked quietly, wiping her face as she drew closer to him.

"I don't know. . . ." She released a long, agonized sob and he gathered her up into his lap and simply held her.

"I will go to Vlad," she said after a moment, pulling back and wiping angrily at her tears.

"He will kill you on sight. I will not allow it."

"No. He will not." She stood and paced back and forth in front of where Sir Rodney sat. "Lady Jung Suk used a coven to try to amass more power than me because she was jealous of the . . . attention . . . and respect that Vlad offered me over her. To him, she was a tool. To him, I was a powerful ally. Being aligned with a coven would give her access to make her own deal with the demons."

Sir Rodney sat back in his chair and dragged his fingers through his disheveled hair. "Go on."

"But she was indebted to Vlad—was to be his assassin forever. That was the deal she and Vlad struck when he gave her Amy's body after she'd fled court. The demon that Empress Lady Jung Suk raised with her possession spell simply wanted a virgin as a sacrifice. Vlad is panicked. Vlad is not thinking. He could give that demon any young girl and get out of his contract."

"If you have a hand in such matters, Cerridwen, I swear we will be done forever." Sir Rodney just stared at her until she looked away. "Do not even tell him that. Promise me, so that someone else's daughter doesn't wind up missing."

"I promise," she said, finally meeting his unblinking gaze. "This is for us to know, not to give Vlad an easy way out . . . but what is critical here is the fact that the only way to override one demon deal is to replace it for another, stronger one. . . . This is where the Erinyes fit in, I'm sure. They did not breach your dungeons for the body of one young woman. No. That had to be the result of a larger deal entered into by Lady Jung Suk—but since the Vampires didn't pay up for her, they could leverage the Vampires. I know she had to do this, because the one thing I'm sure a woman of power like the empress loathed was being indebted eternally to a cruel and worthless bastard." Cerridwen stopped, winded, and stared at Sir Rodney. "Vlad is a cruel and worthless bastard."

Sir Rodney lifted his chin. "I'm sure I've been discussed in as colorful terms."

She shook her head and their gazes locked. "Never."

"Never?"

"I spoke of you in fury. Called you a gallivanting cad . . . but never cruel. Never worthless. Your heart is as large as your castle." She came back to him and stood before him, waiting until he accepted her back into his arms. "Please let me help."

"And should the Vampires decide that you are their sacrifice . . . what then?"

"Then perhaps justice will be served," she said, stroking his dark spill of hair away from his face. "For all the wrongs I have committed against you and mere mortals . . . for the duplicity and back-room deals so numerous I shudder to remember. Maybe it is just my time."

"And what crime have I committed so egregious that my heart be served to the Vampires on a silver platter?"

A rush of air left her lungs as she pulled his head to her breasts and squeezed her eyes shut. "I love you so, milord. Too much to allow you to ruin the House of Inverness once this is all said and done. We may win the battle once the sun comes up but then lose the war once all of this nasty business is unfurled." She looked down at him. "Rodney, they will demand your throne for sending the Seelie to war on behalf of the Unseelie queen whose hands were dirty and who was literally in bed with a Vampire. I shan't allow it."

She stood and walked away from him clutching her heart. "The night I entered this castle, all I could think of was my own self-interest. My empire of ice, my vassals, my constituents—my life. My guards. Garth was right to hate me for that. But . . ." She shook her head as new tears rose to her eyes. "The ice around my heart has thawed and melted away. You did that with your generosity. You even buried my men who were savaged in your dungeons by the Erinyes. I now see your wolves as friends; they held demons at bay and stood with us. I now see, for the very first time, the humans you used to weep for when we were younger . . . how their condition kept you up at nights, just as it did last night. *I saw,* Rodney."

He stood and lifted his chin and swallowed hard, taking his time to find his voice. It was raw but filled with pride when he spoke. "That is all I ever wanted from you, Cerridwen . . . for you to see that part of me. For I have always seen your warmth, that part of you that no one else understood to be there. Is that not what partners do? See the details no one else can, flaws and all, and still love what they see . . . still find it beautiful, regardless, simply because it is a part of the grander mosaic of that person."

"There was a time when I thought your words were the lofty ruminations of a frustrated poet, or a boy king who had too much free time on his hands. I missed the simplistic truth while empire building . . . not realizing that seeing the world and seeing its citizens as you do is the real magick."

They stared at each other for what seemed like a long time and finally she went to him and he gathered her into his arms.

"I will not allow you to go to Vlad to be taken hostage or to be harmed in any way, Cerridwen."

"Then at least let me get word to him that he may have been cuckolded by Lady Jung Suk, who used her relationship with the local dark covens to do a secondary, backdoor deal with the Erinyes. They are the only demons strong enough to have broken her ties to Vlad, and Vlad never gave her a body—so whatever he had was overridden."

Sir Rodney pulled back and stared at Cerridwen. "But how can you know for sure? When we made the empress's twisted spirit leave Amy Chen's body, Sasha Trudeau commended it to the Light."

"But the empress had already gone dark, Rodney. The Devil already owned her soul. No doubt she went to the Light, but the Fair One spit it back." Queen Cerridwen gently extracted herself from Sir Rodney's embrace. "We don't have much time before sunrise. I will compose an ice missive for Vlad. You hold your garrisons; tell them to wait for your strategic command. By day, I will need to work just outside the walls of your sidhe, for the safety of your set demon barriers."

"I don't like it when you get that look in your eyes, Cerridwen. What will you do?"

"I will call in some markers I have in places you don't want to know about."

"It is almost dawn and we must go down into the vault," a breathless Vampire sentry said as he went down on one knee before Elder Vlad. "Caleb never came back. We have searched high and low for him. He could have been injured or killed by our enemies."

"I highly doubt that," Vlad said coolly, feeling his energy waning with the approaching light. "My registers would have informed me of his extinguished existence. Find him, now!"

"Your Excellency?" The bewildered sentry looked up and then glanced at the blue-gray sky through the mansion window.

"Have our human friends hunt for him *by day*. Be gone from my sight before I decide to allow daylight to make you wiser next time."

The sentry stood and quickly backed out of the room. Elder Vlad released a weary sigh and then stood to go to the false wall that would lead him down to the sun-proof vault. But just as he turned, his floor frosted over and the message from Queen Cerridwen Blatant of Hecate was crystal clear.

"Will it always be like this?" Jennifer asked in a tight whisper, pressing her face into the crook of Crow's shoulder.

"No . . . uhm, you mean war? Naaaah . . . things will normal out. Just—"

"War? That, too? Dragons?" she said in a high-pitched whisper. "Plus, all the women in your family, when they saw me they, they, turned into really angry wolves and then your big pack brother, Bear Shadow, he got in between me and them—thank God he was there—then dragons showed up. I thought I was hallucinating, and then everything went black."

"Look, baby, don't mind them. They were just trying to battle-challenge you to see what your rank would be in the pack, you know?"

Jennifer rapidly shook her head. "No! I don't know, Crow! Are you crazy?"

"Uh, well, yeah, I feel you. That probably didn't come out right. But what I meant was, you were new."

She drew back from him and stared at him with wide eyes. "I'm new?" She looked around the beautifully appointed room. "No . . . *this* is new."

"Yeah, the Fae are kinda cool, if I must say so myself. Very fly how they hooked up the room with the Fairy dust and Pixie sprinkles and whatnot, clothes, food, hey . . . and their baths, man . . . wait till you get in the tub."

"Fairies did this?" She squeezed her eyes shut tightly. "Now you're telling me there are actually Fairies?"

"Yeah, girl . . . where you been? Beats Vampires and demons—but, like, we can talk about all that other stuff when you feel better."

When she began to hyperventilate he gave her a kiss and smiled a wolf smile, then took her by the hand to lead her to the bathtub. "So, if the rustic outdoors just isn't you . . . Sir Rodney might be cool with letting us rent a room in the palace or something. He doesn't have a problem with you being a human and me being a wolf. Besides, the more I think about it, this really isn't a bad place to raise a kid."

"You haven't slept at all," Shogun said, spooning Amy in a possessive embrace.

"How can I sleep, Husband? People died because of me . . . my parents—"

"No one died because of you." Shogun climbed over Amy's body and faced her. "No one. You must never think that. This was the doing of demons and Vampires."

"No," Amy said quietly, sitting up. "I can feel her, still, your aunt. She is not in me, but she is still . . . somehow—she exists."

"Sasha sent her to the Light. We killed her in the bayou. What you have left is horrible memories and some of the physical traits that she left in your body when she tried to take you over and possessed you . . . but that is all."

Amy shook her head. "Shogun, just saying something is so doesn't mean that it is. I know what I feel." She hugged herself as though staving off a cold chill. "There is a good witch in the castle . . . the one who became blinded by your aunt when she was helping Sir Rodney help you search for me."

"Esmeralda? Yes, she lives here in the sidhe," Shogun said in a worried tone. "But what would you need—"

"I want to talk to her. She is also psychic, yes?"

"I don't feel comfortable about any of this." Shogun stood and paced at the foot of the bed. "At sunrise, we go to war with the Fae. We will overturn every Vampire grave until there are no more. I will not let them harm you. The sidhe has been sealed to demon breach. I swear upon my life—"

"That's just it," Amy said quietly. "I don't want

you to swear upon your life or to go to war. There must be another way." She stood and searched for a robe. "My decision is final. I want to speak to Esmeralda before anyone else has to die."

Somewhere in the night, Hunter had climbed into bed beside her. But she'd been so exhausted that she never even stirred. Now his warmth soaked into her bones. The steady rise and fall of his chest and his deep breaths kept her hovering in the twilight between being awake and not quite. But she knew she had to get up. Morning was not long away, and if they were going to redress Vampires they would need every moment of available sunlight to lob a strategic offensive.

Yet when she tried to extricate herself from Hunter's arms he slowly tightened his grip on her.

Sasha smiled and yawned. "I thought you were asleep."

"I was," he said in a deep rumble, and kissed the back of her head.

"We have to get up; daylight's about to burn, man."

"You promised you'd kiss my boo-boo, later. It's later."

She chuckled and snuggled back against him. "You do realize we don't have time for that this morning, don't you?"

"Yeah . . . but since I was half-asleep, it was nice to dream."

She snuggled more deeply against him. "How're you feeling?"

"Much improved, can't you tell?"

Her chuckle deepened as she felt his morning salute against her backside. "Uh, yeah. But I've been thinking about this whole demon-deal thing. Something about a fighting force as strong as Erinyes breaching a sidhe stronghold, all over some young woman's body they were promised, seems a lot like overkill. I think we're getting played somehow, and I wanna talk to Rodney and Cerridwen before this thing gets even further out of control."

"Okay, I'm up," Hunter said, sitting up and scratching his head. "But damn, Sasha, can a man get a cup of coffee, first?"

CHAPTER 20

"I feel that after all you've sacrificed, I have no right to even be here asking you to possibly sacrifice more." Amy turned her wedding band around and around on her finger as she spoke quietly, keeping her eyes averted from the pretty, sightless woman who'd not long ago given up her eyes to find her.

"This is more for me than it is for you," Esmeralda said, lifting her chin. "Sir Rodney means the world to me, always has . . . and when he came to me with a just case, I could not refuse him. And now . . . now that the empress has taken my eyes in an act of pure cruelty, any opportunity to foil her—even if it means my life—gives me more joy than you can imagine."

"This could be dangerous," Sasha warned, looking around Garth's magick room at the others.

"You have guards who are adepts," Esmeralda said calmly. "This room is full."

"Aye," Garth said, placing a gnarled hand on her shoulder. "The shaman of the wolves is here,

Silver Hawk, as well as the one they call Doc . . . and I am no novice. Shogun and Hunter, two warrior wolf brothers, are here with their enforcers. Sasha's team: the dark arts specialist, Bradley, and her seer, Clarissa, plus two familiars—Woods and Fisher—and the young computer adept, Winters. And of course my wizards are all here to guide you."

"Thank you for letting me know who was in the room with me," Esmeralda said, and then reached over her shoulder to squeeze Garth's hand. "You always try to casually slip it in and to treat me as though I'm not blind, but I am. However, I have strengthened my other senses since the accident."

Garth gave her a kiss on the cheek and touched her hair. "I understand why Rodney will always love you so."

Silence hung in the room as Garth drew away from the young woman.

"So let us begin and call Lady Jung Suk's spirit from beyond the other side of the veil."

Garth swirled his wand over the gleaming round crystal table as Esmeralda grasped Amy's hands. Others in the room formed a tight circle around Garth, Amy, and Esmeralda. Garth's wizards lit the stone walls, ceiling, and floor with strange-moving protective Celtic symbols and then nodded to Garth.

"Anything that comes in here from the darkness will not escape should it be so foolish to manifest and attack," Garth said. "We begin."

"And what if the Erinyes return while she's in

trance or if Lady Jung Suk comes forward?" Shogun asked, glancing around the room at the warriors present.

"Then I have something for that bitch, just in case the white magick doesn't work," Sasha said, patting an Uzi that was packed with silver shells. "I am so tired of her, you have no idea."

Hunter offered his brother a half smile and a shrug. "She woke up like that this morning, man. What can I say?"

"My queen," Elder Futhark said, going down on one knee before Queen Cerridwen in the castle war room. "A missive from the Unseelie provinces that Vampires are poised for tunnel deployment coming in from overseas," he added breathlessly as the garrison leaders and Sir Rodney listened intently. "Our sources from gnome underground camps say they've felt rumblings coming as far away as the old-country maps—Romania, Bosnia, Croatia, the old Czech Republic, Russia, and of course Transylvania."

"Thank you, Futhark. You have done well. Are my forces in place?"

"Yes," he said, still kneeling. "But suffering terribly in the heat of the swamp."

"As are all of Sir Rodney's men," she said with a dismissive wave of her hand. "Rise and please await further instructions from our monarch."

Elder Futhark stood slowly, sharing confused glances with the Seelie leadership who were present.

Sir Rodney nodded and stood and then began walking around his massive round table. "The Scots, are ye ready? Sir Gordon, I trust you with my life."

"Aye," a ruddy brunette said, glancing around the table and gaining nods from his fellow dragon riders. "Till the last man stands."

"Good man." Sir Rodney went to him and exchanged a hearty warrior handshake. "Glad to have ye with us, Cousin."

"Muldane," Sir Rodney said, turning to a bulky warrior with a thick red beard. "The fighting Irish be with us?"

"Indeed, sire. Wouldn't miss this for the world."

"Nor I," Sir Rodney said, chuckling as he patted Muldane on the back.

"Do not count out the Welsh," a sinewy fighter said, his gaze intense despite his jaunty smile.

"Nor the Brits!" another called out, each receiving a personal handshake of recognition from Sir Rodney.

"Good," Sir Rodney said, after making the rounds. "Seelie ground forces will work with Unseelie Gnomes in the underground ambushes. Gnomes dig up; my infantrymen slash and burn on the surface. Anything that goes airborne gets shot with Unseelie ice to make it fall, and as it's hurtling earth bound our aerial squadrons scorch it. Archers remain in the trees, focus on keeping gargoyles grounded. I want all forces poised to bring the battle to the bayou, not over human populations. Draw the Vampires out and into battle near the UCE courthouse, deep within the swamps, we clear? You wait for my signal. Any questions?"

Nervous glances passed around the room and finally Muldane cleared his throat.

"The Bonnie Isles are with you all the way, sire, but we must confess this is a bit unusual in two ways." Muldane looked around the table. "No disrespect, but me and my men never expected to be fighting side by side with Unseelie forces. I think I speak for the men present when we say this somewhat . . . I don't know what to call it."

Queen Cerridwen lifted her chin and Sir Rodney thrust his shoulders back.

"Whot is to know is that demons and Vampires threaten our collective Fae way of life. Is it not the Fae way to fend off the enemy first, and then sort out our differences behind our own Sidhe walls?"

"Aye," Gordon said, casting a frown toward Muldane. "That is enough of an explanation for me."

Muldane smiled and gave Sir Rodney a curt nod. "Then that be enough for me—no feathers need to fly."

"You said you had a second question," Sir Rodney said, slowly circling the table. "Get them all out before we commence to battle!"

"The timing, sire," Muldane said, nonplussed. "Why wait for nightfall when we can catch these bastards in their lairs asleep?"

"Because we are waiting on séance information—it is not just the Vampires we are dealing with, but also the Erinyes."

* * *

"Colonel Madison, sir, we have to get Sasha Trudeau on the line. We've got local authorities blowing up our phones. Over a hundred and fifty civilians have been abducted since about oh four hundred hours. The base is still going crazy from what we saw last night and we still don't have any clearer answer for the Joint Chiefs this morning than we did last night."

"Tell the local law enforcement to stand down, Commander," Colonel Madison said, wiping the sleep deprivation and tension away from his face. He stared at Captain Davis, totally understanding the commander's quiet panic. "Sometimes Trudeau has to go dark in order to bring us back valuable intel. If a hundred and fifty of New Orleans' citizens have disappeared, the last thing we want to do is get them slaughtered by a misstep."

Esmeralda slumped forward suddenly as Amy's eyes flew open, glowing red. Amy quickly released Esmeralda's hands as Garth held up the semi-conscious psychic. Slowly, Amy's jaw cracked, thickening, contorting as Were Leopard fangs lengthened in her mouth. Digging into the table, Amy's claws scored the crystal, and her voice bottomed out in a demonic rasp.

"Who dares to look into my past dealings with the underworld?" Amy growled.

"We do!" Garth shouted, leveling his wand at

Amy as Bradley took over the task of keeping Esmeralda upright.

"By what right?" Amy replied, smiling as she looked around the room.

"By the right of the Fae," Garth said, holding the demon within his ancient gaze.

"One would have thought you had learned by now," the voice from within Amy replied, snarling. "One pair of eyes was not enough of a loss?"

"You do not frighten us, demon," Silver Hawk said, entering the fray and making Amy's head pivot. "You cannot enter a silver aura. But now we know that you live."

"Yesssss . . . ," Amy said, and then laughed a horrible, screeching cackle.

"Which means you cut a side deal," Sasha said, making the demon completely revolve Amy's head to look at her.

Hunter caught Shogun by the arm to hold him back as Sasha engaged Lady Jung Suk's evil spirit.

"Oh, how fortunate for me," the thing inside Amy said, and then she spun to lunge at Sasha.

A quickly thrown plume of shamanic white sage and silver shavings left Silver Hawk's hands as Hunter body-blocked Sasha. Garth threw up a silver shield between Sasha and Hunter and the now-screeching demon.

"I thought you'd brought me an innocent," Amy said, growling, as she returned to the table, chuckling under her breath.

"That's it—I want Sasha out of this room," Hunter said, panicked. "Right now, séance is over!"

"Too late," Lady Jung Suk cooed, making lewd tongue gestures at Hunter.

"Oh, just let her come on out of Amy's body," Sasha said, sneering. "I wouldn't leave this room if you tried to drag me out by my hair."

"She doesn't know, does she, wolf?"

Sasha gave Hunter a look, but his eyes went from Amy's misshapen body to his grandfather.

"You promised me she'd be protected."

Silver Hawk nodded. "She is. This is just the demon trying to find your soft spot."

"And I found it, Hunter. . . . How do you know these old men are right? What if I get inside Sasha and—"

"No!" Hunter shouted, transforming into his wolf and baring fangs at Amy.

"What are you doing, Brother!" Shogun said, body-blocking Hunter from Amy's body. "Come back to your human!"

"Grandson, come back," Silver Hawk said, slowly moving Shogun aside. He blew a plume of shamanic powder on Hunter and waited. "It is the way of the demon to divide and conquer and to get two brothers to battle while she slips from the room."

Hunter transformed instantly and quickly returned to the circle holding Sasha, but Silver Hawk was too close to Amy's body. She pounced on him, deeply raking his back; however, the old man simply flipped her and pressed her face to the floor on one of the sacred symbols.

Twisting, screaming, Amy screeched out foul

invectives while Silver Hawk struggled with her, yelling for Shogun and the others to stay back. Garth was instantly at Silver Hawk's side, torturing the demon inside Amy with silver-threaded white light until Amy collapsed and a long stream of black smoke exited her nose.

Wizards immediately wrapped Amy's, Sasha's, and Esmeralda's bodies with silver cloaks as the black smoke ricocheted off the walls, screaming.

"Cover all humans," Garth ordered his men, tossing cloaks at Clarissa and Doc, then to Winters and Bradley, who'd kept the demon away from them with liberal plumes of brick dust and holy water.

The moment the demon headed toward Woods and Fisher, Garth hit her with a fistful of silver dust and then tossed them a cloak. Shogun went to Amy's limp, scarred body as Hunter helped his badly ravaged grandfather from the floor. But within the seconds of pandemonium in the room the demon found host in Shogun's body. She threw his head back and laughed, turning his eyes red.

"Oh, now you have a problem, gentlemen," she said, speaking through Shogun's vocal cords. "You forgot, he's a Were, not a Shadow, and owns no silver in his aura. I will live and always wanted this bastard dead . . . and his body is sooo much stronger than Amy's. Go ahead and try to kill me."

Shogun lunged at Hunter, but Garth caught him mid-air in a silver mesh energy net with his wizards straining to hold it down. Shogun twisted and yelled, the silver burning his Werewolf body.

"You'll kill him!" Hunter shouted.

"Fight the beast within, Shogun," Silver Hawk said weakly. "Fight her and make her tell you her bargain. Look on the floor at your wife and summon strength."

Two voices yelled beneath the net: one Shogun's, one Lady Jung Suk's.

"I will die for her, you evil bitch!" Shogun shouted. "There is no pain too great for her. I will burn to death in silver and make my brother hold the net—know that!"

"What was the deal?" Sasha said, coming to the net, circling it. "I'll hold the net. True love never dies. You can't stay in there long. The man will give his life for Amy. You know it; I know it."

"The Erinyes!" the voice of Lady Jung Suk screeched as burning flesh stung Sasha's nose.

"What about the Erinyes, body stealer?" Hunter shouted, holding the edge of the net as he stared into his brother's eyes. "I will allow my brother to die. Believe it. I am Shadow Wolf and I am no liar. I know that is what Shogun is prepared to do."

Shogun's wails escalated. "Tell Amy I love her!"

"I will also hold the net," Silver Hawk said, struggling to touch a section of it. "I am an ancient Shadow. Feel my silver aura; know that I will let one man die the way he so chooses to stop evil and to stop your bargain with the beasts!"

"Tell us!" Sasha shouted, leveling the Uzi at Shogun's head. "And know that I will put this man out of his misery with you in his body, because he's my family and because Amy is his wife."

"The spell of possession was my deal!" Lady Jung Suk's voice screeched. "The Erinyes were promised a virgin by Vlad, but I gave them something better—Fae bodies, if killed by Vampire hands. . . . They want the war, they shall have the war. Fae will die and the Erinyes, like me, will be free!"

"Get that man out of the net!" Garth shouted, making everyone pull back.

Shogun collapsed, unconscious, as the black smoke poured out of his eyes, nose, ears, and mouth, leaving a trail of black blood.

"The demon is weak," Silver Hawk said, collapsing into Hunter's arms. "Finish her now."

Garth and his wizards sent silver tracers from the tips of their wands, gathering up the screaming smoke into a long silver tube and then sending it crashing through the floor. Working quickly, they sealed the floor with white light and then turned to the injured and Doc.

"All able hands, get them to our healing stations!"

Guards drew swords and then lowered them as Sasha burst through the huge double doors of Sir Rodney's war room led by Rupert. All that had been seated at the round table were on their feet, their expectant eyes on her.

"It's a double cross," Sasha said breathlessly. "Queen Cerridwen was right. Lady Jung Suk entered into a stronger, secondary deal with the demons—but the goal is to make the Vampires kill as many Fae as possible by causing what seems like unprovoked Fae attacks. For every Fae killed, Seelie and Unseelie alike, the Erinyes get to possess your bodies so they can roam free of the pit."

"And whot of the Vampires?" Muldane called out, looking around at his countrymen.

"Pawns. Just pawns that the Erinyes could care less about. If they can get the Vamps to do the slaughtering for them, then they could care less how many graves the Fae open to the sun."

"And where's the rest of your team?" Sir Rodney said. "And Hunter and Shogun, all the others?"

"There were a lot of injuries down in that magick room," Sasha said, and then raked her hair. "Silver Hawk was badly mauled . . . Amy and Esmeralda have internal injuries from being body inhabited . . . but the worst is Shogun. We had to silver net him to get the demon out of him."

Queen Cerridwen began running with Sir Rodney, heading for the healing room. Sasha was right behind them.

"Don't worry, lassie!" a big redheaded Dragon rider shouted behind them. "If our monarchs be on it, all will be well!"

CHAPTER 21

"It is well into your daylight hours in your region, Vlad," Elder Kozlov said slowly, "and yet no attack by the Fae against your strongholds."

Elder Vlad opened his eyes within his darkened lair. He hated intercontinental communication when the daylight was against him and was sure that was why Elder Kozlov always delighted in such meetings.

"Your Eminence," Elder Vlad murmured out loud, too weary to force a mind-to-mind exchange. "The Fae have not attacked, simply because we took human hostages from the surrounding towns to ensure they would use restraint. One of their allies, the she-Shadow Sasha Trudeau is still inexplicably wedded to the human condition—and the human military, as all my earlier reports have shown. That is why I believe we have not yet been daylight breached."

"And you are sure this had nothing to do with the Fae's charges of us being manipulated by the Erinyes?"

"That is preposterous, Your Grace, a slap in our faces. First the Fae break open six viceroys' tombs and then feel our wrath, and now it is the cause of Erinyes?"

"This is what they claim," Elder Kozlov said in a lethal tone. "They also assert that the only reason we are in this predicament is your post-court collusion with one Lady Jung Suk, a demon . . . hence our debt that would have been cleared by the assassination in open court of Baron Geoff Montague."

"As I told you in our previous discussion just hours ago, these claims by the Fae are their way of trying to negotiate surrender. They have attacked us, thinking our Vampire forces were weakened by earlier campaigns, only to discover that we own vast resources, and are now questioning the wisdom of drawing us into battle."

"That is a possibility," Elder Kozlov said through a long, wheezing inhale. "But before you attack the Fae and squander resources, I want a meeting in the swamp with the Erinyes. If they have indeed made us to be their serfs . . . there will be hell to pay for any and all involved in the chain of events that led to the Vampire Cartel losing face. If not, and if this is a ruse by the crafty Fae, then they will be obliterated. To ensure that, I have reconsidered your request and have sent troops poised in the tunnels that are awaiting for darkness to fall in your land. They will take your lead; you are their commander. Use them wisely, Vlad. I would hate to see Fae troops felled only to fly up in your face as freed Erinyes. That would disappoint me."

"What are the Fae waiting for, Sister?" Alecto leaned in as she stared into the black scrying bowl filled with human blood that her sister held between her talons.

"I don't know!" Megaera said with a frown. "They should have been blowing the doors off mausoleums and storming mansions in search of vaults by now. Yet they remain crouched in the swamps near the UCE court."

"Maybe the Fae have lost their nerve? Should we provide a little incentive?"

"No. We wait. The Vampires' forces from their old country build in the tunnels; the Harpies are excited, as the old ones are prepared for war. If the Fae have lost their nerve, this bodes well for us. It will be a complete slaughter, for the Vampires will never negotiate."

Alecto laughed, but her cackling was cut short as Tisiphone entered the cavern. "Sisters, there is word that Lady Jung Suk was lured to a séance and destroyed."

Megaera waved her hand and drank down the contents of the scrying bowl. "After we breached their Sidhe, of course the Fae would try to get the last vestiges of the demon out of Amy Chen's body, now that she has become one of their strong allies' wife. The empress was a fool to allow herself to be lured into such an obvious trap. We no longer need her. She gave us the spell, had her dark coven cast it; now all we need is for Fae bodies to fall."

Hours had passed as the Fae healers worked tirelessly on Shogun while Sasha and Hunter used all that they had to bring Silver Hawk around. The elderly shaman's back was raw, but his determination and spirit had never been stronger. Doc ministered to Amy, slowly bringing her around and helping clear out any vestiges of dark energy with Clarissa's and Bradley's help. Esmeralda was the easiest and first to heal, simply because the demon didn't want her—the demon wanted lodging in a member of Shogun's family or with someone who had the power of the Were, something that would hurt her nephew deeply and scar him for life.

The cruel irony was, however, she'd possibly done that, if Shogun lived, by forcing everyone's hand to keep him held and burning beneath a silver net.

"How is he?" Hunter asked, wiping the sweat from his brow.

"Still touch-and-go," Garth said quietly. "It was truly bad going for him this time."

"Then with me, Sasha, maybe even Grandfather . . . we can try to help with his healing," Hunter said anxiously, trying to push past Garth.

Garth shook his head and gently touched Hunter's arm. "You two are almost depleted, and like Amy, Silver Hawk shouldn't do anything but rest for at least twenty-four hours. We will need you on the battle lines, soon. Your man Bear Shadow

has arrived with five thousand wolf soldiers and
you will have to lead them. Shogun's cousins arrived with twenty-five thousand Asian Werewolves
strong, trekking for days through the Arctic and
down through Canada into the U.S. to be at this
battle. We need you there, just as Sasha must lead
her human forces, should they join us again."

"Stay with your brother and grandfather," Sasha said to Hunter. "I'll go to the front. I have to
communicate with Colonel Madison anyway. I
haven't spoken to him all day, and after last night
who knows what has happened on the base?
By now the Joint Chiefs might be ready to launch
ICBMs at Dragons in the air, they could be so
freaked out."

Hunter stepped in front of her. "No, Sasha.
Rather that you be here with Shogun and Grandfather helping them heal . . . I just can't have you
go out there after what almost happened in the
magick room."

"Hunter, I don't know what's gotten into—"

"To the swamps!" a Fae guard yelled, running
down the hallway. "Battle stations! Gargoyles and
Erinyes are positioning in the tunnels for a sunset
strike—so say the Gnomes!"

"Go," Garth urged, grabbing Hunter by both
arms. "What would your brother do? Would he stay
and keep you alive just so that your wife and her
parents could perish once the castle was stormed,
or would he fight?"

Sasha looked at Hunter, touched his face, and
then turned to follow the sounds of chaos. Within

seconds he was at her side, exiting the sidhe through the secret tunnel Garth had shown them.

Fae archers were everywhere. Horsemen thundered toward the dark interior of the bayou as the sun kissed the horizon. Sasha ran beside Hunter with her cell phone pressed to her ear, talking to Colonel Madison in fits and starts.

"Seal off the area to all civilians," she said, panting as she leaped over fallen logs, swamp bog, and branches. "Clear the airspace over New Orleans—yes, sir, the whole area. The sky is gonna be lit up with dogfights like it's the Fourth of July. Dragon air strikes are on our side. But be ready to scramble jets, and our boys might need to come into a situation hot. I will make contact; until then, keep 'em back. They might shoot friendlies and there's no time to explain how to tell the difference, sir." She paused for a moment and stopped running as she listened to the terrible news. "Hostages? How many?"

Hunter skidded to a halt beside her, listening, and then resumed running ahead of her, calling out for Sir Rodney.

Sir Rodney turned back, dismounted from a tree, and landed in front of Sasha and Hunter. "What news from the humans?"

"A hundred and fifty humans were abducted," Sasha huffed, catching her breath. "No doubt an insurance policy by the Vampires to keep us from blowing lairs by day."

"We had no intention of doing that, so—"

"But it means they didn't believe Cerridwen's

missive to Vlad," Hunter said as they jogged deeper into the bayou.

"The Vampires never allow themselves to be backed into a corner without room to negotiate," Queen Cerridwen said, gracefully appearing from behind a tree. She then raced alongside the leadership, finally coming to a halt when they'd reached the dark glen. "We will call the court to rise," she said, slightly winded, "and through our evidence, we will obtain the release of the humans."

"We cannot go to war over New Orleans," Sasha said quietly to Hunter, Sir Rodney, and Queen Cerridwen. "We covered up the other incidents with very thin media spin, but E-3 AWACS and F-16s over the city won't be a flyby training mission no matter how much damage control we attempt . . . and if Dragons and gargoyles start falling from the sky with a hundred fifty dead or missing . . . are you all hearing me?"

"Rodger that," Hunter said, catching his breath and glancing around at the outrageous show of force on the ground, in the trees, and now circling in the air. "Maybe we won't have to, if all goes well in court."

"Precisely," Sir Rodney said. "But it is always good to let them know that if they want a battle, so be it."

"I call the United Council of Entities court to session!" Queen Cerridwen shouted. "May the crone of the court arise up the great hall!"

Thunderous applause greeted Queen Cerridwen's request, and just as swiftly as the building began its laborious ascension from the murky swamp depths Elder Vlad stepped from the shadows with an army flanked by gargoyles.

"Yes, allow the court to rise from the depths so that we may enter into the record the Fae's complicity in attacking six of my viceroys with no evidence of foul play."

Electrified tension hung in the air under the weight of the moon. No one watched the building rise; all eyes were on the other, on the enemy. They waited in the stillness, poised for attack lest anyone cough. The doors of the courthouse eerily creaked open. Frogs and crickets, all nightlife, were deadly silent as the old crone of the courts made her way methodically past the huge columns and down the swamp-slicked marble steps.

"Book!" she screeched. "Bring plenty of ink for the ledger. Tonight what we have here is an unprecedented show of power. Who speaks the first complaint?"

Queen Cerridwen waited until the ancient black tome took its place in the air, hovering above the crone's right hand and beneath the raven quill pen. "I speak," Queen Cerridwen announced, and proudly stepped forward.

"You *dare* to be the first to lob a complaint, Cerridwen—you *traitorous* bitch—after you opened Ariel Beauchamp's tomb to daylight to avoid prosecution in the first trial?"

"I'd advise you to watch your tone, Vampire!" Sir Rodney shouted across the glen amid murmurs of discontent from all camps. "Hiss and spit all you like, Vlad Tempesh, but our fair Fae *queen* has the floor."

"Thank you, Sir Rodney," she said, giving Elder Vlad a glacial stare. "Today we had a séance and called forth Lady Jung Suk—"

"Out of order!" Elder Vlad yelled. "A known criminal—"

"And I'm not concerned with that part of her past," Queen Cerridwen said, keeping her gaze steady on Elder Vlad. "I agree that it is complicated." She paused for effect, watching the ancient Vampire subtly release a breath of relief, admitting neither his wrongdoing nor hers before the assembled armies. "What is of importance is that we learned the Erinyes have a benefit in bringing the Fae to war with the Vampires. We believe they have double-dealt the Vampires and through sleight of hand, using our Unseelie battle tactics, have made it look like we were the culprits in opening your viceroys' graves."

"Preposterous!" Elder Vlad shouted as his army of Vampires and gargoyles jeered.

"If we are right, then you have killed sixty innocent Fae!" Sir Rodney called out once the noise died down. "But we are prepared to offer you a truce. Stand down against the Fae and fight with us against the Erinyes and we will not hold the Vampires accountable for our losses."

Fae soldiers grumbled amongst themselves as Elder Vlad remained passionless.

"Rather that we lose sixty good men at the border, due to mistaken identity," Queen Cerridwen said, "most of whom were from my Unseelie ranks, than lose thousands on this battlefield tonight. What will it be, Vlad, your ego or a rational truce?"

Elder Vlad smiled and shook his head. "Cerridwen, Cerridwen, Cerridwen, so much fire beneath all that ice, till I fear you shall melt away . . . as always in our interactions," he added, baiting Sir Rodney and attempting to embarrass the queen with innuendo.

"I assure you that shan't be the case," she said, sending icicles across the trees and causing mist to puff from her lips as she spoke. "I have reserved a cool head and a cold heart for all of our dealings, Vlad. The only one ever fear that I melt away from his attentions is my king, Sir Rodney."

Chuckles from the Fae ranks followed the queen's statement, but it was clear that both Sir Rodney and Elder Vlad were still rankled.

"I believe your offer of a truce is based upon your understanding that your troops will be decimated, should the Vampires elect to go to war. I believe that you began a campaign that you were ill prepared to continue, once you saw the extent of our wrath . . . so now you have come to grovel."

Sir Rodney swept his arms out to either side. "Does this look like groveling? Be rational and be strategic, old Vampire. From the air there are Dragon squadrons ready to meet your gargoyles and fliers. From the ground, the infantry and cavalries speak for themselves, and many of you that became night embers have already met our archers."

Elder Vlad narrowed his gaze. "As you have met our mercenaries, but have yet to experience our European forces from the Old World. . . . Legions will crush you under their boots."

"To what end, Vlad? That is a complete waste of resources all around and you know it. Stop this folly now and at least be sure you have the correct information," Queen Cerridwen said in a bored tone. "Let us settle this by the only reasonable way one can. Call the Erinyes."

Another collective murmur rippled through the crowd.

"Are you serious?" Vlad said, and then smiled, baring fangs. "You want the crone to call demons up and question them as a matter of record? Then you will owe them, and have nothing substantial to bargain with."

"Correction," the crone said, breaking the stand-off. "The Erinyes will testify for the court and all members of the UCE will have to put in something that they want—unless they are found guilty of a crime against members of this court."

"I'm banking that they are guilty as sin," Queen Cerridwen said coolly. "You know me well enough to know that I wouldn't call demons and be left in a position to owe them unless I thought they'd come away owing me. On this they will owe the sixty Fae lives that were lost due to inciting the Vampires against the Fae. Hence why Sir Rodney and I are willing to allow bygones to be bygones, once we have their testimony."

"It is a good deal, Vampire," the crone said,

shaking her head. "I would take it if I were you. Erinyes, if called by the court for the truth, will not be able to lie—it is the conjuring province of the spells cast for eons by the UCE."

"Then call them," Elder Vlad said between his teeth.

The old crone chuckled. "I thought you would take that sane way out." She walked the perimeter of a small circle and began her ancient incantations as the glen fell silent under the light of the moon. Soon billowing yellow sulfuric smoke rose from the center of the circle that she'd walked off; then a tall burst of green light shot up with a screeching Erinys inside it.

"A complaint has been lodged," the old crone said. "And we ask you—"

Before she could finish her sentence the swamp floor erupted with warring Erinyes. They flew at the Vampires and Fae alike.

Sasha's voice rang out, "Do not kill each other— hit demon targets only!"

"Mirror shields up!" Queen Cerridwen shouted.

Vampires hissed and sent black bolts toward the mirrors.

"Kill no Vampires! Evasive actions only!" Sir Rodney's voice rang out as Dragons spiraled down to hit demon targets.

"You must use the mirrors!" Hunter shouted, tossing a shield to Vlad. "If your legions look at them in the eyes they will go to stone!"

Vlad watched in horror as several hundred of his local men instantly turned to granite, but the

Vampire forces from Europe were prepared and slashed at the beasts, using their telepathic senses to guide them.

"Use the Fae shields!" Vlad called out, and entered the battle with his eyes closed, fighting blindly.

Wolves ripped demon appendages as fleet-footed Fae blasted the injured Erinyes with white-light wand charges. Vampires were merciless, ripping out throats and disemboweling creatures so that wolves could finish the job on the ground. Gargoyles funneled up, mixing in with the Erinyes' flight bursts, savaging them, riding their backs, and sending them to the ground for Dragon consumption. Sasha was liquid motion, moving in and out of the shadows with Hunter as though doing an elaborately choreographed dance.

From the corner of her eye in the flash of a mirrored shield, Sasha remembered the one who had breached the castle as their leader. The screech was the same pitch, her raspy demon voice unforgettable. The moment Sasha was sure she'd identified the one named Megaera, Sasha cut through the battle lines on a mission.

Hunter had a demon by the throat when he saw Sasha break formation and then saw where she was headed. Casting off the gasping demon into the heart rip of a waiting Vampire, he took off after Sasha.

He yelled, "No!" at the same time Megaera turned. Sasha was in mid-air lunging toward her when their eyes met. The stone transformation was instant. Sasha dropped to the ground as granite. Megaera threw her head back and laughed and then called for her Erinyes sister to retreat.

But Hunter tackled Megaera from a sidelong blow and pinned her down on her stomach as Sir Rodney and Queen Cerridwen silver-netted her with Hunter trapped in the mesh.

"Retreat!" Alecto called out.

"Gather Fae bodies so that we shall rise again!" Tisiphone screeched.

And just as quickly as it had begun it had ended. The only things disturbing the stillness were the howling screeches of the demon burning alive in the silver while being savaged by a very angry wolf.

"Get Hunter out of there!" Bear Shadow shouted.

Fae rushed in with Sir Rodney and Vampires hung back from the silver, but Hunter's fury wouldn't allow anyone to get close to the mesh.

"Let him finish that bitch!" Crow Shadow said, weeping as he crouched down beside Sasha. "She killed my sister. Let him tear her up—eat her alive!"

"We need the testimony of the leader," Queen Cerridwen said, and then stunned Hunter with an icy blast from her wand.

Wolves snarled and lunged but stopped just short of an actual attack. Fae soldiers moved quickly to drag Hunter out of the netting but left the screeching demon who was missing an arm, her tail, and most of the lower part of her body.

"Wake him gently," Sir Rodney said, and then pressed his wand to the demon's throat. "Tell this court what you have done. Is it true you would use the Vampires as pawns to kill the Fae and then inhabit their bodies as though they'd been sacrificed for you?"

"Yes!" Megaera screeched. "We already have the spell. There are sixty of you dead, if not more! We will rise again!"

"But if you betrayed the Vampires," Elder Vlad said in a dangerous voice, "then I rescind any sacrifice—those sixty dead Fae are not given unto you, and any dead on this field you cannot claim because my forces never attacked a single Fae."

"Damn you, Vlad Tempesh!" Megaera screeched.

"Too late," he said with a bitter smile, "and you shall so owe me for all of this."

"No," the demon shouted, growing weaker as the effect of the silver depleted her strength, "it is you who still owes me for the body of the young girl! We still have unfinished business."

"I have over a hundred and fifty human hostages scattered around lairs in this state—pick a body, any body," Vlad said, laughing.

"No . . . ," Elder Kozlov said calmly as he stepped out of the shadows and summarily beheaded Elder Vlad with a black death charge from his fingers. "Consider this Vampire head your debt paid in full. It was the best I could do on such short notice." He looked at the legions of Vampires as Elder Vlad's head rolled to his feet. "I have read disturbing testimony from Caleb that was entered in the court dockets just before dawn. Know that the last thing anyone ever wants to do is lie to me."

Elder Kozlov drew himself up and then looked down at Megaera. "Lucifer and I are on a first-name basis . . . care to wager what he might think about your squandering *Vampire* resources for your own personal gain . . . his elite fighting forces of the darkness?"

"You wouldn't," the demon whispered, now seeming to feel every injury she'd sustained.

"But you know that I would," Elder Kozlov said with a tight, fanged smile. "You have forgotten your place, *demon*."

"What do I have to do to make this right, Your Eminence?"

"The first bargain is void, because you double-bargained over it."

"Yes, yes, of course."

"This deal is null, because it was based on fraud." Elder Kozlov looked at the crone. "Enter this into the record."

The crone bowed as the demon nodded.

"You have cost us viceroys. . . . Oh, you will so pay me for that offense, plus however many Fae lives that my misguided Vlad ordered executed."

"Yes," Megaera hissed.

"And you will return the she-wolf to her human form, all of her unharmed, as the wolves have shown restraint throughout and were peacekeepers to the end . . . thus avoiding us having additional casualties."

Megaera lifted her one talon and sent a dark energy charge to Sasha that the Fae quickly rinsed with silver and white light before it entered

Sasha's stone body. Crow Shadow clutched his sister to his chest as her wolf form gave way to a limp, warm, unconscious woman.

"Go to Hell," Elder Kozlov said with a sneer, and then watched Megaera vanish. "We are much more discreet than this. Release the humans so that it does not become a media issue for our region. . . . Leave it to the Fae to spin the story and bespell those poor cattle. We don't play with our food." He nodded and Caleb slipped out of the shadows of the courthouse. Elder Kozlov crooked his finger, and Caleb smiled and then descended the steps to follow him.

Vampires stepped back and within a slow blink of an eye they were mist, swirling away on the night air with a funnel cloud of gargoyles.

"Awake Hunter gently,' Sir Rodney said, and then went to Cerridwen to hug her as a unified Fae and wolf cheer rang out.

EPILOGUE

Two Days Later

Doc stood beside Sasha and then extended his elbow. "You ready?" He turned to her and gave her a smile when she didn't answer. "Me neither, baby. . . . You look beautiful."

She couldn't make her hands stop shaking or get her flowers to stop bouncing. "Thanks, Dad, but I think I'm gonna hurl."

He kissed her through her short white veil. "Just a little morning sickness, it should pass in a couple of months."

"What!" she wheezed, now holding on to his arm for support.

"The Fae give a nice party," Doc said, seeming thoroughly amused as he began the promenade. "Great cake all done up with flowers and such—as the father of the bride, I know this has got to be a hundred-thousand-dollar affair. I never expected to have the luxury to walk my daughter down the aisle, so on my Army salary from years ago I never put away for anything. Things worked out, huh? Smile at the Chens, sweetie," he added. "They're still clueless. Look ahead; smile at Hunter; the poor man is faint."

"You're sure; you're absolutely sure," she whispered, beginning to hyperventilate.

"It's not just because I'm a doctor and did your blood work, but don't you recall Hunter acting really weird? I mean more protective than usual?"

Sasha swallowed hard and kept her eyes straight ahead so she didn't pass out while the Pixies and Fairies flung flower petals in her path. Her bone-hued silk gown felt like it was second skin as perspiration suddenly leaked into the delicate gossamer fabric the Fae had spun. But Queen Cerridwen just gave Sasha a nod as she passed, and the next thing she knew a cool breeze had dried everything.

The entire garrison had come out and the wedding was being held in the gardens just so Sir Rodney could go nuts and show off what a true summer Fae monarch could do. Rupert wept uncontrollably, and even old Garth blinked back moisture from his eyes. But she couldn't think beyond the buzzing in her ears. Pregnant. Pregnant? She was a warrior and pregnant. "How did that happen?" she murmured, not realizing her mouth had engaged what was rattling around in her head.

"None of my business how it happened," Doc said with a quiet chuckle. "And you're too old for me to discuss the birds and the bees with you, baby. Ask your husband later today; I'm sure he'll show you how."

Her father patted her arm, but his wry comment made her smile. Yes . . . now it all made so much sense. She stared at Hunter and watched his Adam's apple bob above his crisply starched tux collar. Cherry blossoms littered the lawn out of season as Sir Rodney waved at the flora like a mad orchestra conductor, changing the flowers upon her every footfall, turning the outer palace gardens into a veritable Fourth of July flower show.

Still, nothing was as handsome as the quiet warrior who waited for her at the end of the garden beneath a natural canopy of interlocked blooming trees. He was her friend. He was her guide. He was her lover. He was her dream partner. He was her rock. He was her champion. He was her breath. He was her spirit. He was now the father of her child. Tears rose in Sasha's eyes. She'd been so blessed, and at different times; both of them had almost never lived to see this day. And that they'd made it this far together was one thing, but that everyone they so dearly loved had made it, caused her to bite her lip to hold back a sob.

Shogun blotted Hunter's forehead with a white cotton handkerchief and then his own. Her brother-in-law had made it. For the close call, after a few days of rest and lots of good Fae fare, Shogun just looked like he had a bad case of sunburn and was peeling. Amy beamed at her and Clarissa dabbed her eyes as both women clutched their bouquets and waited for Sasha to arrive at the front of the garden to stand beside Hunter.

"She's all yours," Doc said quietly as Shogun and Bear Shadow parted.

"I still haven't had a chance to kiss your boo-boo," Sasha whispered as she stepped in closely to Hunter.

He gave her a sidelong glance and a sly half smile, chuckling, and then simply turned to her, lifted her veil, and kissed her hard.

The Fae went nuts. The crowd was on their feet with a rowdy cheer. Jennifer began bawling the moment Hunter moved into place, and Mrs. Chen put a supportive arm over her shoulder.

Silver Hawk just smiled and closed his eyes. "You two will have to give me a moment alone with the Great Spirit before I begin the formal ceremony . . . because witnessing this day, for this old wolf, is truly a miracle."

Experience the dark pleasures and animal passions of

CRIMSON MOON

The acclaimed series
from *New York Times* bestselling author

L.A. BANKS

BAD BLOOD
ISBN: 978-0-312-94911-2

BITE THE BULLET
ISBN: 978-0-312-94912-9

UNDEAD ON ARRIVAL
ISBN: 978-0-312-94913-6

CURSED TO DEATH
ISBN: 978-0-312-94299-1

NEVER CRY WEREWOLF
ISBN: 978-0-312-94300-4

AVAILABLE FROM ST. MARTIN'S PAPERBACKS

Don't miss the Vampire Huntress Legend™ Novels
from *New York Times* Bestselling Author

L. A. BANKS

Available from St. Martin's Paperbacks